M000197069

TEMPTING
THE
DEVIL

QUENTIN SECURITY SERIES
BOOK FIVE

MORGAN JAMES

Tempting the Devil
Copyright © 2021 Morgan James.
ISBN: 978-1-951447-18-2

PROLOGUE

Abby

The figure moved forward, closing the distance between us. "Sitting here all by yourself, little one?"

I nodded up at the deep voice, unable to form words. The man's face was blurry, and I couldn't quite pull it into focus as he moved in front of me.

"You're a good girl, aren't you, Abilene?"

I nodded, a strange sensation taking root deep in my belly. I couldn't quite explain it, but it was the same kind of feeling I'd had once after eating too many cookies. A little sick, a little afraid of what would happen if I were caught.

The bulky figure took a seat on the coffee table in front of me. "I seem to be missing some money, Abilene. Had twenty dollars right on the kitchen counter and now it's gone. You wouldn't know anything about that, now would you?"

I shook my head, fear and something else rising up in my throat, stealing my words as he leaned closer. His features remained obscured, fuzzy but somehow still familiar.

"I think you took it, Abby." Again, I shook my head vehemently, but he cut me off as I tried to speak. "It's okay, I understand. I'll keep your secret."

One huge hand settled on my knee. "No one has to know."

The hand slid up my thigh, and the butterflies in my belly kicked into full flight.

"Such a pretty little thing..."

CHAPTER ONE

Abby

My feet felt heavy as I trudged through the hotel that had served as a home to me for the past two nights. My brother had offered to let me stay with him, but I'd declined. Con had already done enough for me, and I didn't need to add to his burden. He was absorbed in his business, and he'd already taken the time out of his busy schedule to move my things into Violet's place, even enlisting the help of his friend and employee, Cole.

The hotel bar came into sight, and I pushed down the guilt that threatened to swallow me whole. God, I was so tired. Tired of the guilt. Tired of feeling sad and out of control. The last couple of weeks felt like a rollercoaster of activity and emotion. Even now that I was finally off the ride, the world around me was still spinning violently. After the past few days, I just needed a little bit of time to myself and a drink or two to take my mind off of things.

Everything had happened so quickly. Two weeks ago I'd left college in Connecticut to move in with my guardian, Violet. Dallas was home for me, and I'd gone to live with Violet while Con opted to enter the Marines after our parents passed away. Aside from my brother, she was the only other person I had to call family. I should've known something was off, but I was so busy with moving and getting settled that I'd ignored all the signs. Violet seemed to be more forgetful than usual, but I hadn't thought much of it—until the day of the fire.

On Monday morning, I left Violet in the sunroom where she enjoyed drinking her coffee and working on her crossword puzzles. I shopped for groceries then stopped by the drugstore to pick up Violet's prescriptions, completely oblivious to the turmoil unfolding back home. I'll never forget the sight that greeted me as I turned onto the street. Fire trucks had gathered in front of the house, creating a barrier around the burning house, and thick black smoke billowed up from the old brick ranch.

A sobbing Violet greeted me by the ambulance. Though she wasn't hurt, it was glaringly obvious; she couldn't be left alone. While I was gone, Violet had apparently decided to make breakfast. From what we concluded, she'd forgotten about the pan on the stove and the bacon she'd been frying caught fire. Violet threw water on it to put it out, succeeding only in helping the fire to spread. Thank goodness a neighbor two doors down had heard Violet yelling for help. He'd called the fire department and they'd arrived minutes later.

Most of the kitchen was toast—no pun intended—but at least the house had been salvaged. The fire had spread from the kitchen into the surrounding living and dining rooms, scorching the walls and floors. My brother had hired a company to clean the house and renovate the kitchen so we wouldn't have to wait for the insurance check to come through. We would eventually need to replace the flooring in all the rooms, but for now it just needed to be clean and livable.

Two days after the fire, Violet moved into an assisted living facility. She'd apparently been making plans for several months, but I was blindsided by her choice. I couldn't deny her request, and I'd spent the past few days helping to get her settled. I was exhausted mentally, and I couldn't bear to be at home right now. Though I wanted to turn him down, I couldn't refuse Con's offer to put me up in the hotel. Since I hadn't been able to get to work either, I was a little low on funds. I was scheduled to start this past week working for my brother's security company, but with everything going on he'd pushed my start date to next Monday. I was actually looking forward to it, hoping like hell it would give me something else to focus on.

I stepped into the hotel bar and threw a quick glance around. Since it was Friday night, most of the tables were occupied, either with travelers wanting to relax and unwind or locals who'd come to grab a nightcap before heading home for the evening. Sliding onto the tall leather barstool, I allowed my gaze to rove the room. Most of the men were older, overweight, slouched over their drinks, still dressed sloppily in wrinkled suits and ties. Coming down here was a stupid mistake. I should have called my friend Jamie and asked her to come meet me, but I knew she was going out with Brandon tonight, and I didn't want to interrupt their date.

My attention was drawn to the bartender who leaned against the bar in front of me. "What can I get you?"

"Um…" I'd never been a big partier in college, preferring to focus instead on my studies. I'd had big plans back then, none of which had included moving back home the moment I graduated. Shaking off the thought, I forced a smile to my face as I passed him my credit card. "I'll have an apple martini, please."

He moved away with a nod and began to gather up the things he needed to make it. I was always impressed by bartenders' abilities to memorize and make so many different drinks, and I watched fixedly as he shook the liquid, then strained it into a glass before sliding it my way.

"Thank you."

He returned my card, and I added a tip to the receipt before signing it and passing it back to him. I lifted the drink to my lips and took a sip, then settled back in my seat as the sweet liquor exploded over my tongue. I could feel a set of eyes on me, and I glanced around again. An older man, dressed in a wrinkled collared shirt with a light brown stain in the region of his breast pocket, stared at me like he wanted to devour me.

It was bad manners to meet someone's eyes without acknowledging them, but I forced down the urge to flash him a polite smile. I wasn't here to encourage anyone. Studiously avoiding him, I turned my back and tuned out the older gentleman to my right.

My gaze slid over the sea of faces seated sporadically around the room. I was scanning the back wall when I suddenly froze, stunned by the sight of the gorgeous man tucked away in a corner booth. My insides tingled as heat raced through me, and I shifted on my barstool. Focused on the plate of food in front of him, the man didn't seem to be aware of my presence. Story of my life. Suddenly, as if feeling my eyes on him, his gaze lifted. I immediately ducked my head, my heart thundering in my chest as I stared at the green liquid sloshing precariously in my glass. I forced my hand to steady as I drew in a deep breath.

Holy shit, he'd almost caught me ogling him. Heat crept into my cheeks, and I flicked a glance up through my lashes to see if he'd noticed me. My chest tightened a little with disappointment when I found his attention once more focused on the plate in front of him. I turned my body a bit, keeping him in my peripheral vision as I sipped on my own drink. I took the opportunity to look him over as he drank deeply, his Adam's apple bobbing with the motion. The sleeves of his black button up shirt were rolled up, exposing corded, veiny forearms that my fingers itched to touch. Chiseled jaw, dark hair that was cut close to the sides but left longer on top. Broad shoulders and thick biceps. I couldn't see the color of his eyes from here, only the dark look in them, warning everyone else away. Sitting all alone in the corner booth, he practically had the words *fuck off* stamped across his forehead.

A rail-thin blonde approached, and her hip bumped into his table. Her giggle lilted on the air, and my insides tightened with something like jealousy as it reached me. How ridiculous was that? I didn't know this man at all. *But you'd like to*, my subconscious spoke up. That was true enough. I couldn't tear my gaze away as I watched the interaction between the man and the blonde across the room.

He offered her a tight smile, then redirected his gaze to the glass in his hand. But the blonde didn't get the memo. Drink balanced in one hand, she leaned toward him and ran her fingers over his arm. Even from here, I could see him tense. It took guts to hit on a guy who looked like that, so I gave the girl props. But he obviously wasn't having any of it, and he was too nice to tell her to pound salt.

I watched in rapt fascination as the woman jerked away from him and made an agitated gesture with her hand. Her movements became wilder, more pronounced. She was obviously giving him hell for something. The man started to shake his head, but the woman's voice grew louder and louder. The man in the booth looked incredibly uncomfortable as people around them turned to watch the show unfold.

I bit my lip, then made a split decision. I didn't know this man or what had transpired between him and the beautiful woman next to him, but I felt compelled to intervene. Adjusting my purse over my shoulder, I slid from my barstool and made a beeline toward the booth.

Halfway across the room, my steps faltered. What the hell was I doing? My gaze flitted around, looking for the bathroom so I could change my course and escape inside where no one would be the wiser. But the door I sought was nowhere in sight, and I dimly remembered passing it on my way into the bar. Damn it. Drawing in a deep breath, I steeled myself as I continued along my trajectory, straight toward the man seated in the booth and the leggy woman next to him. The closer I got, the more my stomach twisted. Oh, God, this was a terrible idea.

"You just left me!" the woman practically wailed. "I thought I meant something to you!"

A lover's quarrel. Even worse. I couldn't tell why, precisely, but I felt bad for both of them. I felt bad for the woman who obviously believed she and the man had shared something special, only to have him leave. But I felt bad for him, too. She was making an unholy scene—and no one deserved that, regardless of the situation.

My eyes flew back to the man in the booth. He was doing a good job of keeping his emotions in check, but I saw the hard lines of his face, the tight clenching of his jaw as she railed at him. I swallowed hard as I stepped up next to the woman. My head barely came up to her shoulder, and not for the first time since I left my spot across the bar, I was swamped with a sense of insecurity. The man's eyes flicked to where I stood next to the beautiful blonde, and I could practically read the question in their depths.

Who are you, and what the hell are you doing?

Instead of responding, I cleared my throat and brushed lightly against the woman, silently prodding her to move. Still wrapped up in her ongoing tirade, the woman didn't even notice me.

"You asshole! I can't believe you," she fumed. "You promised you would—"

I tapped her on the shoulder. "Excuse me."

"What?" The woman whipped toward me, eyes wide and slightly crazed looking.

"I, um..." I swallowed hard and tried again, forcing myself not to cower under her intense glare. "I think you're mistaken."

Her wide blue eyes flew toward the man in the booth, then back to mine, still filled with a mixture of hurt and anger. "About what?"

I smiled, praying that neither could see my unease. "I think you have the wrong guy."

"No." She shook her head and pointed a finger his way. "He—"

"Trust me." I drew a deep breath. "He's my boyfriend."

CHAPTER TWO

Clay

I knew my past would eventually come back to bite me in the ass. I'd just hoped it wouldn't be somewhere public where the woman was making a scene and drawing attention from everyone in the room, including the man I was tailing.

The blonde—Sheila? Shelly? Hell, I couldn't remember—looked mad enough to spit nails. I opened my mouth to speak, but a second woman materialized next to the table.

Hello.

I was so distracted by the sight of her that I completely missed what she said. Something about being mistaken. Whatever it was, I would gladly set her straight. She turned her attention back to the blonde—Rochelle, that was her name! The word *boyfriend* falling from her lips had me snapping back to reality as she directed her pretty dark eyes to me with a sweet, if slightly wobbly, smile.

"Sorry I'm late. Work was hectic and I finally just got off."

I froze, feeling like I was standing at the wrong end of a scope. Who the hell was this woman? My gaze clashed with hers, the dark depths silently urging me to just go with it. I shrugged good-naturedly. "No problem. Glad you made it."

"I see you started without me." She threw a wry look at my half-empty plate, completely tuning out the blonde who stood by, watching with a sense of bewilderment.

The brunette turned to the blonde, an expression of sympathy on her pretty face. "Sorry for the misunderstanding. He gets this a lot."

Rochelle's gaze jumped between me and the other woman before settling on the brunette. "You're with him?"

"For about eight months now. Right?"

She threw a look my way, and I nodded. "Next week makes nine."

"He gets confused for his brother a lot," the brunette explained to Rochelle. "He's a twin, and sometimes..." She lifted her hands, as if that explained everything.

Rochelle glared at me suspiciously. "Is that true?"

"It is." I fought the urge to glance at the brunette, wondering how the hell she knew about my brother.

"Oh." She blinked several times. "I... I'm so sorry. I thought..."

"It's fine. Sorry I couldn't help." I smiled, still feeling off balance as the brunette slid in next to me and her thigh pressed to mine. She was warm and smelled as sweet as spun sugar, and I couldn't help my reaction to her as my groin tightened. Automatically, my arm moved, wrapping around her shoulders as she leaned into me.

She tipped her head up and threw another of those sweet smiles my way. "Hi, honey."

Looking confused and more than a little embarrassed, Rochelle dipped her head as she turned tail and headed across the bar. Once she was gone, I turned my gaze to the woman next to me. "Well, that was... interesting."

She too had been watching Rochelle make her escape, but now she turned a look on me, her big brown eyes huge in her face. "I'm pretty sure I did you a favor there."

"No doubt. She was out for blood." I suddenly sobered. I knew for certain I'd never met this woman, so how the hell did she know so much about me? It immediately put me on guard. "How did you know about my brother?"

"Hmm?" Her pretty brown eyes searched mine. "What do you mean?"

"You told her my brother was the one she was looking for. How did you know I'm a twin?"

Her gaze widened almost comically. "Oh, my God. There are

two of you wreaking havoc on the female population?"

She'd guessed? Her reaction was too genuine to be anything other than complete and utter surprise at my revelation, and I was stunned into laughing. "Actually, yeah, I do have a twin. We're fraternal, so we don't look much alike. And I promise he's worse than I am."

She let out a little snort when I winked at her. "If you say so, Casanova."

"What? Don't believe me?"

"I haven't decided yet." The pretty brunette next to me settled back against the booth and took another sip of her bright green drink. "Anyway, nice to meet you, Johnny."

It felt like she'd slapped me. "My name's not Johnny."

"I didn't figure. That'd be kind of a coincidence." She turned to face me, her gaze sliding over my torso. "I'm digging the Johnny Cash look, though."

My eyes dropped to the black pants and long-sleeved black shirt I'd worn in the hopes of fitting in with the after-work drink crowd gathered at the bar. "Right. So..." I asked the most obvious question. "Why are you here?"

I watched bemusedly as she stole a fry from my plate and popped it into her pretty mouth. "Like, here at the bar, or here in your booth?"

Either. I definitely wanted to know what had brought her to the bar alone—and how long she planned to be here. But for now, I'd settle for the situation at hand. "Why'd you tell her I was your boyfriend?"

She took a sip of her drink before she turned to face me. "I don't know what transpired between you two, and I don't care. But it's really not very classy to pull something like that in public. I figured you could use some help."

She was pretty—more than pretty, actually. I'd noticed her giant doe eyes and long brown hair the moment she'd walked in and plopped herself down at the bar, but she was even more beautiful up close. Her heart-shaped face was highlighted by those gorgeous eyes and pouty pink lips. A tiny dimple flashed in her chin, and my fingers twitched in their need to touch the tiny divot.

I clenched my hand into a fist where it rested on my thigh. "How could you tell?"

She canted her head to one side and studied me, her chocolate gaze sweeping from the top of my head down to my waist, every place not concealed by the table. "Your posture. Most people probably wouldn't be able to tell, but it was practically screaming 'get the hell away from me.'"

"Yet here you are." I smirked.

"I'll leave in just a sec." She waved a hand dismissively, then paused. "Unless..." Her gaze darted back to mine. "Was I wrong? If you're meeting someone or want me to go, I can—"

"Not a chance in hell." This was way more entertaining. Who gave a shit about the mark I was supposed to be watching tonight when I had this gorgeous woman next to me? The man I was currently tailing would be leaving soon anyway, and I'd already gotten a few pictures of the woman his wife suspected he was having an affair with. He would probably take her to one of the hotel rooms later or he'd go home to his wife where he belonged. Either way, my recon for the night was complete.

"Oh. Okay, good." She looked relieved. "I was worried there for a second. Sometimes I act before I even think about the consequences."

No shit.

Undaunted, she continued. "My brother complains about it all the time, says I have no impulse control." She rolled her eyes like she didn't believe a word, and I couldn't help but side with the brother in question. Then she caught me totally off guard when she leaned toward me and sniffed. "You smell good."

"Um... thanks?" It came out more as a question than a statement, but she nodded regardless.

"I don't like a lot of men's cologne. Some of it is way too strong. I like a guy to smell good, but not bathe in it, you know?"

Jesus. Did she ever stop talking? And her mind—not to mention her mouth—went a hundred miles a minute. She shot me a questioning look and I realized I hadn't answered what I thought was a rhetorical question. "Right."

She turned her attention back to the drink in her hand, and I wondered how many she'd had. It appeared she'd only taken a few sips, but she didn't seem inebriated. Far from it. It seemed like she'd hit the coffee shop across the street and chugged the contents of their espresso machine before striding into the bar and touching down in my booth like a tornado. I felt bad for her brother, whoever he was.

"Speaking of," she continued, undaunted, "did you know that by calculating the current unsolved murder rate, there's a possibility that there may be up to two thousand active serial killers in the US right now?"

How in the hell she'd managed to segue from cologne to killers was beyond me, and I wasn't entirely sure I even wanted to know her train of thought. Not gonna lie, I was both incredibly turned on and a little intimidated. She turned those big brown eyes on me, head tipped slightly to one side as she waited for my response. "Are you one of them?" I asked, only half joking.

She blinked, then let out a laugh. "You think I'm some kind of black widow, preying on men in bars?"

"Never know." I shrugged. "It seems to be working so far. You came over her and pretended to be my girlfriend under the guise of saving me from having my ass chewed out by the Barbie doll."

"Okay, yeah." She grimaced. "It sounds way creepier when you say it out loud like that. I'm just gonna..." She grabbed her drink and made to slide out of the booth, but I grabbed her hip and pulled her back to me.

"You can't leave now. This is just getting good."

She lifted a brow my way. "You compared me to a serial killer."

"In my defense," I replied, "you hit me with the true crime facts first."

Her nose wrinkled. "Fair point."

I found myself wanting to draw out the conversation. "So, what happens now? You lure me in with your pretty face and irresistible knowledge of useless trivia?"

"That's not useless!" Still holding her glass, she used her pinky to point around the room. "What if there's a serial killer in this bar right now?"

I winked. "I'd protect you."

"Please." She rolled her eyes, but a faint smile curved her lips.

"Okay, you're right. I would totally sacrifice you as bait and make a run for it."

"Hey!" She lightly backhanded me, and I laughed.

She was quirky as hell, but I found that I was enjoying myself. I was acutely aware of my hand resting along the curve of her hip, and I fought the urge to curl my fingers into her flesh. "All right. So now that we've broken the ice with talk of homicide, I think I should at least know your name."

"Um…" Although I didn't think it possible, her cheeks turned pink and she fell silent for the first time.

Curiosity piqued, I turned to face her more fully. "You don't want to tell me your name?"

"It's not that," she said, flustered. "It's just… kind of strange." She must have seen my confused expression, because she grimaced. "My name is Abilene."

My brows drew together. "Like the city?"

"Yeah. It's kind of a long story." She let out a beleaguered sigh, and her pretty face twisted as she peered up at me.

Well, I sure as hell wasn't going to let her leave me hanging like that. "By all means, I have all night." Most of the night, anyway. She intrigued me on a level I'd rarely experienced, and everything else was pushed to the back burner as I focused my attention on her.

"Okay, so… my parents were kind of nomads." She paused. "That's not true. I think even nomads have a purpose in life. Mom and Dad were groupies when they were younger, following some eighties band around on tour. They lived in a camper and dragged it from town to town, picking up enough work to pay for their drugs and beer before moving on to the next place."

"That sounds… exciting." In truth, I couldn't begin to imagine. My mom passed when I was young, but my father was the seven-to-three, hard-working, blue-collar type. He didn't have time for fun, let alone his twin boys.

"They hit every major city, and my parents named each of us after the places where we were conceived." Her cheeks burned bright pink. "I guess I'm lucky it was Abilene and not, like, Dallas or something, right?"

"Abilene." I lifted my arm and spread it over the back of the booth, away from the temptation of her mouthwatering curves, and studied her for a moment. Thick, dark hair hung in long waves, framing her beautiful heart-shaped face. Her skin was lightly tanned, or perhaps just naturally olive toned, and it made her expressive, big brown eyes appear even larger and brighter. My gaze skated downward over her high cheekbones and full mouth. Her bottom lip was fuller than the top, but it suited her. She was cool and classy but definitely more than a little peculiar. "I like it."

She rolled her eyes. "No one likes my name. It's a stupid name."

I rolled a lock of that glossy dark hair between my fingers. "I think it's beautiful. Just like you."

She stared at me for a second before a laugh fell from her lips. And not a little giggle, or a chuckle. Oh, no. She let out a loud, bold laugh that penetrated my body and wound around my heart. It was unrepentant, as if she wanted nothing more than to just enjoy life and wouldn't let anything or anyone take that joy from her.

She wiped her eyes as she turned back to me. "Does that work for you?"

I didn't pretend to misunderstand her question about the ridiculous pickup line. I grinned and lifted a shoulder. "Occasionally."

"Uh huh." Her gaze swept over my body once more before taking another sip of her drink.

I scooted closer and extricated the glass from her hand, setting it on the table. "What the—"

Capturing her jaw in one hand, I turned her face toward mine. Deep in those huge doe eyes I saw wariness and hesitation, but I also saw desire. With the pad of my thumb, I traced her full lower lip. "So, Abilene. Now you know my secret."

Her lashes fluttered several times as she blinked up at me. "What secret?"

"That my cheesy pick-up lines don't work."

"Clearly, *Casanova*." She grinned.

"Are you from around here?" I had to know. From time to time I thought I'd caught something of a northern accent, but there was always a chance that she was local. Even if she lived in her namesake of Abilene, that wasn't too far away...

It didn't escape my notice that I was already planning to see her again, but I had a feeling this girl would be worth more than just one visit. Many more.

Those gorgeous eyes searched mine, and her lips opened several times before she rasped out the words. "I'm only here for tonight."

"Shame." I brushed my thumb along her cheekbone. "Up to you, beautiful."

She seemed to know exactly what I was asking because her eyes dropped to my lap before meeting mine again. Her teeth sank into her bottom lip as she studied me. Without a word, she pulled away and slipped from the booth.

My heart hit the floor and disappointment engulfed me. Fuck. I'd pushed her too far, too fast, and now she was running away. I opened my mouth to speak, but she turned back to me and leaned into the booth. Propping one hand on the table and the other on the back of the booth, she caged me in. She dropped a kiss on my cheek, her lips skimming my two-day scruff before her breath hit my ear. "Two-oh-eight."

With that she was gone. My gaze dropped to the table, and I saw the key card she'd left behind, tucked partially beneath the rim of my plate. A slow smile spread across my face as I picked it up and turned it over in my hands. Abandoning my meal, I tossed several bills on the table to cover the tab, then headed for the bank of elevators in the lobby. As soon as the doors closed, I adjusted my hard-on. Tonight may have started out boring as hell, but it was sure looking up.

CHAPTER THREE

Abby

I stared out the window, lost in my thoughts. With the reflection of the lamp beside the bed glaring against the glass, I could barely see the glow of lights outside. A faint click sounded behind me, and I swiveled my head toward the door. My heart stalled in my chest as it swung inward a few inches, then froze.

I held my breath, watching as the giant shadow fell across the wall, the man backlit by the light from the hallway as he paused half a step into the room. Was he going to back out? My offer in the bar had been impulsive; I'd never had a one-night stand before, but I felt this crazy connection to him. If he walked away now, I would be devastated.

As if he'd come to the same conclusion, the man pushed the door open and stepped inside, then quietly closed it behind him.

I slowly let the breath I'd been holding out through my nose as relief flooded me. "You came."

Eyes hooded, he rested against the door for a long moment and just surveyed me. Then, without a word, he pushed away from the door and approached. No, that was wrong—he stalked. Like a panther trailing his prey, he advanced on me. My pulse thundered in my ears as he drew up short only inches away, so close I could practically feel his shoes against the tips of my bare toes. He looked harsh and fierce, and my heart galloped in my chest. For the first time since I'd laid eyes on the man, I was terrified I'd made a horrible mistake.

"Do you want me to stay?" His gaze never left mine, his eyes staring into my soul as if he was trying to pull my thoughts from me. He must've read my indecision, because his head tipped slightly to one side. "Or should I go?"

I swallowed hard. "Would you leave if I asked?"

Hawklike golden-brown eyes stared down at me. "Is that what you want, Dallas?"

"Oh, God." I made a face. "I'm not sure which is worse—Abilene or Dallas."

A tiny smirk tipped the corner of his lips. "I'll call you whatever you want. Better yet... No names. You're only here for one night, so let's just make the most of it. What do you think?"

"Hmm..." With that delicious masculine scent filling my nostrils, I couldn't think clearly, let alone form coherent words.

"I'll be disappointed if you tell me to leave," he murmured. He was so close now that I could feel the heat radiating from his huge body. "But I'll never force you to do anything you don't want."

I barely controlled my flinch as one huge hand moved to cup the side of my face. His fingers halted mere millimeters away, his eyes silently asking permission to touch me. I nodded, and the rough calloused palm landed gently on my cheek. "Do you want me to leave?"

I closed my eyes briefly, forcing myself to look away from his arresting gaze. Was this what I wanted? The heat of his flesh seeped into mine, and I lifted my hands and placed them on his pecs. He was hard and unyielding beneath my fingertips. Yet I trusted what he said; he would leave if I asked.

I shook my head. "Stay."

"You sure?"

I bit back my smile as I curled my fingers into the fabric of his black shirt. "If you leave, I may have to kill you."

Bright white teeth flashed in the dim light. "Can't have that."

His hands moved to my hips and slipped beneath the hem of my shirt. I lifted my arms as he drew the fabric over my head, then dropped it to the floor. His gaze skated over my exposed flesh, setting my nerve endings on fire and my blood racing through my veins with anticipation. "Goddamn. You're so gorgeous."

"I would say the same," I quipped, "but I haven't seen the evidence yet."

His fingers curled into my hips at my challenging words, and he stared me down. "We'll just have to fix that then, won't we?"

Eyes fixed on me, his hands moved to the buttons of his shirt and deftly began to slip them free of their holes. His dark, tanned skin was revealed to me an inch at a time, and I bit my lip. Holy abs. Gorgeous didn't begin to describe this man. The washboard effect of his abdominal muscles was outlined in the dim light, and my fingers tingled with the need to trace every hard line. The fabric of his shirt parted and he shrugged it off over his broad shoulders. Before it even hit the floor, he was on me.

Spinning me away from him, he grabbed my hands and slapped them flat against the wall. I felt his fingers sift through my hair and arrange it in a loose ponytail. Abruptly, he gave a little tug, yanking my head up and causing my back to arch. He made a little sound of approval low in his throat. "Fucking love your hair."

"Yeah?" I could barely form the word as my breaths came faster, my pulse thundering in my ears.

"Mhmm..." He leaned in close and nipped my ear. "Don't ever cut it."

"Okay." I don't know why I agreed, except that he seemed so brutally intent.

His hold on my hair loosened and I felt the long strands tickle my back as he combed my hair with his fingers, carefully arranging it to his liking. When he was finished, his hands skated up my sides, over my ribs, then around to palm my breasts. His huge hands enveloped me, and I sucked in a breath as he worked down the cups of my bra so I was exposed to him. My nipples peaked at the sensation of the cool air hitting them, and my head dropped back as he rolled the tight buds between his fingers.

He nipped my ear again, sending a shiver of pleasure through me, then continued to explore. The rough scruff along his chin abraded my skin as he trailed downward, dropping soft kisses along my throat. A thick, hard ridge pressed against my bottom and I wiggled my hips, eliciting a little growl from him. One arm slipped lower just as he sank his teeth into the soft spot between my neck and shoulder.

I let out a little squeal as liquid fire rushed through me, and my knees buckled. The arm around my waist tightened, pulling me in tighter. Against my shoulder, he chuckled. "There it is."

There what is? Before I could open my mouth to voice the question, he bit the same spot again and stars swam before my eyes.

"Oh, God!"

My neck was my weakness; no one had ever found that sensitive spot so quickly. His questing hand moved lower, popping the fly of my jeans and delving inside. I sucked in a breath as his fingers teased the waistband of my panties before slipping underneath. As he licked and sucked on my neck, he moved downward through the narrow patch of curls until he reached the sensitive bundle of nerves between my legs.

I shifted my feet wider for better access, grinding shamelessly against him. A muffled curse met my ear, and he pulled his hand free. Grabbing my pants, he shoved them down to my ankles. He held me steady as I slipped first one foot free of the material, then the other. I started to adjust my stance, but he wrapped his hands around my thighs, halting me in place.

"Just like this," he said, planting a kiss along my right hamstring.

I shivered as his hands trailed lightly up the backs of my legs until he cupped my bottom. I held my breath, waiting anxiously to see what he would do. In this position, I was absolutely bare to him from the waist down, and he could see every inch of me in the soft lighting.

He palmed my right cheek, kneading it for a moment before I felt his mouth move to the left one. A tiny sigh escaped my lips, stifled when he bit down on the tender spot.

He just bit my ass. I was momentarily stunned, yet exceedingly turned on. His hands moved to spread my cheeks apart and suddenly his mouth was there, his tongue spearing into me.

"Oh, God..." My legs shook, and my hands started to lose their grip on the wallpaper as he took his time tasting me, running his tongue over my folds from bottom to top.

"Yes! Oh, my God, right there!"

His hands tightened on my bottom as he pulled my cheeks apart for better access. Heat built low in my belly as his tongue rasped over the sensitive bundle of nerves. His teeth scraped over my clit, and a shudder rolled down my spine at the sensation.

"More, I need…"

He increased the suction with his mouth, and I let out a little squeak as one hand slid over my bottom and he fingered the rosebud of my back entrance. My denial died on my lips as a feeling I'd never experienced shot through me. It made everything seem sharper and more intense. He sucked harder, pressing inward on the spot, and I slapped one hand over my mouth as I came.

My legs trembled, threatening to give way beneath me and before I knew what was happening, I found myself being swept into his arms. He carried me to the bed and tossed me into the middle of the mattress. I landed with a bounce, the motion momentarily stealing my breath and senses. It was exhilarating and confusing all at the same time. I felt unexpectedly small and feminine in his strong arms. Part of me loved that he could pick me up and throw me around like a ragdoll; the other part of me was instantly furious at the show of dominance. Before I could form a single word, his mouth fastened to my neck and I melted under the delicious assault.

I clutched at his biceps as he kissed his way down my sternum to my breasts, then took the tip of one in his hot mouth. I scraped my nails over his shoulders, needing to mark him the way he'd done to me. I felt every inch of him imprinted on my body, but I needed more.

"Yes…" I drew out the word on a hiss of pleasure as he increased suction almost to the point of pain. "Just like that."

Clay released my nipple. "Stop talking."

I bit my lip as he kissed his way to the other side and flicked the sensitive tip with his tongue. Every tiny touch ate away at my control, and I couldn't stand it any longer.

"Take these off." Reaching between us, I fumbled with his belt and shoved his pants down. I watched as he slid off the edge of the bed and toed off his shoes, then stripped out of his slacks, taking his boxers with then. He fished a condom from his wallet and rolled it over the broad head of his erection, darkened with arousal.

I automatically pulled my knees up, and he pushed them apart as he climbed onto the bed and moved between my thighs. His body was warm and hard against my own, and I reveled in the rightness of it. "God, yes. You feel so good. I want—"

"I said stop talking."

He slapped one hand over my mouth, his fingers digging into my cheeks. The maneuver was designed to capture my attention and show dominance. It served only to piss me off. I thrashed my head and opened my mouth wide, ready to bite down. He pulled his hand back just in time, and my teeth gnashed together.

"Brat." He growled low in his throat. Before I could blink, he'd captured both of my hands in his own and had them pressed to the pillow over my head, his huge body limiting my movement. "You talk too damn much."

Shifting his hips, he lined up the head of his cock with my center and pressed an inch inside. "And if you can still talk"—he drove so hard and deep that it took my breath away—"then I'm not doing my job. I'm going to fuck you so hard"—thrust—"you forget your own damn name."

Under the onslaught of his rough thrusts, I couldn't formulate a single thought. All I could focus on was him, the way he commanded my body and carried me to a place I never knew existed. A keening cry left my mouth as he hit my G-spot again, and I lifted my hips for better access. I opened my mouth to say something, but only a wail bubbled up my throat as ecstasy crashed over me in wave after wave of pleasure.

CHAPTER FOUR

Clay

Holy fuck. This woman was scorching hot.

She gripped my dick tighter than a fist, and I bit back a growl. I wasn't ready to come yet. I wasn't ready for this to be over. I slowed my strokes, drawing out her orgasm until her face contorted and she let out a little whimper, her nails cutting into my skin as she tried to hold me close and push me away at the same time.

Her chest rose and fell on choppy breaths, and her breasts jiggled a little under the motion. I grinned and released her hands, then dipped my head to take one straining peak into my mouth. Her hands flew to my hair, and her legs clenched around my hips. Kissing my way up her sternum, I ran my teeth along the cord of her throat. A sexy little sound filtered from her throat, and I smiled against her skin. Too bad she was only here for the night.

She lifted her head to kiss me, but I gave a little shake of my head. "No kissing, babe."

She looked confused and a little hurt, and I immediately wanted to wipe that look from her face. I turned my head and sank my teeth into the spot that set her off, and her pussy clenched around me where I was still buried deep inside her. Nails scraped along my scalp, and her nipples pressed into my chest as she arched and sucked in a breath.

She smelled light and airy, almost like sunshine and a soft breeze. I inhaled deeply, dragging her scent into my nostrils and committing it to memory. In that moment, I almost wanted to kiss her. I hadn't kissed another woman in nearly ten years. But for this girl... damn, was I tempted.

No kissing, no cuddling. Those were the rules I lived by. Keep my walls up and keep women out. They were conniving and vindictive, and I'd be damned if I let another one betray me the way Samantha had. I enjoyed sex; I didn't need the emotional bullshit. I was too old for that. The fact that I actually felt the desire to break my own rules and kiss her pissed me off. I was always in full control, but this woman pushed me beyond need, beyond desire.

She let out a little whimper as I pulled free of her slick channel. Grabbing her hips, I flipped her to her stomach and yanked her to her hands and knees so she faced away from me.

"Right here, Dallas. Just like this."

She wiggled a little, and I felt a surge of lust shoot straight to my groin. Damn, she was pretty. Her ass was round and full with the perfect amount of give as I sank my fingers into her hips. Christ, she made me so fucking hard.

I barely held back a groan as I sank inside her tight channel once more. I pulled out almost to the tip, anticipation singing through my veins as I drove deep. Abilene jolted forward under the force of the thrust, and another cry ripped from her throat.

I leaned forward, pressing deeper into her. Palming her ass in both hands, I swept my fingers over the soft skin before curling them into her hips for better leverage. Heat enveloped me as I slid all the way in, and I bit back an oath as her flesh tightened around me. Over and over, I pulled out and thrust back in, hard and fast. She let out a strangled cry as her inner walls constricted around me, trying to hold me in. I dug my fingers into her hips and pounded into her, reveling in her body's response to me.

Fuck, she felt so damn good. I could feel every inch of her as her pussy clenched around me, grasping me tight. I didn't know what it was about her, but no woman had ever made me feel the way Abilene did. It wasn't just the sex; it was everything.

Her fingers clutched at the comforter as if to ground herself, and I plunged deeper, harder. A feral grin split my face as she cried out, the sound something between pleasure and pain. It mirrored exactly how I felt. Pleasure, because she felt so goddamn good gripping my cock. Painful, because I was so fucking hard for her, so damn tempted to come but wanting to draw it out, make it last all night long.

"Oh, God!"

She was close. I felt her walls contract as each thrust pushed her closer and closer to the edge. Picking up my pace, I drove into her over and over as hard and fast as I could, intent only on making her come.

Abilene pushed her hips back against me, forcing me even deeper. An unholy groan filled the air as she shattered, her pussy pulsing around me and setting off the beginnings of my orgasm.

"Holy fuck, Abilene..." I clenched my molars together as heat swept up my lower back and every muscle tightened under my impending orgasm. It hit me like a hurricane, stealing my breath and sending a shockwave through my system.

I dropped my forehead against her back and dragged in a breath, willing my head to stop spinning. Christ. I'd never felt anything like that before. I blinked and stretched my jaw, mostly just to make sure I hadn't stroked out. I half-laughed to myself as I peeled away from Abilene and lowered her to the mattress. Not dead, just fucked senseless.

Still a little shaken, I climbed from the bed and made a beeline for the bathroom. Once inside, I stripped off the condom and flushed it down the toilet. I took my time washing my hands, all the while studying my reflection in the mirror above the sink. What the fuck had happened back there? My nerve endings still tingled, like I'd grabbed onto an electric wire.

Warily, I headed back into the bedroom. Abilene lay sprawled out in the bed, arms tucked under the pillow, head turned away from me. The sight halted me in my tracks. She was quiet—too quiet. My eyes narrowed as I studied her prone form. Was she asleep? This was my perfect out. I could pick up my clothes, then slip out the door and be on my way. Except... I didn't want to. The feel of her skin was addictive, and I wasn't ready to walk away yet.

I ran my tongue over my teeth as my gaze swept over the flesh of her back, exposed by the sheet draped low over her hips.

For some reason, this girl affected me more deeply than any other woman I'd been with. We had a connection that I couldn't sever just yet. I propped my knee on the mattress then lay down next to her, hoisting myself up on an elbow and leaning my head into my hand as I watched her. She hadn't moved a single inch.

I reached out and tentatively ran one finger down her spine, feeling the tiny bump of each vertebra, all the way down to the curve of her perfect ass. She shivered slightly at my touch, and a grin lifted the corners of my mouth. I let my hand trail lower until one perfect globe filled my hand, and her head twisted on the pillow to meet my gaze. I lifted a brow, and a coy smile formed on her pretty lips.

"I had fun."

"Me, too." Using my fingers, I dove deeper, nudging her thighs further apart. I nipped her ear as I levered myself over her, already feeling myself get hard again. "But we're not done just yet."

CHAPTER FIVE

Abby

I pulled open the door of the small law office and paused in the vestibule. An older woman smiled at me from behind the glass partition, and she slid one side open to pass me a clipboard. "Sign in here, please."

I scribbled my name on the line, then returned it to her.

"Mr. Grant should be out in just a moment."

She closed the window, and I took a seat in one of the vinyl chairs lining the wall. True to her word, the heavy oak door to my left swung inward a moment later, revealing Harris Grant.

"Abilene." A warm smile wreathed his face as he greeted me. "So good to see you."

"Hey." I stood and moved toward him. "How are you?"

"I'm wonderful, thank you." He smiled and gestured toward the hallway. "Come on back."

Though I knew Harris to be somewhere in his mid-sixties, he was handsome and fit. His hair had grayed, but it gave him a distinguished look, and just seeing him again set me at ease. Harris was Violet's lawyer, but he'd also been a close friend to her over the years. I'd always kind of wondered why they never dated, but I assumed Violet hadn't been able to move on after her husband passed away. It wasn't my place to ask, and Violet wasn't one to speak of romantic matters.

"So tell me, how have things been?"

"Stressful," I admitted.

"I heard about the fire." He threw a sympathetic look my way as he paused next to a doorway. "I'm sorry about that, Abilene."

Outside of Violet, Harris was the only other person who called me by my full name. Why then had I told the man from the hotel? My cheeks heated at the memory of this past weekend. Though I'd told him my name, he'd never offered his. I guessed it was better that way. He was probably passing through, and I'd practically told him the same. Even if he were from around here, what were the odds of us ever seeing each other again? Pretty slim, considering I knew nothing about him. I didn't know what he did for a living or where he lived. A tiny pang ricocheted through my heart. It didn't matter anyway. It was over, and he was gone for good. No matter how much I wished otherwise.

He steered me into a large conference room on the left, and I forced myself to focus on the here and now. "Have a seat anywhere you like. Patrick should be here in just a moment."

"Oh." I tucked my purse on the ground at my feet and turned to look at Harris. "I had no idea he was coming today."

Harris pulled a soft cloth from his breast pocket, then slipped off his glasses, polishing them as he spoke. "Violet wanted me to cover a few things, and it was easier to have both of you come in."

I bit my lip. "Do you think I did the right thing? Letting her go to the assisted living center?"

Harris replaced his glasses on the bridge of his nose and sent a soft smile my way. "It was what she wanted. That's actually part of what I planned to cover today. She knew her health would eventually fail, and she wanted to plan for every contingency. Unfortunately, it happened much sooner than any of us expected."

The knowledge mollified me only the tiniest bit. Knowing that she'd made the decision while still lucid lifted some of the weight of guilt off my conscience, but that tiny niggle in the center of my chest was still there—the one that said I should have tried harder to get her to stay at home. It's where she was most comfortable. She'd spent nearly forty years of her life there; now she was being uprooted, waking every day in an unfamiliar place, surrounded by unfamiliar people.

I knew they would take good care of her, and there was money to cover the cost of the care. But that wasn't what bothered me. I felt like I was somehow letting her down. I'd moved back from college to be with her so she would have someone there if she needed anything. At the time, of course, I wasn't aware that things had gotten as bad as they had.

The phone in the conference room rang, and Harris lifted the receiver to his ear. "Yes?" There was a pause, then—"Send him back."

A minute later Violet's son, Patrick, walked into the room. His eyes widened a bit when he saw me sitting at the table. "Abby."

"Hey." I rose from my seat and offered a hug. Almost two decades older than me, Patrick had been out of the house long before I moved in with Violet. I didn't know him well, but he'd always been nice enough to me when our paths had crossed.

Patrick released me, and we resumed our seats at the table. He greeted Harris, then turned to me. "I thought you were up north for school."

"I was. But with Violet..." I trailed off, letting my words disappear. We all knew about the elephant in the room.

"Well," Harris spoke up, saving me, "thank you both for coming today. Has Violet ever discussed her affairs with you?"

I shook my head and threw a look at Patrick, who did the same. "She told me she updated her will about a year back, but it never came up again and I never pressed."

Heat stained my cheeks. I was glad someone had the foresight to discuss it with her. Although I'd lived with her for nearly ten years, I never really felt like it was my place to bring it up. Not only that, but I had no desire to. I'd lost both of my parents before I turned ten; the thought of discussing Violet's death was too morbid for me to even contemplate. I'd put it off, not wanting to acknowledge that she was getting older. Sitting here now, mortality pressed in on me, turning my breakfast to lead in my stomach.

As if sensing the direction of my thoughts, Harris sent a kind smile my way. "I have something here that she would like you both to see."

Harris turned to the computer in front of him and I clenched my hands together in my lap as the tapping of keys filled the air. Finally, Harris turned the screen toward us. Sitting at a conference table—probably the one we were seated at this very moment—Violet sat across from Harris. A counter in the lower right-hand corner showed the date to be just over a year ago.

On screen, Harris smiled at Violet. "Hello, Violet. We're here today to discuss your estate, is that correct?"

"Yes." She nodded. "I want to make sure all of my affairs are in order and there's no question as to how to proceed once I'm gone."

I swallowed hard against the sting of tears in my eyes at her words. Why hadn't she said anything sooner? Had I known about her dementia, I could have... What? Would anything be different? Her doctor was treating it, but she still had good days and bad. She'd obviously considered this from all angles before updating her will and putting everything into motion.

Aside from Connor, she was the only family I had left. I didn't want to lose her, too, but I knew it was inevitable. Her body was still strong, but her mind was trapped between past and present, and she needed help that I couldn't give her. I knew she was friendly with the other residents, but I vowed to stop in as often as I could.

I watched as Harris asked Violet a series of questions—the date, the name of the current president, her birthdate. She answered all of the questions succinctly, and Harris nodded as if to prove that she was, in fact, in full control of her faculties.

I listened as she named me power of attorney, which wasn't a surprise. The issue had arisen last week when she decided to move into the assisted living facility. What I wasn't prepared for, however, was what she said next. "The house I leave to my ward, Abilene Quentin."

I sat there in shock as silence briefly descended over the room. I felt Patrick jerk beside me in his chair, but I couldn't turn to look at him.

"Rewind that," he demanded.

Harris did as Patrick asked, and I watched in stunned silence as Violet repeated her edict. For some reason, I never imagined inheriting the house. As Violet's only living biological child, not to mention the oldest of us, I thought for sure she would have left it to him.

I turned to Patrick with wide eyes. "I..." What the hell could I say? I'm sorry? I had no idea?

He met my gaze, his own eyes furious and flashing with fire as he slammed his hands down on the arms of the chair. "What the hell is that?"

Harris lifted his chin a bit. "Patrick, your mother—"

"This is a joke." He pointed at the screen. "What the hell is this? She can't leave the house to Abby!"

I sat back in my chair, affronted. I understood his anger, but I couldn't say I wasn't a little hurt that he saw me as so far beneath him. "Patrick—"

"No." Patrick practically vibrated with fury as he rose from his seat. "I won't let this happen."

"This is what Violet wants," Harris replied in his soft but firm tone. "These are her last wishes."

"The hell with that," Patrick snapped back. "This is insane. She's out of her damn mind!"

His words had my hackles rising and anger snaking through my veins. "She's not crazy."

For the first time since his outburst, Patrick whirled toward me. "You did this, didn't you? You came back, and—"

"First of all," I shot back, "this happened well before I moved back. And at least I take care of her. You came all the way into town for this meeting, but I'll bet you haven't even gone to see her. Have you?"

His jaw dropped open a fraction. "Not yet," he sputtered. "But—"

"But what?" My eyes narrowed on him as I rose to face him head on. "She wouldn't know the difference?"

"I—"

"When the hell was the last time you made time to talk with her? Huh?" I poked him in the chest. "I was the one who moved all the way down here because she knew she couldn't count on you."

Harris tried to intervene. "All right, let's just calm down and—"

Patrick's face flared bright red as he glared at me. "I won't let this happen." He turned to Harris. "You can expect a call next week."

With that, he stormed out of the room, leaving Harris and me in stunned, awkward silence. Guilt rose up, along with regret. He was upset and I never should have said the things I did, even if they were true. He was just lashing out, and I happened to be the closest target.

I finally tore my gaze from the empty doorway and swallowed hard. "He's right, I—"

Harris shook his head as he closed the lid of the laptop. "Violet had very specific reasons for doing this. Patrick has his own life, his own family." He offered a little smile. "Violet loves you very much, and she wants you to be taken care of."

I knew she did, and I appreciated it, but... it filled me with guilt at the same time. Violet had given Con money to start QSG. This was her way of taking care of me. I blew out a breath. "Thank you for letting me know."

The house wasn't technically mine yet, not until Violet passed. But one thing was absolutely certain. I couldn't leave now.

CHAPTER SIX

Clay

Con slid a file folder my way and gave me a little nod. I knew as soon as I got back to my computer that I'd find an audio file to match the paper copy I held in my hands. Though most of the words made sense, I occasionally missed something, and I couldn't afford to slip up. Dyslexia was a bitch.

I could memorize anything, and I was full of stupid trivia that no one would ever give a shit about. But hand me a book and tell me to read it? That was a hard no. The more stressed I became, the worse it got. The letters and numbers jumbled together until they were almost unrecognizable. It'd gone undiagnosed for most of my school years without a mother around and a father who didn't give a shit about us as long as my brother and I kept our asses out of juvie.

On top of my inability to decipher words, I'd been a troublemaker. The teachers had shoved me into the special education classes and left me to flounder, unwilling to deal with me. It pissed me off because I knew I wasn't stupid, even though the other kids had teased me mercilessly. I got tossed out of school for more fights than I could count, and I skipped so much school I barely graduated.

I refused to play sports for fear of looking like an idiot if I got confused between my left and right. I could have learned the plays through muscle memory. But to be put on the spot? It was something I hadn't been willing to risk at fourteen.

I hadn't figured out what was wrong with me until my sophomore year of high school. My girlfriend, Samantha, mentioned her brother being dyslexic. When I inquired as to the symptoms, I found that he experienced a lot of the same things I did. I'd looked more into it and finally spoken with the school nurse. She quietly reached out to a teacher willing to tutor me, and with his help, I was able to control it well enough that I got into the military and got the fuck out of Texas the summer after I graduated.

For the first time in my life, I wasn't the kid from the wrong side of the tracks. I did well in the Marines, and Samantha and I planned to get married once my tour was up. Except, it hadn't quite worked out that way. About a year and a half in, I found out she was sneaking around with some other guy. When I confronted her, she blamed me for being gone despite the fact that we'd talked about it repeatedly. After Samantha's betrayal, I turned my focus solely on my work in the military. I had quick, easy hookups but never anything serious. I didn't need that shit in my life. I couldn't stand to be cheated on again, passed over for some other guy who worked an average nine-to-five.

The girl from the hotel came to mind. Those several hours I'd spent with Abilene had played on loop in my mind for the past forty-eight hours. I wasn't sure I'd ever enjoyed a woman so much. She was quirky as hell, definitely a little crazy, but it seriously turned me on.

The way she'd made me feel was dangerous in more ways than one. But maybe it was a sign. She'd stirred something inside me, when I'd thought my heart had no room inside for anything serious. Life growing up had been tumultuous to say the least. With my bipolar mother, we never knew which side of her we would get. My father was constantly on guard. It wasn't really a surprise, but it hurt like hell when she took her own life when Cole and I were twelve.

It seemed like all the women in my life left without a second thought. A woman like Abilene was long gone, and even if she came back through, all it could ever be was a short-lived affair. I wasn't the settling down type. Besides, she was obviously brilliant, and she deserved way better than me. I had a good job but a fuck ton of baggage. I'd never be able to give a woman like that what she needed.

Damn it. I cursed myself again for not getting her information before she left the hotel Saturday morning. But we'd both stuck to the original agreement. She never asked my name, and I hadn't offered it up. But maybe I could find her. There couldn't be too many women named Abilene, right? Even if she lived on the other side of the country, I could...

What? Ask her to consider a long-distance relationship based off one night? Jesus. I must be out of my mind. The sex was good—better than I'd ever had, if I was being entirely honest. But she'd given no indication of wanting more. I had no idea who the woman really was or where she lived. But that didn't stop me from wanting to reach out to her, no matter how crazy it sounded. Maybe she lived close by. Maybe she would—

A pen hit me in the chest, ripping me from my thoughts of the little brunette bombshell. "The fuck, dude?"

I winged the pen back across the table at Con, who hiked up a brow at me. "Nice of you to join us again."

"Sorry." I fought the urge to slouch down in my seat like a kid. "My mind was... somewhere else."

Con nodded. "Any news on Morrison?"

I shook my head. "I spent Friday night at the Hilton, got a few images of them together. Tom Morrison was at the bar for a while before she showed up. I wasn't able to follow them out of the bar."

I'd been too busy stripping Abilene out of her clothes to worry about that worthless cheating fuck.

"Have you gotten anything else so far?" Con asked.

"Caught him making out with the secretary in the parking lot of their building."

"Keep at it. I'll touch base with Mrs. Morrison and let her know. All right," Con continued, "let's break for lunch."

I dipped my head in acknowledgement, and my brother, Cole, leaned in. "Looks like Morrison's getting plenty of action. What about you?"

I fought the urge to react, the memory of the woman from the bar Saturday night flashing to the forefront of my mind. "Why?"

He shrugged. "You were in a hotel bar. Figured you'd have

picked up some chick in town for the night, shown her a good time."

I kept my face neutral as I nodded. "Maybe."

My hand automatically went to my shoulder, and I rubbed the spot where her teeth had left small crescent marks in the flesh. Just thinking of her made me hard.

"Come on," Cole needled as we stood and made our way to the door. "You're seriously gonna hold out on me? Was she that good?"

I bristled at the question. It had been that good; that was precisely why I was keeping my mouth shut. Even though she was probably thousands of miles away at this point, Abilene was mine and mine alone. I wanted to keep those memories locked up in my mind where I could play them back over and over.

My brother could read me like an open book and smell my lies from a mile away. I drew on all my acting skill, letting out a derisive laugh as he pushed open the door that opened into the lobby. "You know how it is. Cheap bar sluts are a dime a dozen. It's not exactly hard to pick them up when they're practically begging to suck your cock."

As soon as the words left my mouth, the hairs on the back of my arms and neck lifted. My head snapped toward the reception area at the front of the lobby, and my body went hot then cold as my gaze collided with a familiar pair of eyes.

Eyes that had stared into my own as I'd fucked her long and hard the other night in the hotel.

Eyes that were soulfully deep and dark—and full of fury.

CHAPTER SEVEN

Abby

Fuck him and the Harley he rode in on.

The asshole I'd hooked up with Friday night—and early Saturday morning—stood across the room, those intense golden eyes fixed on mine. It was no consolation that he looked just as shocked to see me as I was to see him. The motherfucker had called me a bar slut.

Anger simmered in my veins, and my fingers twitched to grab up the scissors in the top right drawer of my desk and cut off the manhood he was so proud of. I was really starting to commiserate with the blonde from the hotel bar. Apparently, everything she'd said was true. He was a prick who used women and discarded them like tissues. All of my thoughts and wishes from this morning dissipated like dust in the wind.

I broke our gaze and turned to Cole, who was currently draped over the counter. "Off to have fun?"

He winked. "Not as much fun as I'd have with you."

I'd first met Cole when he helped Con and me move my things into Violet's place. He flirted shamelessly, even knowing that there would never be anything between us. I started to roll my eyes, then thought better of it. I refused to let asshole over there know he'd hurt me. "What kinda trouble are you gettin' into today?"

"The usual." He turned and waved the new guy over. "Clay, come meet Abby."

I gritted my teeth as he approached but forced a smile to my lips and held out a hand like we'd never met before. "Nice to meet you."

His gaze narrowed as he took my hand in his, giving my fingers a little squeeze. I snatched them away. His face darkened further, but I dismissed it a moment later when Cole's words penetrated my fog of anger. "Abby, this is my brother, Clay."

His *brother*? What in the name of all things holy was happening right now? I stood there slack-jawed for a moment, my brain spinning. "Your brother?"

"Yep." He grinned. "I'm the good looking one, obviously."

"Obviously." My response was half-hearted as my gaze darted over Cole's shoulder to Clay, who looked damn near ready to kill. I couldn't freaking believe it. Cole had never once mentioned his brother's name, and besides—

"Wait." I snapped my gaze back to Cole. "I thought you said you were a twin."

"Yep. Fraternal," he added helpfully.

Oh, my God. Clay had told me he was a twin after the debacle in the bar. Never in a million years did I ever imagine that he was related to Cole Thompson. For whatever reason, I'd imagined an exact duplicate of him—not the man who continued to glower my way across the counter.

I tried desperately not to glare at Cole, because that information would have been super helpful a few days ago. I cleared my throat. "Awesome. Well, I should l let you guys get going."

"You're more than welcome to join us," Cole teased. "The more the merrier."

"I—" I jumped as my brother shoved another file into my hands, jerking me out of my stupor.

"Stop flirting with my guys."

I rolled my eyes. "No one's flirting." And I most certainly did not have an insanely hot one-night stand with the new guy.

"Good, cuz I'd have to kill them for putting hands on my baby sister."

My jaw dropped at his declaration. "Oh, my God, you're such an—"

"Clay, this is my sister, Abby," Con said, cutting off my tirade.

Clay dipped his head, his sharp golden eyes unreadable, mask firmly back in place. "We've met."

I glared at him, but it was short-lived as my brother continued. "You need any help getting settled, let her know. She'll be more than happy to help."

"I'll keep that in mind." His eyes never left mine, and I felt my pulse kick up. I needed to get the hell away from all of them before I lost my mind. My brother would probably kill Clay if he found out about our night at the hotel. He'd practically raised me and acted more like a parent than my big brother sometimes.

"Excuse me," I said, pushing past the three men currently crowding my space and being general nuisances. "I've got to take care of these."

I pulled my phone out of my pocket as I made my way to the back office where the files were kept, then pulled up Jamie's number. We'd been friends all through high school and had reconnected via Facebook when I told her I was moving back to Texas. She'd graduated from cosmetology school a couple of years ago and now had her own small salon on the west end of town.

"Hey, girl, what's up?" she asked when she picked up.

"I need an emergency session with you tonight if you're free."

"Sure. Stop by around seven?"

"You got it." I shoved the files into their places, then slammed the drawer.

I wasn't sure why every life change required women to do something drastic to their hair, but here I was. I was fucking tired of Con treating me like a little girl. I was tired of assholes like Clay telling me what to do. It was time for a change.

Three hours later, I sat in Jamie's kitchen, her shears at the ready. "Are you sure you want to do this?" she asked, her fingers sifting through my long locks. "You're not going to freak out afterward, right?"

"No way." I laughed. "The guys like it long, but this is for me. I want something shorter, more mature. Easy to take care of."

"Hmm..." Jamie circled me, looking at my face and rearranging my hair. She opened her phone and flipped to a picture of a woman with a sleek bob that barely brushed her shoulders and handed it to me. "Is this too short?"

"That's perfect," I said. "Let's get to it."

I watched as long locks of brown hair fell to the floor around me, and I waited anxiously for her to finish so I could see. Finally, she turned me around to face the huge mirror hanging on her wall. "What do you think?"

"Holy crap." It was short, but it felt so light and playful. "I love it!"

Longer in front and a little shorter in the back, the cut framed my face and made me look older. Now if only I could be a little wiser... No more hookups with alpha bodyguards, I promised myself as I studied my reflection.

I hugged Jamie, then headed to my car. Slowing for a red light, I glanced at my reflection in the rearview mirror and ran my fingers through my dramatically shorter locks. A bitter smile curved my face. Clay could eat his heart out, because I was done being that girl back at the hotel. He thought I was some cheap slut he could use and throw away like yesterday's trash. Driven by anger, I hadn't allowed them to come before, but tears now pricked my eyes. I refused to let another man make me feel like that ever again. I'd wanted him, and I'd gone after him. What was so wrong with that?

We'd both enjoyed the sex, so why was it okay for him to hook up with a stranger while I was considered a whore? Never mind the fact that Friday night was the first time I'd ever slept with a man I'd just met. It was a stupid mistake I would never make again, that was for sure.

Now I had to work with the asshole every day. I couldn't let him see that he'd affected me at all. Unfortunately, that was easier said than done. My heart clenched a little bit when I thought back to our time together. He was witty and smart, and hot as hell. I'd almost stupidly admitted to him that I actually lived in the area, but he was gone by the time I woke up.

I'd never asked him where he was from, assuming—probably the same as he had—that he was just visiting. It was a cruel twist of fate that I had to see him every day, with the memory of his touch haunting me.

The more distance I put between us, the better. Soon enough, whatever was between us would fade. In another few weeks, maybe a month, it would be like it'd never happened. He obviously wasn't interested in me, so I had nothing to worry about. I'd just avoid him until I had my feelings under control—maybe start seeing someone else.

Just the thought made me sick. Images of Clay in the hotel room, his lips on my neck, hands leaving fire in their wake as they traveled over my skin, assaulted me. I wasn't the type to just hook up with another guy to get my mind off Clay.

What I needed was a little bit of time, then maybe I'd find a nice guy to date. Someone who actually cared about me and didn't work with me. Someone who wouldn't make me cry.

CHAPTER EIGHT

Clay

My heart raced as I walked toward QSG headquarters, my feet eating up the sidewalk in my haste to get inside. Abby had ignored me for the rest of the afternoon yesterday, and I needed to talk with her—now.

I needed to clear the air, explain to her exactly what she'd heard. I'd felt a true connection with Abby, stronger than anything I'd ever felt with my ex. I regretted saying what I had. It was horrible of me and incredibly immature. Instead of being upfront with my brother, I'd played it off like it was no big deal. But it was a huge deal. Abby was a huge deal.

She'd swept into my life like a pint-sized hurricane, whisking my feet right out from under me. How the hell had she gotten so deeply under my skin when no one else had ever come close? Con was a good friend, and I felt like shit for doing this to him even if it hadn't been intentional.

Over the past twenty-four hours I'd thought of nothing but her. Now that we would be working together, I was faced with a really tough decision. Did I force myself to walk away, knowing how good things were between us? Or did I pursue her, try to change her initial impression of me and risk losing a friendship?

Con would be pissed, there was no question of that. I didn't even really know this woman, but damn... I couldn't walk away from her. Not now. I'd come up with a thousand ways to tell him

I'd hooked up with Abby. Most of them ended up with me either being knocked out or fired, neither of which was a good option. But I thought he deserved to know. Especially because I wanted more of Abby... A lot more.

I knew it was wrong to want her, but I couldn't find it in me to care. I'd tried to talk myself out of it—God knew I had—but I couldn't leave this thing between us unexplored. I'd never felt like this before, completely on the edge of reason and rational thought where nothing really mattered but her. No matter what happened between Con and me, I had to see this thing with Abby through.

I wasn't entirely sure when I'd come to that conclusion, I just had. It was a thought that had been simmering in the back of my brain since I left her cuddled up in bed Saturday morning, still warm and sated from our lovemaking. I'd wanted to get her number then; I should have. Now that I knew exactly who she was, it felt like everything was falling into place.

I stepped inside and scanned the lobby, disappointment coiling in my stomach when I found the room empty. Almost belatedly, my skin tingled with heat and a sense of intuition, and less than a second later the woman in question rounded the corner.

I started to step toward her, then froze. "Holy fucking hell."

Her gorgeous long hair had been shorn up to her shoulders. It showed off that defiant little chin of hers, those high, perfect cheek-bones and full, sexy lips. I thought she couldn't get more beautiful; I was wrong.

Something like challenge entered her eyes as she teased the fluttery ends of her hair with one hand. "Like it?"

Did I like it? Hell, no, I didn't like it. It exposed her elegant neck, that secret little spot no one knew about but me. Now every fucking guy within a hundred goddamn miles was going to want her. "What the hell did you do?"

She rolled her eyes as she continued behind the counter of the reception desk. "What difference does it make to you?"

Because she was fucking *mine*—she just didn't know it yet. I changed the subject. "Why did you lie to me at the hotel?"

Her mouth dropped open in a combination of shock and indignation. "I never lied!"

"You said you were there for one night," I retorted as I leaned across the counter, never taking my gaze from hers. "That kind of implies you're not from around here."

Something like regret flashed across her features, and her eyes dropped to the desk in front of her as she busied herself with the papers strewn across the top. "Not my fault you misread it."

Inwardly I seethed. She'd omitted the truth and I was still fucking pissed about that. "You also told me your name was Abilene."

"It is."

Would it have made a difference if she told me her name was Abby? Probably not. I should have pressed and asked for her last name, but never in my wildest dreams had I ever imagined she'd be the baby sister of one of my closest friends. I'd heard about her over the years when Con spoke about her, but the image I remembered was that of a teen, a young girl who bore little resemblance to the woman Abby was today.

"Anything else you didn't tell me?"

She threw a dark look my way. "Such as?"

I had to fucking know. "And what about my brother?"

Those pretty dark eyes bore into mine, filled with curiosity and wariness. "What about him?"

"You're too smart to play dumb, Abilene." She glared at me, and I fought the urge to round the desk and crowd her more. "There something going on with the two of you?"

She tipped her chin up, effectively looking down her nose at me. "And what if there is? What the hell would it matter to you?"

Every cell in my body flashed hot and cold with pure rage. "Because I'm not about to share a woman with my brother."

"I'm not yours—or anyone else's—to share." I could practically feel the anger vibrating off her tiny body from where I stood. "And you sure as hell don't get to tell me what to do."

Goddamn, the woman just had a way of getting under my skin and riling me. She just fucking loved to contradict me, do the exact opposite of what I told her. She would push and push until—

Suddenly, something clicked in the back of my brain as I recalled our night together. "Your hair."

She tossed her head and propped one hand on her hip as she speared with me another exasperated look. "What about it?"

Had she cut her hair because I told her how much I loved it long—because I'd forbidden her to ever cut it? "You cut it because of me, because of what I said."

She inhaled sharply, her eyes widening slightly. A second later she blinked, her *I don't give a shit what you think* façade firmly back in place. "Wow. Conceited much?" She let out a very unladylike little snort. "I wanted to cut my hair, so I did. That's all there is to it."

Yeah, right. I had to fight the smile that tugged at my mouth. My comment from Friday night, coupled with my asinine remark yesterday, had pushed her buttons. I had every intention of apologizing for the latter, but I reveled in the knowledge that I'd affected her on such a deep level. "You look beautiful."

She jerked back as if I'd slapped her, her expression confused. "Oh. I... thank you."

"You're welcome." And now it was time to eat shit. "Listen, I need to talk to you about what you overheard yesterday. It—"

She lifted one shoulder. "Doesn't make a difference to me."

"It does," I insisted. I needed to make her understand I hadn't meant it. "It was a stupid thing to say, and I'm sorry."

She cocked a brow as she peered up at me. "Then why'd you say it?"

I let out a growl of frustration. "Because I'm a fucking idiot. Because my brother was jumping my ass about dating, and—"

"Sure." She rolled her eyes. "Blame it on him instead of taking responsibility. Classic."

"That's not... Jesus, never mind." I raked one hand through my hair. "I want to apologize. We work together, Abilene. We—"

"We what?" Her dark eyes blazed with molten anger, but she lowered her voice to barely a hiss. "We hooked up? Yeah, we did. It happened, and now it's over. I have no intention of repeating it, so you can shelve your guilt or"—she waved one hand in my direction—"whatever it is you're feeling."

I blinked, blindsided by her vehement response. I knew I'd hurt her, but she seemed absolutely adamant that it never happen again. But what if that wasn't what I wanted? I opened my mouth to speak, but I didn't get a chance.

"No one can ever know about that night at the hotel. *Ever.*"

Harsh, but I got it. Her eyes implored me to agree, and something settled heavily in my gut. I nodded at her statement, but that didn't mean I agreed—far from it. "I understand where you're coming from."

She nodded a little and straightened, sweeping one hand over her hair. "Okay. Good. Thank you."

"You're welcome." But she didn't move, and neither did I. For several seconds, we stared at each other, caught in our momentary truce. I knew she felt the same attraction I did, but she refused to acknowledge it. Because of my stupid statement, or was it something else?

Con's voice broke the moment. "Abby, where's that file on Mickelson?"

She threw one last glare my way before snatching up a manila file folder. "Coming."

"You said that the other night, too." I kept my voice low so only she could hear it, and her head snapped my way, her cheeks flaring bright pink, dark eyes snapping with fire.

"Fuck you."

I grinned, thoroughly enjoying the rise I'd gotten out of her. "Looking forward to it, princess."

CHAPTER NINE

Abby

The figure leaned forward, and his smell filled my nostrils. It was a combination of smoke and something faintly sweet, and it made my stomach churn.

"You sure you didn't take my money, Abilene?"

His features remained obscured, blurry but somehow still familiar. I shook my head, fear and something else rising up in my throat, stealing my words as a second hand landed on my other knee.

"It's okay if you did. Really. I need you to tell me the truth. Good girls tell the truth, Abilene."

I shook my head. "I didn't take it."

"I think you're lying to me, Abilene." The huge hands felt heavy on my thighs as they slid upward, sending my heart into my throat. "Now, what are we going to do about that?"

I bolted upright in bed, cold sweat facing my body. Heart still racing, I drew in several deep breaths and tried to bring my body back under control. What the hell was it with these crazy dreams? For the past few weeks, they had plagued me incessantly. It was the same thing over and over—a strange, faceless man who would approach me in the middle of the night. I could still feel his clammy, fleshy palms on my skin, and I rubbed briskly at the blanket covering my thighs to dispel the sensation.

I felt sick to my stomach, unable to fathom why my mind conjured these images night after night. And it felt so *real*. What the hell was wrong with me? I grabbed up my phone where it was charging on the nightstand, and the numbers on the home screen read that it was a little after 3:00 AM. I wouldn't be able to go back to sleep. Not yet. I was always too shaken after these episodes to rest easy.

Instead, I slipped from the bed and headed out to the kitchen. On nights like these, I desperately wished I wasn't alone. At almost twenty-four, it was more than a little ridiculous of me. I'd spent several years up north in college all alone. I didn't need a man around. But sometimes, even I had to admit that it might be nice. Nearly two years had passed since my last serious relationship ended. I'd met Brandon while attending college and had immediately fallen for him. But after almost three years together, things began to fizzle out. He wanted to settle down, take me home to meet his family. I wasn't ready for that. Not that it wouldn't be nice... someday. But then, at twenty-one, marriage and kids weren't in my immediate future. I'd had dreams of doing something big with my life. I hadn't worked out all the details, but I knew I wanted more than what I grew up with.

Like I had told Clay at the hotel, my childhood had been spent mostly in a state of upheaval. My mother worked whatever odd jobs she could find, typically cleaning houses or waitressing. My father moved around as a migrant worker, following the harvest. Sometimes it was citrus, other times avocado. But he traveled all over the south, working whenever we needed money. When he moved around, my mother typically followed. That left my brother and me alone sometimes for months at a time.

And when my parents weren't working, they were partying. They loved the music scene, reveled in the drink and drugs it offered. It was as if my parents had never really grown up, only gotten older as the years passed. They focused on having fun, seeming to forget that they had two children at home. When I was eight, two officers showed up at the house one evening to inform us that our parents had perished in a car accident. I don't even remember crying for them. I didn't know them well enough to feel any kind of deep emotion that they were gone. If Con felt differently, he never showed it. He told the officers we had relatives who would step up and take care of us. It was a blatant lie. My mother's family had disowned her when she married my father, and I'd never met my paternal grandparents or any of his family.

Con had been more a father to me than a brother. I owed him for taking care of me at seventeen when he should have been out with his friends having fun. Instead, he'd been raising a nine-year-old girl. He'd never once complained, and we made it through several months together before the authorities threatened to remove me from his care.

The summer he turned eighteen, Con enlisted in the Marines and found me a home with Violet, a friend of my maternal grandparents. My mother's parents had cut her off when she married my father, and his parents were God knew where. In the end, we'd had little choice in the matter. Though my maternal grandparents were still alive, they had neither the ability nor the desire to take in a nine-year-old girl. Instead, they'd reached out to Violet, who had welcomed me in with open arms and treated me like her very own.

Violet had seen her fair share of grief. Her own daughter, Lily, had committed suicide at just sixteen, just a couple years before I was born. A few months after I moved in with her, she'd insisted I speak with a child psychologist. I'd thought it silly at the time but, looking back, I was certain she didn't want a repeat of what had happened with Lily. Losing one's parents was bound to do some emotional damage, but as I'd told Dr. Vance then, I was mostly just relieved to finally be in a home with someone who cared for me and was present all the time. I'd spoken with another doctor as well, but both had apparently told Violet that I was resilient and well-adjusted.

Though she was still overprotective, she began to relax her guard a bit as time went on. Still, she mourned her daughter deeply. There was a row of lilies planted along the fence in the back yard that commemorated her life, and Violet had tended them diligently, almost as if they were a living extension of the real Lily. I felt like it was my responsibility to take care of the house Violet had loved so much.

It had never been my plan to stay in Dallas, even though it was home. I'd gone to school for computer science, and I'd always wanted to move out west where technology reined and make a name for myself. But when Con had offered me a job with QSG I hadn't been able to say no.

Honestly, I wasn't sure what I wanted to do. I vacillated daily between staying in Dallas or staging the house and putting it on the market. A slice of pain zinged through my chest, compounding my guilt. Violet had willed me the house, and it felt wrong somehow to sell it when it seemed to mean so much to her that I stay here. I felt like I owed both her and my brother for all they'd done for me over the years.

I flipped on the light to the kitchen and looked around the room. It was still so similar to the place where I'd grown up, yet different now too. After the fire last week, the recovery team had scrubbed the entire room and now the smell of industrial cleaning agents hung in the air. The kitchen looked bare without the cabinets, and I rubbed the little space over my heart as a pang of hurt ricocheted through my chest.

I still couldn't believe I hadn't seen the signs of Violet's rapid downward spiral. Were they there and I had just ignored them? I didn't want to believe that was the case. Either way, the damage was done and Violet was safe in the assisted living facility. I planned to visit Morningside before heading into work in the morning. I wanted to make sure that Violet was settling in okay. After everything that had happened, even though it was her choice to go, I still felt responsible for her wellbeing.

I moved toward the refrigerator, the one thing in the room that hadn't been damaged by the fire, and pulled out the pitcher of sweet tea. I carried it into the adjacent dining room and poured myself a glass of the sweet liquid. It was exactly the way Violet had made it, and the reminder of my childhood brought tears to my eyes.

I pulled out a chair and sat, staring at the glass of brown liquid in front of me. I couldn't stem the guilt I felt rising up like a tide inside me. The only reprieve I'd had recently was the night at the hotel. With *him*. Asshole. Every muscle in my body went tight as I pulled the memory into focus. It had been... incredible. I could still remember with startling clarity the feel of Clay's hands on me.

I couldn't quite reconcile what had happened the other morning, and I'd spent the past several days ignoring him as much as humanly possible. He had seemed truly apologetic, and a huge part of me felt bad for shooting him down. On the heels of that came the immediate self-recrimination. I couldn't begin to understand Clay's obsession with me, or why he wouldn't let it go. He hadn't even kissed me, for Christ's sake. He hadn't wanted anything serious a week ago. Why would it be different now? Just because we worked together didn't mean anything. I was going to put my time with him behind me and move on. But I was sure the memory of that night would stay burned on my brain for a long time to come.

I smiled as the words from one of my friends came to mind. *The best way to get over a man is to get under a new one.* It wasn't my typical way of getting over a breakup—that usually involved P.F. Chang's and ice cream. But in Clay's case, maybe it was for the best. For some reason, he had affected me on an unreasonably deep level, and I needed to exorcise him from my brain. At least going on a date might help. God, I needed to do anything other than sitting around at three in the morning, wallowing in guilt and self-pity, thinking of him.

Feeling not a whole hell of a lot better about myself, but at least no longer unsettled from my dream, I put the sweet tea away, then headed back to bed to get a few more hours of sleep before I went to visit Violet.

My alarm jangled at seven o'clock, tearing me from an exhausted, disturbed slumber. Though I'd been able to fall back to sleep, I hadn't rested well. With a sigh, I turned off the alarm and sank back into the cushions. I was tempted to just close my eyes but I knew if I did, I would fall back to sleep and not resurface until noon. Forcing my muscles to move, I slid from the bed and practically fell into the shower. An hour later, clean and slightly refreshed, I pulled into Morningside and steered the car toward the left side of the lot. Violet's favorite place was the garden, and I had a feeling that, even this early in the day, I could find her there.

After signing in at the desk I made my way through the sunny garden, trailing my fingers over the lush spring flowers blooming brightly in the flowerbeds scattered across the property. The nurse at the desk confirmed that Violet had gone outside to enjoy the weather, and I knew I would find her by the fountain. Although I constantly worried about her, the nurses here were better equipped to help her, and they assured me that Violet had already made several friends.

Leaving the brick pathway, I cut across the yard, a smile lifting my mouth as I saw her seated on a bench scattering feed for the birds. Her head lifted, and a huge smile split her face as I approached. My heart swelled. Today was a good day. Thank God.

Violet welcomed me with a warm hug, and I couldn't help the grin that covered my face. These moments of lucidity were becoming more and more rare, and I felt incredibly fortunate that I was lucky enough to get a few more precious moments with her. The minutes quickly ticked away as we reminisced, and I realized with regret that I was already running late. Con had been extremely lenient with me, allowing me to make up my own hours. I hated to leave him hanging though, especially with everything he had going on.

"I have to get to work, but I'll stop back in a few days."

Violet smiled. "Of course, dear. I have plenty of things to keep me occupied. You go enjoy yourself."

I hugged her goodbye and headed toward the parking lot. I climbed into my car and headed to QSG headquarters. The whole way, Clay's face tortured me. I'd avoided him as much as possible for the past few days, but he was always hovering close by, his eyes locked on me. I could literally feel his gaze on me. What the hell was I going to do about him?

It still boggled my mind, seeing Clay and Cole side by side. They were so different yet so very much the same. They both had the same cocky tilt to their head, the same sexy dimples. But that was where the similarities ended. While Cole's features were slightly darker, Clay's were a stark contrast with his light brown hair and hawk-like golden eyes. Cole was constantly smiling and flirting. Clay's face was always set in a harsh line, a cloak of stoicism resting on his expression.

God, the man was infuriating. Why, then, couldn't I get him off my mind? I knew the reason, of course. He'd stirred feelings deep inside, made me feel something no one else ever had. The way I'd felt in his arms was... indescribable. The sex between us had been passionate, explosive, intense. The way he'd spoken about me, as if I meant nothing...

Tears burned the backs of my eyes. It hurt, damn it. I hadn't dwelled on it, instead focusing on ignoring him and keeping my chin held high. Now, though, the emotions that had taken root curled upward, and a tear slipped free.

He was an egotistical prick. He'd used me just as he'd used the woman at the bar that night. I'd willingly gone along with it, so I had no one to blame but myself. I knew the angry tears were irrational, but I couldn't help them as they fell one after the other. I wanted a connection like that with someone—someone who would actually care about me. Not someone who would casually toss me aside once he'd gotten what he wanted.

Now I was stuck seeing him every single day at work, a constant reminder of what we'd shared and how he made me feel. I needed to find a way to get over him, and fast, before I did something stupid like cave and give in to him again.

CHAPTER TEN

Clay

Cole fixed his attention on Abby as she extended a file to him. "Thanks, beautiful." He winked at her, and she slapped his upper arm with the manila folder she held.

"That shit won't work with me." She gave a little shake of her head, then turned to Xander as she passed an identical folder his way. But my brother didn't let up.

"When you gonna let me take you out, Abs?"

She bared her teeth in a wicked smile. "You gonna make it worth my while?"

I scowled at their banter filled with sexual inuendo. "Always do."

"Knock that shit off," I barked. Jesus Christ. He might be my own flesh and blood, but I wouldn't fucking hesitate to kill him if he ever laid a hand on Abby. Unless she wanted it. Had she been lying to me the other day when she told me there was nothing between them? My knee jumped beneath the table as my hand curled into a fist to keep from dragging him from his chair and beating the truth out of him.

I could feel half a dozen pairs of eyes on me, but I studiously ignored them as I flipped open the file. It was hard to focus, and I listened with half an ear as Con outlined the plan for this week's assignment. Xander and I had been charged with staking out an antiquities shop suspected of fencing high-end items and auctioning them online. In addition to the recon there, I was responsible for an upcoming qualifications class for those who wanted to get their CCW.

I was acutely aware of the moment Abby slipped from the room. I waited for an interminably long time before I finally excused myself, unable to wait another second. I bolted from the conference room after making an excuse to Xander that I was going to go do some research. Instead of heading to my cubicle in the bullpen, though, I turned toward the lobby. Empty. I held back a growl of frustration and headed toward the file room instead.

I could hear her moving around inside before I even reached the doorway, and a strange sensation filled my chest as I stepped inside. Her back was to me, and I spent a few seconds watching her move quickly and efficiently as she organized the folders in the drawer.

Silently I moved up behind Abby, pinning her between me and the filing cabinet. "You fucking love to torture me, don't you?"

Abby jumped a little at my low growl, her shoulders snapping straight. "I don't know what you're talking about."

"No?" I pressed closer, placing a hand on either side of her, caging her between the filing cabinet and my body. I felt the heat rolling off of her in waves, and her body trembled—with rage or anticipation, I wasn't sure. "You keep flirting with my brother. Why is that?"

"I don't flirt," she said breathlessly.

I snorted. "I beg to differ, and I think you know exactly what the hell you're doing. The question is why?"

She lifted one shoulder, and her hair tickled my chin under the movement. "Not my problem you're reading too much into it."

"So, you're not doing it to spite me?" I asked, leaning in close. My lips were bare millimeters from the shell of her ear, and her sweet scent wafted up to me, like sunshine and flowers, a balm to my soul. Christ, what the hell was this woman doing to me?

"Why would I do that?"

"Because you like getting a rise out of me. Because you know you want me as much as I want you. Because you love to see me all fucking worked up over you."

"I admit nothing."

I could practically hear the smirk in her voice, and I leaned closer so I was pressed against her from thigh to chest. I slipped my knee between her legs, forcing them further apart as I nipped her ear. She let out a soft squeak and shuddered, and my body vibrated under the force of it. I settled my hands on her hips and curled my fingers into her flesh. "Admit it. You love torturing me."

"I—"

Whatever she was about to say was immediately cut off as I traced the shell of her ear with my tongue. She let out a little sigh, and I couldn't help but smile. She was so responsive, so fucking sweet.

"Have I told you recently how much that sexy new haircut of yours turns me on?"

She stiffened, her entire body going rigid. "I thought you liked my hair long," she challenged.

"I did. You looked gorgeous then, too. But this..." I settled one hand at the base of her neck, then slid it upward into the silky soft strands. "It's sassy. Sophisticated. It suits you. Plus..." I dipped my head so my mouth hovered near the base of her neck. "I love easy access."

"Easy access—?"

Comprehension dawned a second too late, and her knees buckled as I bit down in that little spot that turned her on so much. She melted into me, seeming to have momentarily lost the ability to control her muscles. I clutched her close, loving the way she fit against me.

All too soon she recovered, forcing her legs to cooperate as she straightened. She arched her hips forward in a vain attempt to put distance between her body and mine. "That's cheating."

"I beg to differ. I found the spot..." I allowed my teeth to graze over the sensitive skin once more as I pulled her back to me again. "Now it's mine."

"*Yours*? I'm sorry—"

"You should be." I cut her off, lightly massaging her scalp, and a tiny tremor racked her body. "Did you really think that cutting your hair was going to turn me off?"

She licked her lips before she answered. "It was worth a try."

I chuckled at her stubborn response. She felt this as much as I did; I knew she did. "Do you really want me to go away, Abilene?"

Her lids closed as I continued to knead my fingers into the base of her skull. "That would probably be for the best."

Had there been any conviction in her voice, I would've let her go. But her words were low and breathy, and her muscles relaxed as she pushed her head against my hand like a kitten seeking to be petted. I curled one hand into her hip and pulled her into me so my mouth was next to her ear. "Better for you, maybe. Why are you fighting this? You know you want it as much as I do."

Her head brushed my chin as it shook back and forth. "You had your chance. One time."

Once would never be enough. This thing between us was real. Intense. It was never just a fling. "That won't work for me. I want a hell of a lot more."

From my vantage point, I watched her throat ripple as she swallowed hard. "I... I can't."

"You can," I encouraged. My lips traveled over the shell of her ear before I kissed my way along her jaw and down her throat. Sliding my hand from her hip around to her belly, I pulled her fully against me. She inhaled sharply as I lightly bit down on her neck, and her hands flew to the arm I'd wrapped around her. Instead of pushing me away, her fingers curled into my skin, holding me close. I nipped the same spot a second time, then licked her skin to soothe away the sting.

"Come on, Abilene." My lips brushed her throat as I spoke, her heady scent filling my nostrils. "Let me prove it to you. Give me another chance."

Her fingers curled into my arm, and her lips parted slightly. Her resistance was wavering, I could feel it. "I—"

"Abby?"

At the sound of her name being called, Abby ripped herself from my arms with a gasp, eyes flying open wide. My jaw clenched, and I could practically hear her heart racing from where she now stood several feet away. I fished a folder out of the cabinet just as Con stepped through the doorway.

His gaze bounced between us before moving back to Abby. "You good?"

She nodded shakily. "Fine."

Con looked suspicious as hell, so I spoke up before he could question it further. "I came in to file this and scared her."

Con flicked a look at Abby, who nodded, looking grateful for the excuse. "Yeah. Sorry, he just startled me."

Con nodded. "He's a sneaky fuck. Hey, can you confirm with Mrs. Howenstein?"

"Sure." She smiled. "I'll take care of it."

"Thanks." He rapped twice on the door jamb, then disappeared.

We remained frozen in silence until his footsteps had receded down the hallway. Then I turned to her. She looked shaken, abnormally pale, something akin to humiliation or regret etched deeply into her features. I needed her to look at me. I needed her to know that what we'd done—what we were doing—was okay. "Abilene."

Avoiding my gaze, she backed toward the door, already shaking her head, her eyes full of apprehension.

Goddamn it. "Abby..."

She held up one hand in my direction as if to ward me off, then fled from the room. I watched her go, mentally cursing Con and his shit timing. I'd been so close to convincing her to give me a second shot, and his intrusion may have spooked her for good. I'd be damned if I would give up, though. I wasn't going to let her go without a fight.

CHAPTER ELEVEN

Abby

Fool me once, shame on you. Fool me twice, shame on me.

Heat climbed into my cheeks as the old adage sprang to mind. I couldn't freaking believe I'd almost fallen into the same trap. But the second Clay got near, I swear my hormones went into overdrive and shut down my brain function. I didn't want to still want him— but I did. And he knew it, damn it.

Inwardly I seethed as I stomped toward the grocery store. Why the hell couldn't he just take a hint and leave me the hell alone?

Is that what you really want? a little voice at the back of my brain asked. *Do you really want him to leave you alone? You could give him another chance, see where it goes...*

I mentally batted away the suggestion. No, damn it. He didn't deserve a second chance, no matter how tempted I was to give in. I had to admit, he'd apologized several times and he seemed determined to work his way back into my good graces.

Why?

It was the one thing that had been bothering me for nearly the past week. Why was he doing all this? He claimed to have said what he did in an attempt to keep Cole out of his business. Part of me could understand that. The other part of me was still too furious to acknowledge his attempts to reassure me.

I let out a little growl of frustration as the automatic doors whooshed open and a blast of icy air conditioning hit my skin.

Damn, damn, damn. Thank God it was Friday and I had the next two days to myself where I wouldn't have to see him. I was going to forget all about Clay Thompson—starting right now.

Grabbing a cart, I steered it into the store toward the produce section. Admittedly, I was pretty excited that I had a real kitchen of my own now. The cabinets had been replaced and everything was now back in order. For the past few years I'd lived mostly off of cafeteria food, coffee, and microwave dinners, so I looked forward to grocery shopping now with no small amount of enthusiasm. It sounded ridiculous, but it was a kind of initiation into adulthood for me.

Violet had cooked every night during my teenage years, and I missed those homemade meals. I wasn't about to delude myself into thinking that my food would be anywhere near as good as hers, but I was willing to try. I grabbed up some veggies I knew I could cook—carrots, potatoes, peppers—and tossed them into the cart, then moved toward the fruits.

I'd come into the store with no real plan, so I was just winging it, buying whatever looked or sounded good. At home, I would finally pull out some of Vi's old cookbooks and recipe cards. Mentally, I ticked off everything I wanted to try. Chicken alfredo, meatloaf, lasagna. I was so lost in thought that I didn't notice the man right in front of me. I jolted in surprise as my cart slammed into his. "Oh, God, I'm so sorry!"

His surprise melted away as he did a kind of double-take. "Oh, hey. Hi."

"Hi." He had pretty, bright blue eyes that bored into mine, and I shifted a little under the intense scrutiny. "Sorry again, I wasn't watching where I was going."

He smiled. "No harm done."

I started to move away, pleasantly surprised when I tossed a quick look over my shoulder and caught him watching me. I turned back, fighting a smile. He was handsome in an All-American kind of way, with short, dirty blonde hair and straight, beautiful white teeth. Though on the shorter side, he was still taller than me, and definitely not bad to look at. Why, then, didn't I feel a spark? Another man's face popped into my head, pushing away the image of the stranger. Damn Clay for ruining everything. I shook my head, intent on leaving him in the past where he belonged.

Refocusing on my shopping list, I headed deeper into the store to grab pasta and bread. As I wound my way around an endcap, I was brought up short again by someone coming right at me—the same man from earlier.

I let out a little laugh, and he gave an incredulous shake of his head. "We've got to stop meeting like this."

I grinned back. "Maybe we should suggest mirrors like they have in high-traffic areas."

He chuckled. "I guess so. I'm just going to..." He pointed down the aisle, a smile on his face, and I returned it.

"Proceed with caution."

My last stop was the dairy and frozen foods section, because, hey, every girl needed to keep a quart of ice cream on hand. I perused the cartons of Ben and Jerry's, then finally selected a flavor I hadn't tried before. As soon as the glass door swung closed, I became aware of someone right behind me. The man was bent over, sifting through the frozen pizzas, but there was no mistaking who it was. Turning, I placed the ice cream in the cart, then crossed my arms over my chest and quirked a brow at the guy.

His eyes widened as he straightened. "Third time's a charm, right?" He grinned sheepishly and held out a hand. "I guess at this point, I should introduce myself. I'm Trevor."

Trying to suppress my smile, I took his hand and shook. "Abby."

"Nice to meet you."

"So, are you stalking me or just incredibly unlucky to keep running into me?" I teased.

A faint blush spread over his cheeks. "I wouldn't exactly call it unlucky..."

My smile grew. "So just a stalker, then?"

He opened his mouth, then snapped it shut. After a second, he finally spoke. "I don't think anything I could say at this point would help my case."

I laughed, enjoying our banter. "Probably not. But if it's any consolation, this has definitely been an improvement to my afternoon."

"In that case, I'm glad I could help." He paused for a long moment, his sea-blue eyes darting away before meeting mine again. "So, I know this is a little... sudden." He cleared his throat. "But if you're free next weekend, my Saturday is wide open."

I thought it over for a second, taking in his tense posture, his discomfort. I could tell he wasn't the kind of person who picked up random women. Unlike someone else I knew...

The more distance I put between Clay and myself the better. Although I didn't feel a spark with Trevor yet, maybe that would come in time. I decided to go for it. "That sounds great."

His eyes snapped wide. "Really?"

I laughed. "Sure. Why not?"

"Awesome. I'll text you next week."

We swapped numbers, and I found myself smiling as I moved toward the front of the store. He seemed nice enough at least, if a little on the shy side. That was a point in Trevor's favor. Between my brother and the guys at QSG, I was around alpha males all day long. I hoped he was different, that he was as studious and sweet as he seemed. Definitely nothing like Clay.

But at the memory of our night at the hotel, his dominant personality taking control, had my cheeks burning. I couldn't deny that I'd enjoyed it, but he was most certainly not the guy for me. I was ready to let sleeping dogs lie and move on. And going out with Trevor would be the first step forward in putting Clay behind me once and for all.

CHAPTER TWELVE

Clay

I adjusted my shades as I watched Abby push the cart out the front doors and approach her car. She popped the trunk and started to load the groceries without so much as glancing around, and I let out a little growl as I pushed off the fender of my truck and strode toward her.

She still hadn't noticed my presence by the time I was two feet away from her, and I settled my hands on her hips. She let out a stifled shriek as she spun toward me, her eyes wide. The surprise leeched away, turning to recognition then anger as she stared up at me.

"Damn it, Clay!" She punched my chest, but the effect was minimized because she stood too close to put any oomph behind it. "What the hell are you doing sneaking up on me like that?"

I glared at her. "Do you not pay attention to a damn thing, woman? You've gotta watch your surroundings."

"Thanks, Captain Asshole," she shot back. "I'll keep that in mind next time someone tries to kidnap me."

"As much as you like to think you are, you're not invincible, Abby." I scowled. "You're a tiny little thing."

"To you, maybe," she snapped.

"Doesn't matter," I continued, undaunted. "You know how easy it would have been for me to knock you out and toss your ass in the trunk? You'd have been long gone before anyone realized what happened."

She rolled her eyes. "I can take care of myself."

"Obviously. One of these days you're going to invite the wrong kind of trouble," I warned.

She smiled sweetly, a cutting look in her eyes as she stared up at me. "Kind of like inviting strange men to my hotel room?"

"That was different," I cut in. "Thank God it was me and not someone else."

She let out a little laugh that held zero humor. "Oh, yes. That was such a relief."

Her tone was full of sarcasm, and I stiffened. "Goddamn it, Abby, how many times do I have to apologize? I didn't mean it the way it sounded."

"You only apologized because you got caught," she retorted. "Besides, it doesn't matter. It was a mistake, and one I have no intention of ever repeating."

This had devolved way more quickly than I intended, and she was out of her damn mind if she thought we were just going to go on our merry way. Hell no. I'd been rattled since that night, and I felt like I needed another go with her to set my world right. "Damn it, Abby, I—"

"See you around, Clay." She slammed the trunk, then shoved the cart in my direction, and I deftly rounded it and reached for her just as she grabbed the door handle.

"Would you stop?" I hissed. "We still have to work together, at least."

Although I wanted a hell of a lot more from her than to just be her coworker. I knew she'd felt the same connection between us that I had. I wasn't sure exactly what the hell I planned to do about it, but I knew I wanted more of her. Abby's taste had haunted me for the past six days, and I swore I could feel the silky smoothness of her skin every time I closed my eyes. This morning in the file room, surrounded by her intoxicating smell, able to taste her again, I felt more at ease than I had since I'd stupidly walked out of that hotel room.

"So?"

"What do you mean, so?" I fought the urge to shake her.

"You're my friend's little sister. I don't want to see you get hurt."

If anything, her expression darkened further. "In case you missed it, I'm an adult. I'm more than just Con's sister, more than some easy hotel lay."

Christ Almighty. This woman pushed every single button I had. "That's not—"

"Whatever, Clay."

"Fucking stop already." My tone was harder than I intended, and Abby whirled toward me, fire in her eyes.

"Did you have an aneurysm? I don't know what your problem is or why the hell you're doing this, but I said no. We had one night together. Leave it at that and move on, just like I have."

She didn't wait for my reply, just slid inside and slammed the door, locking it before I had a chance to maneuver in between. "Damn it, Abby, I swear to God..."

My words were drowned out by the sound of the engine turning over, and I smacked one hand on the window. "Abilene..."

She didn't so much as glance at me as she flicked a glance in the rearview mirror to ensure the cart was out of her way before putting it in gear and started backing up. I stepped back to avoid having my foot run over, cursing her all the while. Damn stubborn woman wouldn't give me two fucking seconds to explain.

Explain what, I still wasn't sure. Every time I rehearsed the conversation in my head, it got more and more muddled. What the hell could I even say to make her understand? One throwaway comment had turned her completely against me, so much that she wasn't willing to listen at all. I knew I was wrong; I'd regretted the words as soon as they left my mouth.

Stupidly, I'd made things worse the following day by accusing her of lying to me. She threw me completely off balance, instilled a simmering need every time I found myself in the same room with her. I still wasn't sure why she'd told me she was only in town for one night. Maybe it was her way of staying detached from a man she thought she'd never see again. That I could understand.

But we had seen each other again. We worked together, and we were going to have to come to some term of agreement. She seemed dead set against me, and it made me see red. She'd avoided me like the plague for the past three-and-a-half days, and it only made me want her more. Goddamn, I was a glutton for punishment. But that only solidified my resolve.

Come hell or high water, Abilene Quentin was going to be mine.

CHAPTER THIRTEEN

Abby

Men. I slammed the cupboard door with a growl of frustration. Where the hell did Clay get off thinking he could boss me around like that? Asshole. Although those dominant tendencies had been appealing as hell in the bedroom, the real-life application was less than desirable. I was so damn tired of being under men's thumbs. I was a grown ass woman, and it was damn time they started treating me like it.

In times like these, there were only two men I could count on. Snatching up the carton of Ben and Jerry's, I pulled a clean spoon from the dishrack and stabbed it into the creamy mixture. I settled on the couch and flipped on the TV, content to zone out to some mindless show for a bit until bedtime.

I had a list of shit to do tomorrow, not the least of which was to get the house back in order and clean it from top to bottom. The workers had cleaned the vents and it smelled immeasurably better, but I needed to wash all of the walls to see if the saturated smoke smell came out.

A slamming sound from outside had me jumping practically a foot off the couch and almost spilling my ice cream. Disaster narrowly averted, I set the carton on the coffee table and pushed off, then made my way to the window to peek into the back yard.

I laughed at myself when I saw the door to the shed in the corner of the yard swinging wildly in the wind, the latch clanging loudly each time it slammed against the clasp. I thought I'd closed it up last time I was out there, which was... I couldn't quite remember. Two days ago, maybe? I'd been so busy cleaning inside that I hadn't paid much attention to the flowers. I knew Violet would be disappointed. I would have to dedicate some time to pruning them this weekend.

Grabbing up the ice cream, I detoured into the kitchen and stowed it in the freezer before making my way out the back door onto the small deck. Curving my arms around my waist to guard against the cool wind, I hopped down the stairs then cut across the lawn toward the shed. The wind had picked up since I got home, bringing with it a storm of epic proportions. The sky had already darkened far beyond what it normally looked like at this time of night, and I hurried to lock up the shed before the rain came.

Violet's late husband had used the small shed as a workshop when he was alive. He'd enjoyed tinkering around with electronics and small engines, and the space was still cluttered with paraphernalia lining the shelves and floor. As I approached, I noticed a small, flat disc-shaped object sitting on the counter.

Even though the light was dim, I recognized it immediately. Harris had purchased the small garden plaque for Violet on the twentieth anniversary of Lily's death. I traced the flowers on the stone, sliding my fingers over the quote she'd loved so much. Now a huge crack split the stone right down the middle.

I wasn't sure how long it'd been damaged, but Violet obviously hadn't gotten around to fixing it, or she'd forgotten all about it. Sympathy seized my heart. It was faded with time, but it held a sentimentality that couldn't be replaced. I tucked the two halves under my arm, making a mental note to buy some industrial strength glue next time I was at the store.

Stepping outside, I closed and locked the shed before returning to the house. As I reached the back deck, the first drops of rain fell from the sky, splattering over my cheeks and forehead. I dodged them deftly, making it inside just as the sky opened up and poured downward.

I'd just returned to the kitchen when the doorbell rang. I peeked out the window over the sink, but I couldn't see to the front of the house. I cut through the living room, depositing the plaque on the coffee table before making my way to the front door. I peered through the peephole, and my heart jumped in my chest when I saw Patrick standing on the walkway. Rain was slanting sideways in sheets, thrown around by gusts of wind, and I bit my lip. No matter what had happened Monday, I couldn't let him stand out there and get soaked.

I reluctantly opened the door, then stood back to let him in. He hurried by, then tossed a grateful look my way. "Thanks."

"Sure." I closed the door, then turned my attention to him. "Let me grab you a towel."

"It's fine." He held up one hand. "Don't worry about it."

I nodded a little as I moved toward the couch and took a seat. Why the hell was he here?

He seemed to read my mind because a regretful expression crossed his face. "I wanted to stop by to apologize. For the way I acted," he clarified. "I... It was wrong of me. Harris's news caught me off guard and I... blew it out of proportion."

I offered a small smile. "I understand. It was a surprise for me, too."

Patrick gestured to the cushion next to me. "Do you mind if I sit?"

"Of course not." I tugged a throw pillow out of the way and tossed it to the side to make room for him.

"Thanks." He fell silent for a minute, and his gaze snagged on the plaque I'd set on the coffee table. "Shame."

"I know." I watched him as he studied it, a sad expression on his face. "I'm going to get some glue and fix it up."

He threw a little smile my way. "She would like that."

Silence descended for a minute before he spoke again. "My mother loves you like her own. After Lily..." He gave his head a little shake. "Having you around breathed life back into her."

"She means the world to me," I said, meaning it with my whole heart. "She was the only real parent I've ever had."

"I know." He turned a sad smile my way. "You deserve to have the house. I'm sure this wasn't what you had planned for yourself after college, but I'm glad she has you around. I just... I hope you'll keep it."

A sharp little pang ricocheted through my heart. I didn't really have a choice. I couldn't in good conscience sell it, and neither could I leave Violet. I was stuck here for the time being. It was incredibly uncharitable of me to even consider it. Violet was all I had left, aside from Con. I couldn't risk moving away and something happening. I knew Con went to see her from time to time, but he'd never been as close to her as I had. Though I'd lived with Violet for a little over ten years, Con had spent that time in the Marines. He'd dedicated his time to serving our country, coming home only once or twice a year to check on me before shipping out again. He'd never really had a chance to get to know her the way I had. It was my obligation to take care of her now the way she'd taken me in and cared for me.

He glanced around at the boxes piled around the room. "What do you plan to do with everything?"

"Put it in storage." I couldn't get rid of it. I knew she probably wouldn't mind, but I couldn't part with everything just yet.

He nodded. "Thank you for doing all of this. You've had to take on a lot, and I can't imagine how hard it is for you."

I lifted one shoulder. "It's not so bad."

Patrick studied me for a moment like he knew full well I was lying but wasn't willing to dispute my statement. "Well, if you ever need anything, you know where to find me."

"I appreciate it," I said, meaning it.

"Anyway." He placed his palms on his thighs, then pushed to his feet. "I just wanted to stop by and apologize, see how you were doing."

I followed suit and hopped up, then headed for the front door. "I appreciate it."

He jerked a thumb toward the boxes. "If you need any help with that, let me know."

"I will, thanks."

Patrick wrapped one arm around my shoulders in a quick, friendly hug. "Good to see you, Abby. I'm glad you're back."

"Thanks." I smiled and sent up a little wave as he headed out to his car, dodging the raindrops that still fell steadily outside.

Once he was gone, I closed and locked the door then turned to the boxes stacked around the room. No time like the present, right?

I pushed off the door, then grabbed my phone and pulled up my favorite playlist, cranking the music as I went to work boxing up reminders of the past.

CHAPTER FOURTEEN

Clay

I led the way into the conference room, then gestured to the table. "Please, have a seat."

Mrs. Morrison slid into the seat closest to the door, her entire body tight with tension.

Taking the seat across from her, I set the manilla folder on the table between us. Her eyes were drawn to the folder, and I watched as her knuckles turned white where she clutched her purse in her lap.

I slid it her way. "I was able to do what you asked."

Inside the folder were dozens of photos I'd captured of her husband last week in the arms of his secretary. In the car, outside her house, in the hotel bar; they weren't terribly selective of where they chose to hook up, nor did they find any apparent need to keep it secret.

Mrs. Morrison flipped open the folder and stared at the first photograph. In the passenger seat of her small SUV, Jackie Newell straddled Tom Morrison's lap, stripped down to her bra. Mrs. Morrison's face didn't change as she flipped to the next photo. Then the next. Finally, after a few minutes of tense silence, she closed the folder and shook her head. "That's not Tom."

I stared at the woman. "Ma'am, I can assure you, that's him. I took those photos myself. I—"

"That could be anyone." She stood, her gaze still fixed on the folder. "The angle is terrible and it's all grainy."

I tried again, unable to fathom that she refused to believe the evidence I'd placed right in front of her. She'd hired us to find this very information, but she chose to stick her head in the sand and pretend it didn't exist. I hated cheaters above all else, and I couldn't stand to let this woman be degraded by her husband. "As you can tell from the photos, he's been with Ms. Newell several times in various places, and—"

She shook her head and gestured agitatedly toward the folder on the table. "It could have been edited, or..."

"Mrs. Morrison?" The sound of Abby's voice drew our attention to the doorway, and she offered the older woman a small smile. "The photos are yours to keep. Why don't you take them home and if you need anything else from us, just let us know."

A brittle smile curved the woman's lips and she snatched up the folder, then strode past Abby.

"What the hell was that?" I stood slowly, and Abby's gaze returned to me.

Sympathy lined her face. "She wasn't ready to admit it yet."

"You know those photos were real," I said, pointing after the woman.

"You know what else is real? What she's going through," Abby said. "Can you imagine how she feels right now? The man she loves has been sneaking around behind her back for God knows how long."

Yeah, I knew exactly how that felt. "Even more reason for her to nail his ass to the wall."

Abby shook her head. "You can't just tell people how they should feel. She's hurt. Betrayed. It's easier for her to deny it than accept the fact that the man who promised his life to her couldn't keep his word."

I let out a mirthless laugh. "Newsflash, Abilene, people lie all the damn time. Especially when they're in relationships. She should move on and forget about the asshole."

"It's not that easy," Abby argued. "She loved him before. She probably still does."

"Don't be naïve." I crossed my arms over my chest. "He's a

cheater, and she'd be better off without him."

"I'm not disputing that," Abby returned. "But you can't just flip a switch and turn off your love for someone. It doesn't work like that."

"And how did he return the favor? By fucking his secretary, right out in the open where anyone could see."

Annoyance flared in her gaze. "What he did was wrong, I'm not denying that. All I'm saying is, from her perspective, this is a huge shock. Even if he wasn't faithful to her, she was loyal to him. She trusted him never to hurt her, and she's not willing to believe her love could have just been thrown away like that."

I scoffed. "Love is bullshit."

She stared at me for a long moment. "I'm sorry you feel that way."

Her words sent a little pang through my heart. Without another word, she turned and left the room. I took a step, already going after her before I realized what I was doing.

Abby truly believed what she said... and I hated to admit that she might be right. I'd never known that kind of trust. I thought I'd loved Samantha. I thought we would get married and live happily ever after. Instead, she'd written me a Dear John and told me I'd been replaced. I expected other women to be the same. It was easier to turn off my emotions and focus solely on finding temporary pleasure instead. If I never let anyone in, then I couldn't be hurt again.

I thought about what she'd said. A decade ago, I'd believed in love. I'd believed in trust and honesty. I would admit that I was jaded, and that was no way to live, either. Was I happy with my life? Sure. But it felt like something was missing, and it was more than just sex.

I thought back to Abby's reaction, her defense that love did exist. I hadn't kissed a woman since I broke up with Samantha ten years ago. It was too intimate, too revealing. There was an emotion in kissing that I couldn't afford to offer another woman. At least, I hadn't. I'd never been more tempted to kiss a woman than I had Abilene. She made me want things I didn't think were in the cards for me.

Growing up, I thought I'd be a normal guy. I'd get a job, get married and have a couple kids. But the first three decades of my life had quietly slipped away and I had nothing to show for them. Maybe it was time to move on, to leave the past behind. God knew I wanted Abby. But could we ever have more? Would she ever truly let me in after everything that had happened? Would I ever trust her enough to find happiness?

I wanted to ask all of those questions and more, but Abby still wasn't inclined to give me the time of day. I needed to talk with her—really talk with her—and see where she stood. Did we have a chance at all? I know we'd only spent one night together, but I truly enjoyed Abby. She was quirky and funny, and this most recent conversation revealed to me a side of her I didn't know existed. If Abby gave herself to someone, she would do so whole-heartedly. And it surprised the hell out of me how desperately I wanted to be that man.

CHAPTER FIFTEEN

Abby

I stared at my reflection in the fogged-up mirror of the bathroom, wondering just what the hell I was doing. Going out with Trevor had seemed like a good idea at the time. Now I wasn't so sure.

In the two weeks since I'd met Clay, I hadn't come any closer to understanding him. My thoughts turned back to our conversation two days ago. Did he really feel that way? Was he truly so cold and unfeeling? All of the evidence I'd seen so far said yes. He refused to kiss me, a fact that still rankled. What the hell kind of rule was that anyway? Everyone kissed. Grandmothers, friends—hell, kissing was the standard greeting in multiple countries. Yet Clay wanted none of it because it was too intimate. God, the man was so infuriating.

I let out a sigh and wiped the remaining condensation from the glass, then began to dry my hair. Half-heartedly, I applied my makeup and styled my hair, then dressed. I'd just slipped on a pair of wedge sandals when the bell rang. My stomach flipped, and the knots in my belly felt tighter than ever as I strode through the living room toward the front door.

Peeking through the side window, I made sure that it was Trevor before unlocking the door and swinging it open. "Hey."

He greeted me with a wide smile. "Hey. You look nice."

"Thanks." I smiled, and he glanced over my shoulder into the living room. Before he could try to invite himself in, I took a small step forward. "Are you ready to go?"

"Sure."

I closed and locked the door behind me, then followed Trevor to his car. He moved to the passenger side and held the door for me, and I shot him a smile. "Thank you."

I couldn't remember the last time a man had opened or held the door for me. It was little things like that that showed the measure of a man. It wasn't that I couldn't do it myself, but it said a lot about the fact that he was willing to put me first. It was a promising start to the date, at least.

After closing up, he rounded the car and climbed inside. "Seafood or steak?"

I lifted one shoulder. "Either is fine with me."

We made small talk on the way downtown, the conversation stilted and awkward. I felt antsy, and the more nervous I became, the more I rambled. Trevor seemed a little overwhelmed, not entirely sure how to respond, so I forced myself to keep my mouth closed for the remainder of the drive.

Once we were seated and the waiter had brought us a basket of bread, I looked around the restaurant. "This is nice. Have you been here before?"

He threw a sheepish glance my way. "Actually, no. I just moved here."

"Really?" I folded my arms on the table and leaned forward. "How long ago?"

"Ah..." He picked up his glass and took a sip before regarding me. "A little over two weeks now."

"Did you come here for work?"

He shook his head. "I'm originally from Colorado. Back home, I worked as a dispatcher for 911."

"That's awesome." I'd never really thought of the people on the other end of the line who took those phone calls. "That must've been stressful."

"Sometimes," he admitted. "Occasionally, we got some really funny calls too."

I grinned. "I can only imagine."

For the next thirty minutes, he regaled me with stories.

"So what brought you to Texas?" I asked.

His gaze dropped to the table. "I needed a change. I reached a point in my life where I had more questions than answers, and I thought a change of environment would help me figure things out."

I nodded a little. "I can understand that. I actually went to school up in Massachusetts. When I left, I had no intention of ever coming back. I always had these dreams of working for the FBI or creating a computer program that would make lives easier. But... here I am."

He tipped his head in question. "Why did you come back?"

"Family," I said simply. "They needed me, so I came. I haven't given up on my dreams, I just... put them on hold for a while."

"When did you move back?"

"Actually," I said, "I've only been back for a couple of weeks too. The spring semester ended, and my brother came up to help me move down. It's been... hectic." I didn't want to get into all the details with Violet just yet, so I closed my mouth.

"I'm sure," he replied. "Are you renting the place you're at now?"

I shook my head. "It actually belongs to a family friend."

"Cool. Kind of like a roommate situation?" A sharp pain ricocheted through my chest at the thought of Violet.

"Not exactly. My parents died when I was young, and Violet took me in. She was good friends with my grandmother, and she didn't have any family, so she offered to let me stay with her."

I skipped over the details of Violet's history, not wanting to get too deeply into family dirty laundry on the first date. "I actually came back home because she has dementia. She wasn't able to live by herself anymore, and Violet decided that she would rather live in an assisted living facility."

"Couldn't she have hired live-in help?"

The question stung, and I felt almost as if he were judging me, wondering why I wasn't taking care of her. My response came out a little harsher than I intended. "That was her choice. I tried to convince her otherwise, but she said she didn't want to be a burden."

"I'm sorry," he said. "That must be hard."

"Yeah, but you know how it is." I smiled a little. "We just take it day by day."

"Does she have any family besides you?"

I shook my head. "Violet has been through a lot. Her daughter died when she was young, and her husband died only a few years after they married. She has a son, but he's busy with his own family."

Trevor made a little face. "It sounds like she's had a pretty rough life."

"She has," I agreed.

The whole conversation was starting to feel like an interview, and I was desperate to change the subject. For the next hour as we ate dinner, we talked about our interests, everything from books to music to movies. Trevor liked to travel, while I was more of a homebody. He enjoyed concerts while I preferred a quiet night in watching TV or reading a book.

After the date was over, we headed back to my place. Trevor put the car in park and reached for my hand. Reluctantly, I laid my palm inside his and shifted in the seat, turning to face him more fully. "I had a great time tonight."

I offered him a polite smile. "Me too."

"I'd like to take you out again."

I didn't like the way his eyes raked over me, as if trying to see what lay beneath my clothes. I curled my lips into what I hoped resembled a smile. "Just text me."

I kind of regretted giving him my phone number now, but if he did call, I would just put him off and tell him I was too busy.

Trevor started to lean forward, and I snatched up the door handle. "Thanks for the ride."

Noticing my obvious discomfort, he lifted our joined hands to his mouth and pressed a kiss to the back of mine. "Talk to you soon."

"See you." I extricated myself from his grasp and slid out of the car before he could say anything else. I threw a little wave his way as I let myself in the back door.

I didn't know what about the kiss was so revolting, but I couldn't stand the lingering feel of his lips on my skin. I managed to resist until I was out of sight and as soon as I stepped inside, I wiped the back of my hand on my jeans. "Ick."

I slipped out of my shoes, then dropped my keys and purse on the counter as I wound my way through the kitchen on the way to the living room. I was halfway across the darkened room when I froze, suddenly aware of a presence. The large figure rose from the chair in the corner, looming like a specter in the dark, sending my heart rate into a tailspin and stealing my breath. I whirled to my right and grabbed up the closest thing at hand, which happened to be a dish sitting on the end table. I flung it across the room, already sprinting away as the crash of porcelain met my ears.

From behind me, a low growl sounded, and two strong arms wrapped around my waist. I let out a scream as the man pulled me against him, and I drove my elbow into his midsection as hard as I could. A muffled oath met my ears as I struggled to get him to release me.

"Goddamn it, stop!"

Through the terror clouding my vision and muddling my ears, the voice didn't sink in right away.

"Abilene!"

Clay's voice penetrated the fog that surrounded my brain, and I let out a little whimper as he relaxed his hold. Relief turned my muscles to jelly. It wasn't an intruder—not exactly.

My initial relief turned to fury and I spun to face him, already swinging. "You asshole!"

I got three good hits to his chest before he grabbed my wrists and shoved me backward, pinning me to the wall. I jabbed upward with my knee, but he dodged it. "Watch it!"

That served only to infuriate me further, and I kicked out at him. "Are you kidding me right now?"

Clay leaned into me, using all of his weight to keep me still. I could feel his golden gaze boring into me even in the dark. "You done yet?"

"Hell no, I'm not done!" I shrieked. "You fucking asshole, I swear to God, I—"

My next words were stolen as his weight lifted off of me and he moved quicker than lightning. Adjusting his grip on my wrists,

Clay spun me around once more until I was wrapped in his embrace, his thick arms securing me in place. "You think I was going to let you go without a fight?"

He wanted a fight? Well, he was about to get one. "You broke into my fucking house!" I stomped on his foot, eliciting another low growl from him. "You scared the life out of me!"

His grip tightened infinitesimally, then loosened. "I know, babe. I'm sorry."

He released me and I whirled to face him. "What the hell were you thinking?"

Citrine eyes glowed like a cat's in the dim light. "I had to see you."

Incredulousness rendered me speechless for a second. "So you broke into my house and waited for me in the dark like a crazy person? What the hell is wrong with you?" When he failed to answer, I smacked his chest once more. "Answer me! What if I had company over?"

At that, Clay took a step forward. "I don't want you seeing him."

I'm sorry, what? "You don't get to tell me what to do." I shoved at him, but he didn't budge an inch.

He peered down at me, his face only inches from mine. "Did you kiss him?"

My mouth dropped open at the jealousy tingeing his tone. "What the hell do you care?"

One hand settled on the curve of my waist, and his thumb stroked over my stomach. "Because I want you. I thought I made that crystal clear."

"Too damn bad. You had your chance," I spat. "I'll go out with whoever the hell I want."

His fingers curled into my flesh where he held me. "Over my dead body."

I let out a half laugh. "You and your stupid rules. You're so worried about another guy kissing me, but you won't do it yourself." I stared at him. "Isn't that right? You wouldn't kiss me that night at the hotel. Well, do it now. You want me that bad? Prove it."

He hesitated, a muscle ticking in his jaw. For a second, I

thought he would do it—I'd hoped he would. Silence spread between us, and the hot flush of shame rose over my body.

"That's what I thought."

Tears pricked my eyes as I pulled back a step, my heart crumbling to dust in my chest.

CHAPTER SIXTEEN

Clay

She was right, I hadn't kissed her; I couldn't. I hadn't kissed a woman in ten years, but this tiny little spitfire tempted me to break my most steadfast rule. Sex was sex, but kisses spoke of intimacy and passion. The sex between us was explosive, but I was terrified that her kiss would tear me apart. She saw too much of me as it was. If I kissed her, that last boundary would be gone, and I knew I could lose myself to this girl. She was funny, smart, and I loved that wicked sense of humor. If I let her kiss me, if I really let her in, I had a feeling it would be the end of the world as I knew it. It wouldn't just be another soulless encounter with Abby, and I wasn't sure I was ready for the change that might bring.

But my window of opportunity rapidly narrowed as her eyes filled with hurt and she turned away. Without conscious thought, my hand shot out and grasped the back of her neck. Her gaze snapped with fire as I spun her back to me, and her mouth parted to let loose the string of oaths I knew hovered on her tongue. If I did this, if I kissed her, everything would change. I would never be the same; Abilene had the power to wreck me. My gaze dropped to those perfect cherry lips, and I knew then I had a split second to make a decision. Stay or go? Give every piece of myself to her or walk away forever? The thought of never feeling her next to me again cut through me like a knife, and I couldn't bear the thought. Eyes fixed on her lips, I dipped my head and accepted my fate.

A little squeak of surprise escaped her lips as I hauled her up against me and crushed my mouth to hers. Her fingers dug into the muscle of my chest, then pressed flat as if trying to put distance between us. Instead of releasing her, I locked my arm around her lower back, pressing our bodies even closer, and increased the pressure of the kiss. She tasted better than the sweetest treat, a mixture of sweetness and spice, sin and desire. I couldn't get enough.

Sliding my hand up her to the silky strands of her hair, I cupped the back of her skull and angled her head to the side. I curled my tongue around hers, intent on exploring every inch of her hot, sweet mouth. Before I had the chance, she pulled back.

Without warning, her teeth sank into my lower lip, and I reeled back as a growl welled up and out of my throat. "Little bitch."

I fisted my hand tighter in her hair and met her fiery glare. My cock swelled as I stared down at her. I fucking loved her feisty, loved the way her cheeks flushed pink and her eyes glazed with pent-up emotion. I wanted to harness that passion, wring it out of her one orgasm at a time. "What the hell was that for?"

"Making me wait." She curled her arms around my shoulders, attacking my mouth as she lifted one leg and hooked it around my thigh.

I coasted my hands downward to cup her bottom, then hoisted her up against my chest. She locked her ankles together above my ass as I headed toward the bedroom. I spoke between kisses. "Done waiting. Need to be inside you, now."

Not breaking the kiss, her hands moved between our bodies and tore at my shirt, pulling it free of the waistband until it got stuck under my armpit. I paused in the hallway and pinned her to the wall, then lifted my arms and allowed her to strip it off over my head. The second it came off, I grasped the hem of her tank top and drew it upward, then tossed it over my shoulder. Her tits were encased in a pink bra spattered with rhinestones, and she arched her back, allowing me access to flick open the clasp and draw it down her arms. Tight little nipples scraped my chest as she wrapped her arms around my neck and melded her lips to mine.

My dick pulsed against my zipper, painfully hard, eager to sink into her. I had to find out if it really was as good as I remembered or if I'd built it up in my mind. I stopped next to the bed and let her slide down my body until she was on her feet, our mouths still fused. I broke away then, cupping her breasts as I kissed my way down her throat and over her collarbone. Her hands came up and gripped my biceps as I sucked the tip of one peak into my mouth, and a soft, sweet sigh left her lips as her head dropped back in pleasure.

I brushed the other nipple with my thumb, the straining tip hard beneath my touch. I rolled it between my fingers, teasing and tweaking, enjoying the convulsion of her body beneath my touch. I circled the tip of her, then laved it my tongue, then lightly bit down, hard enough to make her jump.

"Clay!" My name ripped from her throat, both an admonishment and a plea.

Kissing my way over to the other breast, I let my hands wander down to the waistband of her skirt. I popped the button, and she shimmied her hips until the fabric came free and hit the ground with a whisper. I released her nipple with a soft pop, then leaned back slightly to take her in. She stood in front of me, clad only in a pair of tiny pink panties, looking good enough to eat. A grin split my face as I dipped one finger into the waistband and pulled downward.

"I need you," Abby said, her words breathless as she delved her fingers into my hair. "Please, Clay."

I loved the sound of her begging, and I wanted more of it. "Say it again," I commanded.

She sucked in a breath as I lightly touched her core, and her head dropped back as her teeth cut into her lower lip. "Tell me. I want to hear you say it."

Her fingers tightened in my hair, but she didn't open her eyes. Even her brows furrowed in confusion. "What?"

Yanking the fabric of her panties to one side, I lightly brushed the sensitive little nub with my thumb, causing her to jerk. "Say it again. Beg for it."

I increased the pressure slightly, moving in a circular motion, and she thrust her hips forward, seeking release. I pulled my hand free. "Beg, Abilene."

"Please!" The word burst from her lips. "Please, Clay, I need you!"

Raw desire swept through me, and I fisted the delicate panties, then yanked hard. The material gave way, and I tore the lacy scraps from her body. She stumbled backwards and her bottom hit the mattress. She teetered for a second before I gave her a tiny shove, and she collapsed onto her elbows on the bed. I used the position to my advantage, dropping to my knees and hooking her knees over my shoulders, opening her to my perusal. Her pretty pink folds glistened in the moonlight, and I breathed deeply as her musky feminine scent wafted up to me.

Using my thumb and forefinger to spread her wide, I speared my tongue deep inside. Her high-pitched cry bounced off the walls of the room, and her essence exploded over my tongue as I lapped up her juices, licking up her slit from bottom to top, then taking her clit and sucking it into my mouth. Her thighs trembled were they rested over my shoulders, and her heels dug into my back as her hands curled into the fabric of the comforter.

"Clay! I'm... Oh, God!"

I sank my fingers inside just in time to feel the faint pulses of her inner walls. I sucked harder, and her flesh tightened before she released on a scream, flooding my mouth with her sweetness. She writhed beneath me as I plunged my fingers in and out, massaging her swollen flesh.

Rough pants left her lungs, and she pressed against my head and shoulders, trying to push me away. "Stop! I can't... It's... it's too much!"

Taking pity on her, I lifted my mouth and gentled my strokes. As I levered myself over her, my chest brushed hers, and she blinked her eyes open to meet my gaze. "I'm just getting started, baby."

My eyes dropped to her mouth, and I dipped my head, nipping at her bottom lip. Her mouth trembled beneath mine, and the overwhelming urge to dominate her ripped through me. I wanted her to taste herself on me, and I slanted my lips over hers, my tongue probing deep. Her legs wound around my hips, holding me close as her tongue dueled with mine. Tiny hands moved across my shoulders and down my back, the feeling of her blunt nails scraping along my skin sending a pulse of heat to my groin and making my dick swell. I had to be inside her. I couldn't wait any longer.

Lifting my hips away without breaking the kiss, I freed the button and worked the material down my hips. I'd gone commando, so I dropped my jeans to the floor and toed out of my shoes in one smooth motion. Sliding one hand beneath her hips, I scooped her upward and shifted us toward the middle of the bed.

I was done holding back.

CHAPTER SEVENTEEN

Abby

Curling one hand into his hair, I yanked his head back down, and our teeth clashed under the raw force of the kiss. His large palms stroked up my back, down over my bottom, lighting every inch of my skin on fire. I shifted, trying to get closer, needing to alleviate the ache between my legs. I opened my mouth to him, and his tongue swept inside, curling over mine. His lips were warm and firm as he captured my mouth with an almost bruising force.

Propping a knee between my legs, he levered himself over me, caging me in his arms. I curled my fingers into the thick, hard muscles that covered his back and nipped at his bottom lip as he started to pull away.

He returned the favor, capturing my lower lip between perfect white teeth. I arched upward, needing to feel every hard inch of him against me. He obliged by settling his heavy weight in the cradle of my hips, the hard ridge of his arousal pressing against my stomach.

A low whimper left my mouth when he lifted away from me again, and he let out a strained chuckle. "Right here, babe. I'm not going anywhere."

I watched as he snatched up his jeans, then dug out a condom and rolled it on. I lifted a brow, and a wicked grin split his face. "No way was I gonna let you slip through my fingers again."

Anticipation and desire kicked my heart into high gear, and I grabbed at him as he climbed back onto the bed. He leaned over me, pressing me into the mattress with the weight of his body. "You ready for me?"

"Why don't you find out for yourself?" I lifted my chin at Clay, daring him.

I didn't have to wait long. One thick finger moved to the tiny nub at the apex of my thighs, and I bit my lip at the sharp bolt of pleasure that streaked through me. He rubbed in a tiny circular motion, pressing ever so gently before slipping inside. More surprised than anything, I gasped at the sensation. My body was still hypersensitive from the orgasm that had ripped through me only moments ago, but I was primed and ready to go again. My legs fell open, and my breath came in pants as he dipped in and out, sliding a second finger inside. He lubricated the folds with my arousal, gently rubbing my clit in a circular motion. I lifted my hips, moving with him, the friction pushing me closer to the edge with every stroke.

A soft cry ripped from my throat as he sank his fingers deep.

"Come for me, baby."

His thumb pressed down on my clit, and another hard thrust of his fingers sent me spiraling upward in a shower of stars.

"Oh, God... Holy..." I couldn't even string together a coherent sentence, my mind was so jumbled with pleasure.

His lips came down on mine, soft at first, then more force-fully as he rolled his tongue over mine. Tension drained from my muscles, and my head dropped back as he kissed his way over my jaw, scraping his teeth along my throat, sending tingles of pleasure to the tips of my toes. For a man who claimed not to kiss... Holy shit. I'd never experienced anything like it. The way his mouth felt on mine, the way we connected... Every past encounter disappeared in the blink of an eye as Clay claimed me for himself. And there was no other word for it. His touch was firm and demanding, yet somehow tender at the same time.

He braced his hands on the mattress beside my shoulders, and I felt his arousal brush my sensitive folds as he stretched his body over mine. My hips lifted of their own accord, inviting him in. His lips covered mine, and he swallowed my gasp as he thrust hard, seating himself deeply inside me. The sensation was almost overwhelming, bordering on painful as he stretched every inch of me.

He didn't give me time to adjust, just pulled out and slammed back in again, stealing my breath. My already heightened awareness tipped me over the edge, and the sensation within me boiled over, rocketing toward another orgasm. I clutched his shoulders as heat raced through my body, and I let go on a silent scream. Clay pumped into me several more times before emptying his seed into the condom with a ragged groan and slumping over me.

He lay heavily on my chest, covering me from head to toe, and I absorbed the heat from his body. His lips brushed over my collarbone, and I shivered as the tingles of pleasure fanned outward, down to the deepest recess of my body, spurring me on. He was still inside me, and I couldn't bear to break that connection with him just yet. I needed more time—I needed him.

"Damn."

I rolled my head his way, brows drawn slightly together at the incredulousness saturating his tone. "What?"

His honeyed eyes met mine. "I think that was better than the first time."

A hot blushed raced over my cheeks. "I think so, too."

Pushing up on an elbow, he dropped a quick kiss on my lips and climbed from the bed. I watched him stride into the bathroom, every hard muscle rippling in the moonlight. Yanking the covers up to my chest, I snuggled into the pillow as I listened to the water running in the bathroom. I imagined Clay taking care of necessities before he came back to me. A sense of contentment settled over me as I closed my eyes.

God. Being with Clay felt... incredible. It was almost too good to be true. I fought a smile and lost at the memory of him kissing me for the first time. It had totally been worth it. My nerve endings still felt like they were on fire, and a little shiver raced through my body.

I never dreamed I could feel this way with another person. But with Clay... It was stronger. More intense. It was maybe the forever kind of feeling people searched for their entire lives. I wanted more of his kisses, his touch, his loving, over and over again—every single day.

CHAPTER EIGHTEEN

Clay

As I turned off the light and left the bathroom, my gaze imme-diately fell on Abby where she lay curled up in the middle of the bed. She looked so content. So sweet. So... perfect. Too perfect for me. A familiar foreboding tingle began at the base of my spine and crept upward. An overwhelming emotion clawed up my throat, threatening to choke me.

Oh, God. I had to get out of here, clear my head. Grabbing up my clothes, I watched Abby's still form as I moved toward the door. She was snuggled up on her side, one arm tucked under the pillow, looking exactly the way I had when I'd left her at the hotel. That seemed like a lifetime ago, yet at the same time it seemed as if it were just yesterday.

I slid out of the room, not bothering to close the door behind me. I crossed the house at a fast clip, tugging on my shirt as I went. At the back door, I tugged on my jeans and shoved my feet into my shoes. I was out on the porch before I even knew what I was doing and I paused, resting against the railing as I drew in my first full breath in minutes.

I'd tucked my bike close to the porch, and the chrome gleamed in the moonlight. I could climb on, take off without a backward glance. My mind whirled, and my heart raced as I took a step toward the stairs, then stopped. What the hell was I doing?

I dropped my head and closed my eyes, willing everything to

just... stop for a second. I needed to think. I needed to... Hell, I didn't know what I needed. A huge part of me wanted to climb on my bike and escape. The other part of me wanted to crawl right back into bed with Abby and not surface for days.

I locked my fingers together behind my head and paced the length of the narrow porch. I paused by the door, staring up at the inky black sky. If I walked away now, things would be over between us. Abby would never forgive me. Fear grasped at me, and I battled it down, drawing in several deep breaths. I'd be lying if I said I wasn't scared shitless by the things I felt when I was with Abby. Everything with her was just so... different. She made me want more, made me want to be better.

For years I'd resisted anything even resembling a relationship. Now that it was right here in front of me, all I had to do was reach out and grab it. But I was being a fucking coward. I let out a half laugh. Of all the things I'd faced in my life, this thing with Abby concerned me the most. My initial instinct was right on. This girl could ruin me, and that terrified me. I wasn't sure which was worse; that this might actually work out between us, or that it could crash and burn two days from now. All I knew was the past couple of weeks without her had been painful. I couldn't bear the idea of never giving things between us a chance and letting her slip through my fingers.

I was never one to turn down a challenge, and I hated the idea of being a coward—yet here I was, ready to run again. I couldn't do it. She sure as hell deserved better than me, but I couldn't let her go. The idea of never having her again hurt too badly to contemplate.

Fuck. What the hell would Abby think? I'd literally pulled out of her and bolted. Guilt slammed into me, and I yanked open the door to the house. I kicked off my shoes next to Abby's and crept back to the bedroom, praying to God she hadn't noticed. Maybe she was asleep. She lay in the exact same spot, except her body was now turned away from me. I quickly shed my clothes before climbing in behind her.

But I knew the second I touched her that everything was wrong. Her body tensed, and she shifted away. But I wasn't going to let her go again. "I'm sorry, Abby. I freaked out."

She shook her head but didn't say a word, and I knew I had to explain. "I've never felt like this before. I just... It caught up to me all of a sudden and I couldn't breathe. I just had to get out for a second."

Her body shuddered next to mine, but she refused to acknowledge my words. I grasped her bicep and tried to roll her toward me, but she resisted. "God, babe. You'll never know how sorry I am."

Finally, she relented and rolled toward me. The tear tracks cutting down her cheeks threatened to slay me. "Fuck, Abby."

I dipped my head so it was next to hers and pulled her tightly to me, tucking her head into my chest and cuddling her close. "Don't you cry for me, baby. I'm not worth it."

She hiccupped a little as she fought to stifle a sob but didn't say a word.

"I promise, sweetheart. Never again." I held her even tighter, hoping to hell that she would believe me. "I'll never leave you again."

Finally, her arms came around my waist and she clung to me as I kissed her forehead and held her close. "I'm sorry, baby," I whispered next to her ear. "I knew the second I walked out I'd fucked up. I just... I can't let you go, Abby. You hear me?"

Her head bobbed against my chest in what I assumed—hoped—was a nod, and I kissed the top of her head. "I'm not leaving you again. You're too good for me, but I won't let you go."

Her breathing eventually slowed and evened out as she slipped into slumber, but I lay awake for what felt like hours, just watching her as she slept in my arms. My heart seized in my chest at the thought of how close I'd come to losing her tonight. I couldn't explain why she was so damn important to me; she just was. It was more than the fact that we'd had sex before. It was more, even, than the fact that she was my friend's little sister and I wanted to keep her safe.

There was something about Abby that just made me... crazy. I wanted to possess her. Claim her. Protect her. I wanted to be as important to her as she was to me. I closed my eyes and eventually fell asleep, that last lingering thought clinging to my brain.

Most of the following day was spent packing up Violet's belongings and stacking the boxes in the living room to be moved to the storage unit later. I didn't care that it was boring as hell, I just wanted to spend every second with Abby that I could. I offered to run home and swap my bike for the truck, but she declined.

She threw a curious look my way. "Where did you park? I know you didn't drive your truck, and I don't remember seeing your bike anywhere."

Shame caused heat to rise in my cheeks, and I cleared my throat. "I tucked it around back, by the porch. I didn't want you to see it and throw a fit before I had the chance to talk to you."

One dark eyebrow arched, and I shifted uncomfortably. Admittedly, waiting in the dark for her hadn't exactly been my best idea. At all. But it had worked, and she'd finally dropped her guard and given in to the attraction I knew she felt for me. At least temporarily.

I could feel her putting distance between us with each minute that passed, and I hated it. Although I tried to fight it, she told me I should go back to my place and spend the night. It made sense in a way since I didn't have any clothes, but I hated to leave her when I'd screwed up again, leaving things so tumultuous between us. Reluctantly, I did as she asked and gave her space.

It was a mistake. The next day at work was even worse. Gone was the warm, open, passionate woman I'd spent the night with. This Abby ignored me at every turn. Any time I got within twenty feet of her, she turned tail and ran away like she didn't even want to be in the same room with me. After yesterday, it stung more than I was willing to admit. I knew she still didn't fully trust me after I'd almost walked out the other night, but I'd spent the past twenty-four hours trying to alleviate her fears and prove to her that it wouldn't happen again.

By the end of the day, I could stand it no longer. Only Cole, Con, and myself were left, and I didn't want to put off the inevitable another minute. I headed downstairs and cut across the lobby to look for Abby. Her eyes widened when she saw me coming, but she was trapped behind the front desk and couldn't escape me this time.

I was intent on exploring things with Abby. After the taste of her I'd gotten this weekend, I wanted the opportunity to see where things could go. But the first step in that was coming clean. I wanted to tell Con man-to-man that I was dating his sister.

Abby darted a quick look around as I moved beside her. "What are you doing?"

"I want to talk to your brother."

She tipped her chin up to look at me, wariness evident in her pretty brown eyes. "About what?"

I threw her a hard look. "I've known him for years. I won't disrespect him by dating you without his knowledge."

Already, Abby was shaking her head. "Please don't say anything. Not—" She rested one hand on my chest when she saw the dark look on my face. "Not yet. Everything is still so new."

I couldn't help but feel like a dirty little secret. I took a step backward. "You don't want him to know about us?"

Something like regret crossed Abby's face, and her gaze swept the room before returning to me. "Can we not talk about this here?"

From the tone of her voice, it sounded like she didn't want talk about it ever. I fell back another step. I wasn't going to lie. I kind of felt used, and it wasn't a good feeling. I could feel the walls going back up, could feel myself pulling away from her. I'd thought we were on the same page; apparently, I was wrong.

Abby reached for me, her face pleading. "Let's just talk about this later. You can come over or I can come to your place, whichever. Please."

It was that single word that she tacked onto the end that had me reconsidering. I had to meet up with Xander to do some recon, but I'd meant every word I told her Saturday night, and I wanted to prove that she could rely on me. "I'll be there after I'm done."

Before she could say another word, I turned and headed for the bullpen. Heart racing, I made a beeline for my desk to grab my keys. I knew I'd hurt her, but she refused to give me a chance to redeem myself. Every time I took one step forward, she took two steps back. I knew she was into me, but I couldn't figure out for the life of me how to get her to trust me. I'd have to keep picking away at that hardened reserve and hope she would eventually listen.

CHAPTER NINETEEN

Abby

I let out a huge sigh as Clay left through the front door, not sparing me another glance. I couldn't tell if this strange feeling in my stomach was relief or disappointment. Up until he'd cornered me a few minutes ago, I'd somehow managed to avoid him all day.

I couldn't forget his reaction Saturday night. Part of me still couldn't believe he'd run out on me. It was like a dagger to the heart. One minute, everything was perfect. The next, the front door had slammed, sending a spear of agony straight through my soul.

I'd been crushed. My heart still felt a little tender, truth be told. He'd seemed so sincere, apologizing over and over after he'd come back to bed. But could I trust him? It was eerily similar to the night at the hotel. I'd woken just after dawn, and the bed where he'd lain next to me half the night was cold and empty. What if it happened again? Would he just decide one day that I wasn't enough, that he didn't want to be with me and walk out just as he had Saturday night?

I'd caught both Con and Cole eyeing me through the day today, watching as if they thought something was different with me. I'd managed to avoid both of them too for the most part. I couldn't bear to answer any questions. I knew Clay wanted to tell my brother about us, and I understood where he was coming from. But I wasn't ready—especially after this weekend. What was the point in telling everyone we were dating if it wasn't going to last?

"What do you have going on tonight?"

I jumped at the sound of my brother's voice and pasted on a smile as I turned toward him. "Just heading home. Gonna chill and pack some more."

"How that's going?" He leaned one hip against the desk and studied me.

I shrugged. "It's kind of a process. There's so much stuff I don't know where to begin."

"Want some help? I can grab a pizza and swing by."

I thought about that for a second. It'd been a while since I'd had some time alone with Con. "Actually, that'd be nice. Thanks."

"Meet you at six?"

"Sure." I'd make sure to text Clay when I left and let him know that Con was coming over so he wouldn't show up. He wouldn't like it, I was sure of that, but I couldn't help it. I should tell my brother—and I would. If things worked out between Clay and me, and when the time was right.

I gathered up my stuff and headed home to wait for Con. True to his word, he was there less than a half hour later. His eyes widened as he stepped inside. "Damn. You've been busy."

I glanced around at the boxes as I closed up behind him. "I know. I've been getting stuff boxed up, but I haven't had a chance to take most of it to the storage unit yet."

"We can take a load in the SUV tomorrow," he offered.

I grinned. "You're useful once in a while, you know that?"

Con snorted. "Whatever. You don't know what you'd do without me."

"I don't," I agreed. "You're pretty much the best big brother ever."

"I know." His cocky smile reappeared, and I rolled my eyes.

"Good thing you're so humble."

His smile slid away, replaced once more with his patented serious expression. "I hope you know you can talk to me if you ever need to."

Piercing dark eyes stared into mine, and I fought the urge to spill my guts to him on the spot. "I know."

"Okay." He studied me again. "You just... haven't seemed like yourself recently. I know you've got a lot going on, I just want to make sure you're okay."

"I'm just a little overwhelmed," I admitted. "I mean, with the house and Violet and everything..."

Not to mention the drama with Clay, but there wasn't a snowball's chance in hell that I would ask my brother for advice on that. *Ever*. I trailed off, and thank God Con picked up on the excuse. "It's a lot for one person to handle. I'd be more than happy to help you with whatever you need."

"I appreciate that, and I might take you up on the offer." I gestured to the subfloor we stood on. The workers had pulled up the damaged flooring after the fire, but I'd yet to fix them. "If I stay here, I'll eventually replace the floors, paint, that kind of thing."

"Makes sense." He nodded a little. "Is there still a question of you staying here?"

I watched as Con flipped open the lid of the pizza box and extracted a slice, all while contemplating his question. "I don't think so, not anymore."

"You sure?" He took a bite and chewed. "No one would blame you, you know. You went to school for a reason. Hell, you left the state because you wanted bigger and better things. No one wants to hold you back. If you want to go back up north, or if you want to travel, you should do it."

"I know, but..." I bit my lip. "I feel guilty.

"Don't." Con shook his head. "You can't live your life based on someone else. I understand that you want to be here for Violet, and I commend you on that. But you don't have to put your life plans on hold. I mean, I'm your brother so I obviously want you to be safe. I'd prefer you be here, but I understand that you need to find your own way, too. If you're not happy here, you should go do what you want to do. You can always come back. You can visit, or you can move."

"I don't think I want to leave." I shook my head. "It's just... I know it doesn't make much sense. This feels like home. I love it here, and a lot of my friends are still here. You're here. It's just that I never quite pictured this when I went away to school. I always thought that I would go to work somewhere big and important, and do big things."

"You still can," Con said softly.

"I could," I agreed. "When I was up north in school, I felt like I belonged. But then I came back her and this fits, too. I just can't decide what I like better."

"Well, just so you know," Con said as he lifted his pizza and took another bite, "I'm going to do everything in my power to make sure you're happy here so you stick around for a while."

I lifted a brow. "Maybe give me a raise?"

"Eh, except that." Con grinned, and I lightly backhanded him. "Come on, I'm putting you to work."

For the next couple of hours, Con and I sorted through Lily's old bedroom. Violet hadn't had the heart to get rid of her things, so for years it had remained a sort of enshrinement to her deceased daughter. After a long conversation, Con and I decided to keep only the important things in storage in case Violet or Patrick ever wanted them and either donate or toss the rest. It was a blast from the past, seeing all of the nineties décor as we packed all of her things into boxes and bags.

Tucked between the frame and box spring of the twin-sized bed, I found an old book. I fished it out and turned it over in my hands. The cover was faded and cracked, and I opened it to find childish handwriting. As I flipped through the pages, the hand-writing got neater, but the content became darker and bleaker.

"Whatcha got?" Con peered over my shoulder, and I held up the journal.

"I think it's Lily's diary," I said.

His brows drew together. "I wonder if there's anything in it?"

I had no idea. I felt like an interloper reading Lily's personal thoughts, especially since she'd later killed herself. There was no question that Lily had been damaged, disturbed. I set it aside to go through later and decide what to do with it. I wasn't sure whether I wanted to bring it up to Violet or not.

I glanced around the nearly empty room. "Thanks for your help. I think I'm going to relax for a bit."

"Sounds good. I'll take these out on my way," he replied, gesturing toward the bags we'd gathered.

We dragged them out to the curb, and Con threw an arm

around my shoulders in a brotherly hug. "I'll see you at work in the morning."

"Sounds good."

"Think about those floors," he said. "I'm sure we can find something relatively inexpensive and easy to install."

"I will."

With that, he was gone and I headed into the house. I hadn't heard from Clay yet, but I was fairly certain he'd be stopping by later. I fished my phone from my pocket, disappointed to find I didn't have a response to my earlier message. I could tell he'd been upset with me earlier, and I bit my lip as I typed out a new one asking if he'd be over. I hoped fervently that I hadn't screwed things up.

My heart gave a little leap when his response came a couple of minutes later, telling me he'd be there in an hour.

I wandered back into Lily's room, then picked up the diary again. I felt like I was violating her privacy, but she'd been gone for more than twenty-five years. Besides, I couldn't deny that I was intensely curious about what was inside. Had she written about what was bothering her? Maybe there was something in there that could give Violet closure.

I took the book into the living room and opened it, losing myself in the words of a troubled teen as I waited for Clay to arrive.

CHAPTER TWENTY

Clay

I left QSG, ignoring the call from Cole. I caught him looking at me twice earlier, and I knew he'd noticed something was different. I wasn't sure I was ready to say anything, especially given Abby's reticence. Part of me wanted to tell my brother everything. He was my twin, the only person in the world that I could typically count on. I texted him to let him know I was headed out for recon and that I'd talk to him later. That at least would buy me a little time to decide whether or not to tell him.

I swung through a fast-food joint and ate as I drove over to meet up with Xander. For the next hour, we watched our mark. And I stewed over my situation with Abby. Why was she so afraid to tell her brother we'd hooked up? I didn't think she was afraid of him, exactly. It seemed like she was more... embarrassed. And that fucking stung. I didn't want to be anyone's second choice, and I refused to be some dirty little secret. Was she ashamed of me, of the time we'd spent together? I wanted to corner her and ask, but every time I got within ten feet of her, I lost my fucking head. It was like the chemistry between us took over, and I had the urge to push her up against the wall, take her like I had in the hotel. I wanted to feel that one more time—a hundred more times. I didn't know what it was about her, but I couldn't get enough.

"You good?" Xander threw a curious look my way, and I

nodded.

"Yeah. Sorry." I shifted in my seat, cracking my neck to relieve some of the tension there. "Just... a lot on my mind."

"You seem a little on edge," he remarked.

If he only knew. "A little," I admitted.

"If you need anything, you know where to find me."

I appreciated the offer, but Xander had female troubles of his own. "I'm good. Thanks, though."

My brother called just as Xander and I were packing it in for the night, and I thumbed the screen to answer. "Yeah?"

"Meet me for a drink."

Christ. That was the last thing I wanted to do right now. "Nah, I think—"

"Come on, don't be a pussy. Meet me at Van's in thirty."

The line went dead and I rolled my eyes. "Fucking Cole." I threw a look Xander's way. "Wanna grab a beer?"

"I would, but I'm headed to Lydia's."

Part of me wanted to ask how that situation was going, but the tone of his voice stopped me. I couldn't tell exactly what I detected there. Maybe the same possessiveness I felt for Abby. I thanked him as he dropped me back at my bike, then headed toward Van's Bar downtown.

I scanned the room, and my eyes were immediately drawn to my brother sitting at the corner of the long bar, a dark brown bottle in front of him. Winding through the maze of tables, I approached and slid onto the stool next to him.

Beer bottle to his lips, he sent a little half-nod my way, then wiped the moisture from his mouth. "Hey, man."

"Hey." I flicked a look at the bartender and gestured toward the bottle in Cole's hand. The younger guy nodded and reached into a cooler, then cracked the top before passing me the bottle.

I could feel my brother's eyes on me as I chugged half of it before setting it on the bar. "You been stressed lately."

It was more of a statement than a question, but I nodded regardless. "Just a lot on my mind."

Namely the gorgeous little brunette I'd fallen into bed with a week ago and hadn't been able to get my mind off since. I saw her every single day at work, but she avoided me like the plague. It left me frustrated and, ironically, even more crazy for her. The woman knew exactly what she was doing, making me work for it. Why the hell I was going along with it was beyond me.

That wasn't true. I knew exactly why I was ass over tea kettle for her. She drove me crazy—in the best and worst of ways. She was quirky. Crazy. Maybe a little unstable. And she intrigued the hell out of me. There were so many layers to Abby that I wasn't sure I'd ever reveal them all. And the craziest part of this whole thing was that I actually wanted to. I wanted to know everything about her. I wanted to taste her again, feel her soft skin under my hands. There was just something about her that revved my engine, and I wanted more of it.

"Well," my brother said, pulling me from my introspection, "plenty of ways to forget it tonight."

I followed his line of sight as his gaze swept hungrily over the single woman sporadically placed throughout the bar. I grunted. "Not in the mood."

"Since when?" He lifted a brow my way, and I rolled my eyes.

"I don't need to get laid to make myself feel better."

"Never hurts," he countered.

And he was partially correct. Months, even weeks ago, he probably would've been correct. I enjoyed having fun, especially with women. I enjoyed everything about them from their sweet lips to their soft skin. But I couldn't remember a single damn woman I'd slept with in the past. Their faces had all been replaced by Abby's bright countenance, her dark eyes and sweetly curving mouth.

"Maybe," I replied, but my tone held no conviction. I had no intention of pursuing anyone but Abby.

He stared at me. "What's going on?"

I picked at the label on the bottle, scraping at the glue with my thumbnail. "I've kinda been seeing someone."

"No shit?" Cole tipped his chin. "Where'd you find her?"

"The hotel."

He grinned. "I fucking knew there was something up with you. So, what's the deal?"

"I'm not sure." I sighed. "It's complicated."

"You like her," he said slowly.

"This girl is..." Beautiful. Smart. Fucking crazy—in the best way possible. "God, I don't even know how to explain it."

"So, what's the problem?"

"Most immediately?" I lifted a brow. "Her brother. She doesn't want to tell him about us, and I... I get it, but I hate it."

Cole stared at me. "Why doesn't she want him to know?"

I drew in a breath. "Because we work together."

I watched the pieces of the puzzle fall into place, and Cole's eyes widened. He dropped one foot to the floor and leaned forward on his stool. "Abby?"

I nodded, and he shook his head a little. "How?"

I told him about meeting her at the hotel while I was tailing out Morrison, and everything that had happened since.

"Damn." He blew out a breath. "So Con doesn't know?"

"Not yet." I pinned him with a hard stare. "She wants to tell him, so I swear to God I'll murder you if you fuck this up and say something."

He waved one hand. "I won't say a word."

"Thanks." I felt immensely better telling Cole about us, and we sipped our beers in silence for a few minutes until he changed the subject.

"Talked to Dad last night."

Not at all what I wanted to discuss. I couldn't help the sarcasm dripping from my voice when I responded. "Good for you."

Cole studied me. "You should call him—"

"No, thanks." I cut him off before he could finish whatever well-meaning thought was going through his head. "I took his advice years ago and took off without a look backward. Not gonna start now."

"Come on, man. I'm sure he'd like to see you."

"Well, I don't want to see him. And I'm pretty fucking sure he couldn't give a damn about me one way or the other. In fact, I'm almost positive those were his words to me the day I left."

Cole sighed. "You guys have never seen eye-to-eye."

My father never had any criticism for Cole. He saved that for me. "No fucking shit. You were always the golden one. I was the failure, the stupid one."

"You're not fucking stupid." Cole's eyes flashed as he stared at me.

I shrugged. "Doesn't change the past. You were smart and talented. I wasn't. At least he got one good son."

I'd shed the insecurities of my youth—mostly. But sometimes they rose up, threatening to choke me. I'd never been good enough, smart enough. While Cole had aced his classes and played first string football and baseball, I'd been the slacker. After a while, I'd stopped giving a shit about trying to impress my father. All I wanted was to graduate and get the fuck out of the house the minute I turned eighteen.

Cole could have gone to college—he should have, with his grades. Instead, he'd followed me to the military. It was kind of a twin thing. I felt better with him by my side, the way it'd always been. He was a huge pain in my ass, but he was still my brother, my flesh and blood. There was a connection between us that few people understood. We were different as night and day, but as I grew, I discovered that we each had our strengths and weaknesses. While he was good with the analytic stuff, I was a hell of a Marine. I loved the physical aspect of it, and Cole had helped me pass all the tests I needed to get into the military.

"I was no better than you. I just argued less," my brother responded.

I snorted. "That's an understatement."

"He's not doing so great." My brother raked one hand through his hair. "He won't say anything, but I think it's serious."

"Yeah?" I took a swig of my beer. "Well, that's what happens when you chug a twenty-four pack every night after work. The bastard's lucky he's lasted this long."

"I just..." Cole hesitated, looking torn. I knew he hated having to choose sides. "I just... I don't want you to regret not talking to him while you still have the chance."

I knew where he was coming from, and I appreciated his concern, even if I knew there was no hope for the situation. "I'll think about it."

"I'm going to see him next week. Maybe you can come with

me," he offered.

"Keep me posted." I drained the rest of my beer and pushed it away, then fist-bumped him. "I'm out. See you in the morning."

With that, I slid off the stool and headed out into the humid night. I rang the bell at a little after ten, and Abby swung the door open with a smile. "What, not going to break in this time?"

I offered her a half-hearted smile, and her face fell at my lack of enthusiasm. Abby closed the door as I stepped inside and shoved my hands into my pockets. "What's on your mind?" I asked.

Abby fiddled with the hem of her shirt, looking uncomfortable as hell. "Look, I'm sorry about earlier. I just... He's my brother. I feel like I owe it to him to tell him personally."

"I fucking hate sneaking around like teenagers." I sighed. "Why don't we just tell him?"

Her teeth dug into her bottom lip. "I'll tell him soon, I promise. I just... With everything going on recently, it hasn't felt like the right time."

I studied her for a moment. "The longer we wait, the harder it will be."

"I know. But... For as long as I can remember, Con's been like a parent to me. Even before our parents passed away, they were never really... active in our lives. I spent time with Con when I was little, so much so that I hardly remember my mom and dad. He's all I have left, and I just..."

I could understand that. I even respected her choice. I knew how much Con cared about her, so I completely understood her need to tell him personally. I also knew that my actions the other night had set us back a few steps, and I hated myself for that. I wanted to show her how much I wanted to be with her, and the best way I knew to do that was to come clean and tell everyone she was mine.

"I know, babe. But hiding it is going to make it a thousand times worse. Trust me. He's gonna flip the fuck out if he thinks we've been hiding it from him."

I dropped my hands to my sides. "Just promise me you won't wait too long."

She shook her head. "I promise."

I held out a hand to her, and she moved into my arms, automatically tipping her head up for a kiss. I cupped her neck, sliding my thumb under her jaw. "I meant what I said. I won't run out on you again. All I want is a chance to find out where things can go."

"I know," she whispered. "Me too."

Her mouth twisted in consternation, and I pulled her into me. "I can take care of it if you want. Or we can do it together."

"No." She shook her head. "I want to tell him myself. He needs to hear it from me."

"If you're sure."

"I am." Abby let out a little sigh as she pressed her face to my chest, and I wrapped an arm around her waist, pulling her close.

"For tonight, let's just forget about everything else."

Her brown eyes lifted to mine, full of heat. "I can do that."

CHAPTER TWENTY-ONE

Abby

I walked through the lobby of Morningside, lost in thought. I shot a quick smile at the nurse sitting behind the desk before I signed in, then turned toward the garden. I drew up short as a person rounded the corner, nearly running into me.

"I'm sorry, I—" I blinked, dumbfounded. "Trevor?"

His expression morphed from embarrassed to surprised, then finally pleased as he recognized me. "Abby, hey."

"Hey." I stared at him for a second, feeling off balance. "What are you doing here?"

He seemed to tense at my question. "Visiting an old family friend. What about you?"

I couldn't believe he was here. It was more than a little awkward considering our date the other night. I hadn't had the guts yet to tell him I wasn't interested in seeing him again. Instead of just biting the bullet and getting it over with, I'd ignored him for the past several days and now it had finally caught up to me.

"Is everything okay?" Trevor studied me intently, and I realized I hadn't responded yet.

"I'm sorry, I'm fine." I waved off his concern. "I just stopped in to see my grandmother."

"Cool." He nodded. "How's she doing?"

"Good days and bad." I adjusted my purse on my shoulder. "But I hear she's been making friends and she seems to be happy overall."

"That's good."

Silence descended over us for a second, and I forced a smile. I was just about to tell him goodbye when he spoke again.

"I'm actually really glad I ran into you." He stared at me, and my stomach twisted. I already knew what was coming. "You haven't responded to any of my messages or anything..."

He trailed off, and guilt ate away at my insides. He looked so sincere, so sweet. I hated to hurt his feelings, but the quicker I got this over with, the quicker he'd leave me alone. "I'm sorry I've been kind of flighty here recently. I just... I think you're a great guy, but I don't think things are going to work out between us."

His face fell, and he gave a little nod. "I had a good time on our date," he offered. "Maybe we could still be friends?"

I aimed for a smile but knew it fell flat. I knew how those things worked. "I want to be totally transparent with you." I took a deep breath. "I think you should know that I'm interested in somebody else."

"Oh." My heart twisted as his face fell further. "I understand."

I was sure it was hard for him being in a completely new place, knowing hardly anyone. He looked so damn pitiful that I couldn't help but apologize. "I'm sorry," I said softly.

"It's not your fault." He shook his head and smiled, though it was strained. "You're a great girl, and whoever the guy is, he's lucky to have you."

"Thanks." I felt a pang of uncertainty as memories from the other night came rushing back, watching Clay flee like his heels were on fire. I shook the thought from my head. Over the past few days, he'd been more attentive than ever, though he continued to keep his distance at work like I'd asked. He'd practically begged to tell my brother about us, and that more than anything told me how serious he was.

He tipped his head toward the exit. "Well, I should get going."

I smiled at Trevor and offered a little wave. "See you around."

I headed toward the garden, a strange sensation causing my stomach to flutter. It was odd running into Trevor here, of all places. My steps slowed. Why would he be here? During our date he said he'd only been here for a couple of weeks. I'd assumed from the context of the conversation that all of his family was back in Colorado.

A tiny shiver moved down my spine, and I couldn't help but toss a look over my shoulder. The place where Trevor had stood was now empty, but I had to wonder... Was he following me? Almost as quickly as it'd come, I dismissed the possibility, laughing at the ridiculous direction of my thoughts. He'd been here first; there was no possible way he could have followed me.

I exhaled deeply as I headed toward Violet's favorite spot. I hated hurting people, especially nice guys like Trevor. He seemed like a truly good person; I just... wasn't attracted to him.

Violet's familiar face came into view, and I braced myself for whatever greeted me. She sat in the shade, a book spread open in her lap, and I approached cautiously. "Violet?"

Her head lifted, and the clarity in her eyes made my heart dance in my chest. "Abby! So good to see you, sweetheart."

"You, too." I bent to give her a hug. "Sorry I haven't been by for a couple of days."

Violet snapped the book shut and set it beside her. "You're young and busy. You have better things to do than spend your time with an old woman like me. Sit, sit." She waved me over to join her before I could even respond. "Tell me, how do you like your new job?"

"It's been great." Drama with Clay aside, that was. But I didn't mention that.

She eyed me. "Is Con treating you well?"

"Always," I promised. "He's the best big brother."

"He's a good man." Violet nodded concisely. "All those military men are."

"Yes, they are," I murmured, thinking of Clay.

Her face took on a dreamy quality as her gaze slid over the lawn. "Eugene was so handsome in his uniform. I'll never forget the day he shipped out..."

I listened for several minutes, enraptured, as Violet talked about her late husband. I knew of him, of course, but he'd passed away years before Violet had taken me in. She'd spoken of him only briefly from time to time, but for the most part their relationship was a mystery to me. It was so good to see her happy.

Violet's smile grew as she turned to me. "Remember that?"

I jerked back to attention. "What's that?"

"Those men were two peas in a pod, weren't they, Edna?"

I blinked, feeling as if I were floundering. "I—"

And suddenly it hit me. She thought I was an old friend, someone named Edna. It was on the tip of my tongue to correct her, but I swallowed it down as she stared at me expectantly. My heart hurt as I nodded and smiled. "They were."

I turned my gaze away, hoping she wouldn't see the tears glazing my eyes. But she didn't seem to notice. Violet rambled on about days gone by, while I mourned the woman who'd raised me—but didn't even recognize me.

CHAPTER TWENTY-TWO

Clay

I woke with a start, my body attuned to Abby's. Immediately, I registered her panting, uneven breaths, her chest rising and falling rapidly.

Propping myself up on an elbow, I settled my hand on the curve of her shoulder. "Abby. Wake up, baby."

Her head rolled on the pillow next to mine, and she made an agitated gesture with one hand, her fingers curled tightly into the sheets.

I shook her a little harder. "Abilene."

She woke with a start, tearing herself away from me and drawing in a sharp gasp as her eyes flew open wide. She looked disoriented as her gaze flew around the room before landing on me. Her chest still heaved, and terror creased her face in the moonlight. I gave her a second to collect herself, carefully cataloging her reactions. "You okay?"

She nodded shakily and swallowed hard as she rubbed her chest with one hand, as if the motion could physically slow down her heart rate. "Yeah. Just... a bad dream."

I pushed to a sitting position. "Want to talk about it?"

"I..." She dropped her chin to her chest, and she practically folded in on herself right before my eyes.

"Come here, babe." Moving slowly, I looped one arm around her shoulders and drew her close to me. Her entire body trembled, and I dropped a kiss on the top of her head. Whatever she'd been dreaming of had rattled her—hard.

"Everything's fine," I murmured against her hair. "Just relax."

The tension gradually drained from her muscles as she melted into me, and I tightened my hold on her hip, letting her know I was right there with her. With my left hand, I drew the backs of my fingers up and down her arm in a soothing motion.

"They started once I moved back in," she finally confessed. "I was here—in the living room. It was the same... but different. I don't know how to explain it. Like, I could tell it was the living room, but it just felt different."

"What happened?" I asked softly.

She hesitated, her teeth cutting into her bottom lip. "There's a guy... A man. Tonight was the first time I was able to make out his face. He..."

Another shiver racked her body, and I nuzzled her temple. "It's okay, sweetheart. It was just a dream."

"I know." I felt her swallow hard. "It's just... God, it felt so real."

"They do sometimes." I turned my head and kissed her temple. "Do you know who he is?"

She lifted one shoulder. "No one familiar."

"Did he hurt you?" I ventured warily.

Her lips rolled together. "Not... Not like that. He accused me of stealing from him. Then he... touched my leg. Like this." She grabbed my hand and settled it on her knee, then slowly slid it upward almost to the juncture of her thighs.

I fought to keep myself from recoiling. Why the hell would she have dreams like that? My stomach clenched. "Has anyone ever...?"

She shook her head. "No. I mean, my parents weren't great, but I wasn't abused or anything. That's what makes it so weird."

Relief ricocheted through me, and I couldn't help but pull her into my arms. Even though it was only a dream, I found myself wanting to protect her from everything, anything. We sat that way for a long time, just enjoying the feel of each other. For once, Abby wasn't inclined to fill the silence.

"I'll be right back," I said as I dropped a kiss on her temple.

"I'm going to grab a drink. Need anything else?"

She shook her head and yawned. "Just you."

Unable to help myself, I kissed her once more. "You already have me."

I pushed up from the bed and silently made my way through the darkened house to the kitchen. It was a fairly long walk through the ranch, but I felt like I knew every inch of Abby's house as well as my own. I'd spent nearly every night here for the past week, and I was looking forward to many more nights just like this.

Standing next to the sink, I opened the cupboard and pulled down a glass, then filled it with tap water. I leaned against the counter and sipped at it, lost in thought. Abby still hadn't talked with Con about us, and I hadn't pressed. I hoped she would hurry up and tell him so we didn't have to tiptoe around anymore. I wanted—

Motion in the backyard caught my attention, and I froze. Every instinct went on full alert as I watched the man's form skulking around the back porch, outlined in the moonlight. I dashed back into the bedroom as quickly and quietly as I could, then yanked on a pair of jeans.

Abby bolted upright. "What's wrong?"

"Someone's out back. I need you to stay in here and lock the door behind me." I swiped up my side piece so I would have it if needed. "If I'm not back in five minutes, call the police."

The person was still skulking around the backyard, and I slipped outside, then yelled out to him. "Freeze!"

He did, for about half a second. Then he bolted toward the side of the yard. I darted after him and tackled him to the ground.

The guy kicked and begged as he fought to get away. "Please, I—"

There was nothing he could say at the moment that would make a damn difference. We could settle this inside—once he was secure and we had some privacy to work. I cocked back and delivered a jab that snapped his teeth together and finally shut him up. I grabbed him in a chokehold and pulled him toward the backdoor. His feet left twin depressions in the dewy grass as we cut across the moonlit lawn, and I heard the slide of the door behind me.

"Clay?"

Abby's soft voice floated over my shoulder, and I rolled my eyes. I swear, arguing with this woman was useless. I should have known she wouldn't stay in the bedroom. "Grab a chair, babe. We have a guest."

CHAPTER TWENTY-THREE

Abby

I hurried to turn the light on and watched, eyes wide, as Clay dragged the guy inside, then slammed him into a chair. My mouth dropped open when the light hit his face. "Trevor!"

He glanced up at me sheepishly. "Sorry, Abby."

Anger welled up and took over. "What the hell are you doing here? Are you crazy, sneaking around my house in the middle of the night? You could have been shot!"

I flicked a look at Clay, who stood just off to Trevor's side, looking very much like he hadn't quite ruled out the possibility.

"Why the hell are you sneaking around my house in the middle of the night?"

He threw an apologetic glance my way. "I know it looks bad."

From my left, Clay snorted. "You fucking think?"

I slanted a glare at him before turning my attention back to Trevor. "You better have a really good excuse for this, otherwise you'll be pleading your case to the police."

Trevor shook his head emphatically. "Please don't. Just... let me explain."

I lifted a brow and crossed my arms over my chest. "I can't wait."

Trevor's face twisted at my sarcasm. "I was adopted as a baby, literally the day I was born. My birth mother had nothing to do with me except for a couple of letters a lawyer sent on her behalf.

The first one came on my eighteenth birthday when my parents finally told me I was adopted. The second came just a few months ago on my twenty-fifth birthday.

"When I got that first letter, I wanted nothing to do with it. I didn't want to know about my biological parents. I was mad that my mother cut me from her life completely, hadn't even tried to get in touch with me."

"She sent you a letter," Clay pointed out in his no-nonsense tone.

I couldn't disagree with that. Still, I kind of understood where Trevor was coming from. "I'm sure that was hard for you," I offered. "But I'm not sure how that explains anything."

"I know. I'm getting there, I promise. It's kind of a long story." He took a deep breath. "Anyway, the second letter came a couple months back on my birthday. I didn't want to open it, but my parents—my adoptive parents—insisted I should at least give it a try. My birthmother had left me a decent inheritance."

My eyes widened, surprised at the turn the story taken. "Maybe that's all she thought she could offer you," I said slowly. "I'm sure she wouldn't have given you up for adoption without a good reason."

"I know that now." Trevor nodded. "That's kind of what spurred this whole thing. I started looking into her, and I wanted to talk with her, wanted to know what had happened. Why she put me up for adoption. I found my biological mother's name listed on the adoption paperwork, but there was no mention of my father. It was a good place to start, though, and I decided to reach out to her. Unfortunately, when I pulled up her name, I found out that she died shortly after I was born."

"That sucks," I said softly. "I'm sorry."

He peered up at me. "Apparently it was too much. She committed suicide."

The way he phrased that... "Wait." I rocked back on my heels, stunned. "Are you saying...? Is...?"

Trevor nodded, picking up on my train of thought. "Lily was my mother."

A million thoughts flew through my brain, and I latched onto the first thing that solidified in my mind. "That's why you went out with me," I accused. "You were trying to get information about Lily and her family."

Trevor shifted uneasily. "Not completely, but yes."

And suddenly it clicked. Trevor showing up at the grocery story, running into him at Morningside the day I went to visit Violet... "Violet's the 'old family friend' you mentioned. You went to see her." Anger simmered in my stomach. "When the hell were you going to tell me?"

"Soon." He looked sincere, but I was still furious that he'd used me. "But I had a feeling you were avoiding me after our date, and by the time I got to see you again, you broke things off."

"Because I was with Clay," I murmured.

Trevor nodded. "Obviously, I came to speak with Violet, but I found out that you were living here instead. I arranged to run into you in the store so I could talk with you a bit. When you told me Violet was in the nursing home..." He exhaled deeply. "I went to see her, but she wasn't in the best frame of mind."

I couldn't begin to wrap my mind around what had happened. "I... don't know what to say."

"I'm sorry." His eyes pleaded with me. "Really, I am. I should have been upfront with you and told you the truth from the beginning."

I folded my arms over my chest. "Well, I can't really help you. Violet talked about her from time to time, but other than that... You might have better luck with her brother, Patrick."

"Thanks. I just... I don't know how to explain it, but I got the feeling from her letters that her pregnancy was unwanted."

"I can imagine. Lily was young," I put in. "Maybe she just regretted it."

"Could be," Trevor admitted. "But the whole tone of the letter was just... sad. She said something once that she felt trapped where she was."

Almost immediately, Lily's diary came to mind. I'd read a handful of passages, but the whole thing was depressing. She'd lamented being ridiculed by classmates, unable to speak to anyone. She'd mentioned that she had no one to talk to; no one would believe her if she told the truth. She'd apparently considered taking her life several times but couldn't bring herself to hurt the baby.

I threw a quick glance at Clay, but his expression remained impassive, and I knew he was waiting for my cue. I wasn't sure exactly what Trevor's intentions were, so I decided it was best to keep that to myself for now.

"Do you have these letters?" Clay looked skeptical, not that I could blame him.

"They're back in my hotel room."

Clay's lips pressed into a firm line as he regarded Trevor. "So we've determined that Lily was your birth mother and you came here looking for information. The question is why. Why keep looking for her after you knew she was gone?"

"Right. So, that's where it gets interesting," Trevor said. He turned to me. "I tried reaching out to Violet first but when that failed, I looked for Charlie."

At my blank look, he tipped his head. "Do you remember Charlie?"

Should I? I racked my brain, but I couldn't think of anyone close to Violet with that name. "I don't know who that is."

Trevor studied me. "She never mentioned him?"

I had no idea who he was talking about, or why. "No. Why does it matter?"

"Charlie was Violet's second husband."

I shrugged a little, lost. "If she remarried, it was long before I even came around. It obviously didn't last long, because she never mentioned him to me. Besides, what does that have to do with anything?"

"Charlie was married to Violet for almost a decade before they divorced. He came into the picture not long before Lily— my mother—got pregnant."

"And...?" I drew out the question, wondering what the hell he was getting at.

"I think he had something to do with it."

He couldn't have shocked me more if he tried. "You think...?" I shook my head, unable to fathom the implication. "No way."

Trevor lifted his shoulders. "I can't be sure of anything

without evidence. That's why I've been poking around here. I talked to Violet, but she claimed not to remember. Besides, I didn't want to push too hard. I wasn't sure how she would react if I accused her husband of raping her daughter."

I could only imagine. I focused once more on Trevor. "Have you spoken with him?"

"I can't."

The way he said it both piqued my curiosity and filled me with a sense of dread, but Clay spoke up before I could voice my questions.

"Why not?" Clay asked. "Were you not able to contact him?"

Trevor stared up at me. "I've looked everywhere, followed every lead but there's absolute no record of him anywhere."

I exchanged a quick glance with Clay as I let that sink in. "You think he's dead?"

Trevor shook his head, looking serious. "I think he was murdered."

CHAPTER TWENTY-FOUR

Clay

I steered into a parking spot alongside the hotel and turned to Abby, who was in the process of unbuckling her seat belt.

"I go first. Stay behind me and to the left."

She threw a bewildered look my way. "Seriously? You think he's going to attack me or something?"

Personally, I thought the guy was either completely full of shit or out of his damn mind. But if Abby wanted to give him a shot, then that's what we were going to do. Didn't mean I was gonna be happy about it, or slack off. I had no idea what his agenda was. This whole thing could be some kind of trap, and I'd be damned if I would put Abby in danger. He'd been casing the house; who knew what he would have done if we weren't there. My bike was in the garage next to Abby's car, so it looked like no one was home. If she'd been there alone... Christ, I couldn't fathom. Fury surged through my veins.

"I never joke about your safety. Despite what he told us earlier, we don't know anything about him."

That was another issue I planned to rectify soon. As soon as we got to QSG in the morning, I would have Abby run background on both Trevor and whoever the hell this Charlie guy was.

Abby stared at me for a second, then finally nodded. "All right, you win."

I smirked. "I like that you say that like you have a choice."

One dark brow lifted. "You're such a cocky prick."

I winked at her as I settled my hand on her thigh and squeezed. "Bet your pretty ass. Now, let's get this over with so we can get back to bed."

After Trevor had dropped that last bomb—that he assumed Charlie, his father, was dead—he insisted we come to the hotel so he could prove it. I had no idea what we were going to find inside, and a huge part of me didn't really give a shit. If the guy had knocked up his fifteen-year-old stepdaughter, he probably deserved whatever had happened to him.

So, here we were, a little after midnight. I didn't trust this guy as far as I could throw him, and I was more than a little cranky about the whole situation. Abby seemed intent on listening to his explanation though, and I owed it to her to at least give him half an hour of our time. My Smith and Wesson was warm and familiar at my lower back, and though Abby had given me hell when I tucked it into my waistband, I didn't care. I never went anywhere without it, and I wasn't going to start now. Besides, I wasn't entirely convinced that this guy wasn't mentally unbalanced.

I made my way around Abby's car and opened the door for her. I wasn't about to drag her around on my bike in the middle of the night, so we'd opted to take hers instead. Once she was on her feet, I locked up again and tucked her partially behind my body as we made our way toward the seedy hotel. Trevor must've seen us coming, because he flung the door open seconds later. The inside of the room was lit up like a beacon, which seemed to be a good omen at least.

I still wasn't exactly sure what the hell we were doing here in the middle of the night. All I knew was that when Abby got an idea in her head, it was damn near impossible to get her to veer from her course. I'd tried to tell her no fewer than a dozen times on the way over that we could do this tomorrow—or, you know, never—but she'd insisted we at least check out what he had to say.

Keeping my eyes forward, I directed my voice over my shoulder, just loud enough that Abby could hear me. "You owe me for this."

She slipped her hand into mine and gave it a little squeeze. I stepped into the hotel room first, still shielding Abby with my body as I turned to Trevor. "Show us what you've got."

He closed and locked the door, then strode across the room to a small table in the corner that doubled as a desk. I was momentarily stupefied by the number of post-its and newspaper clippings stuck to the wall around it.

"I've been going through everything I can think of," Trevor started. "The last address listed for Charlie was in New Orleans."

I nodded, playing along. "Not the worst choice." It was close enough to Texas that he could come back and visit if he wanted, but far enough away to start fresh. "So I'm assuming he wasn't at home when you went to visit him?"

"Not just that," he replied. "The address listed on the paperwork doesn't even exist."

Abby's hand tensed where it still rested in mine. "How is that possible?"

Trevor gave a little shrug and picked up a paper on the desk, then passed it to me. "Remember that inheritance I told you about?" Neither of us bothered to answer the rhetorical question, and Trevor continued. "I used a little bit of it to hire a private investigator before I came here. This is everything he was able to dig up on the man."

I scanned the list as he spoke. "The phone number goes to an automated message that states the number is no longer in service, and the physical address is literally nonexistent. I went to New Orleans myself to try to find it. It's a rundown old building."

"Doesn't mean he didn't live there at one point," I countered.

Trevor shook his head. "For the past thirty-six years it was a delicatessen. The owner passed away last winter, and it's been empty ever since."

Interesting. "What about family and friends?"

"I've talked to a few, but no one has seen or heard from him."

He picked up another sheet of paper and passed it to Abby. "According to state records, this is when the divorce was finalized. When did you move in with Violet?"

"Summertime," she said softly as she skimmed the paper. "It was right after school let out and Con went into the Marines."

Trevor nodded. "The records show the divorce paperwork was filed almost six months after that, in the middle of winter. It was finalized soon after."

Her eyes lifted to him, filled with confusion. "I don't understand. Why would she not say anything about him?"

Trevor lifted one shoulder. "I don't know. But there has to be a reason."

"Maybe they separated after Lily's suicide," I offered.

Abby tipped her head to one side like she was considering every angle. She drifted toward the table and began to sift through some of the papers. "It just makes no sense. She never once mentioned him, and there was no trace of him—or any man—in the house that I could ever remember."

"It's like he just vanished," Trevor agreed.

"He could have wanted to just disappear," I said, playing Devil's advocate. Granted, it would be hard as hell to not leave some kind of footprint these days, but nothing was impossible.

"Still," Abby insisted as she riffled through the papers. "Why wait that long to divorce him? And why—?"

I watched intently as she cut off midsentence, her entire body stiffening. She held up a small picture and showed it to Trevor. "Who is this?"

"That's Charlie."

Her eyes flew to mine. "That's him."

My brows drew together as I watched a thousand emotions flight across her face. "It's who, babe?"

"Charlie," Trevor reiterated at the same time Abby spoke.

"The man from my dreams."

I stiffened. "Do you think that's him?"

She nodded shakily. "That's definitely him. Maybe..." One hand flew to her throat. "Maybe it wasn't a dream. Maybe it was..."

A memory. She didn't have to say the words out loud, but I knew that was exactly what she was thinking. The heat of fury raced over my body. If Charlie had abused and impregnated Lily, then come after Abby... Red clouded my vision as the implication sank in. "That could very well explain why he's gone."

Trevor's gaze bounced between the two of us. "What

happened?"

Abby still looked unsettled, so I spoke up for her. "Ever since Abby moved back into the house, she's been having a dream about a strange man approaching her. Now that we know who he is…"

Trevor's eyes widened. "You think it was Charlie."

I eased Abby against my side, curling my fingers into her hip as she leaned into me. "What else happened in your dream?"

She shook her head, lost in thought. "I… I don't know. It never finishes. It's like my mind just cuts off."

Christ. Had something terrible happened to Abby, something so horrible that she'd shut it out? I prayed not. The thought had my stomach roiling. If her dream was actually a repressed memory, I couldn't help but wonder what had happened afterward. And if Violet had discovered that he'd raped her Lily, then come after Abby, could she have been pushed to take drastic measures? I knew what I would've done if it were my daughter, but I didn't say that aloud.

"Maybe he was murdered," I finally conceded.

"By who?" Abby asked. "I don't think Violet could do it."

"Maybe not by herself," Trevor stated slowly, "but maybe she knows who did."

Trevor and I exchanged a look over Abby's head. One thing for certain—we had to talk to Violet.

CHAPTER TWENTY-FIVE

Abby

I repressed a yawn as the printer spit out the final sheet of paper, then tucked it into the folder for Clay to look over. I'd run background on both Trevor and Charlie per his request, even though I was more certain than ever that Trevor was genuinely telling the truth.

I couldn't get the memory of seeing that photo last night out of my mind. It was eerie seeing the face from my dream in a photograph. I'd felt cold all day, unable to shake the chills plaguing me. Worse, I couldn't even go to Clay the way I wanted. He'd kept his distance the way we always did at work, and my heart constricted. He was right; I needed to tell Con.

It was something else that weighed heavily on my conscience. Things had been absolutely chaotic around here, and I didn't want to heap more concerns on my brother's plate. I vowed to tell him soon—just as soon as everything calmed down and we could have a rational discussion one-on-one.

I closed up the folder, then slipped into the bullpen and moved toward Clay's desk. My heart kicked up at the sight of him, and I fought to cover my reaction. In the middle of a discussion with Blake, he paused and glanced my way as I extended the folder.

"Thanks."

He accepted it with that single word and nothing else. I didn't know what I was expecting, but it hurt a little that he was so blasé about the whole thing. It was irrational, I knew, since I was the one who asked to keep things quiet at work, but his indifference stung.

I'd told my brother that I was taking off a little early to go check on Violet, so I strode back to the front desk where I grabbed my keys, logged out of the computer, and headed out to my car. I stopped by the bakery to pick up a slice of Violet's favorite Key lime pie before turning toward to Morningside Assisted Living Facility.

Since it was another gorgeous, sunny day, I decided to check outside first. After looking around for a minute, I saw one of the nurses with another patient. "Hi, Robin, have you seen Violet today?"

She shook her head. "Not yet. Why don't you check her room?"

"Thanks." I smiled and headed inside. As soon as I stepped into Violet's room, I knew today was a bad one. She sat huddled in a chair in the corner, her raggedy old shawl wrapped around her shoulders, a blank expression on her face.

She turned to me as I entered the room. "Hello."

I never knew exactly where her mind was, so I offered a tiny smile but didn't move any further. "How are you feeling today?"

"Fine, thank you."

She appraised me for a second, like her mind was trying to connect the dots, wondering if she knew me and why I was here. "Would you like to come in for a minute?"

"That would be great, thank you." Ignoring the sharp dagger of pain spearing through my heart, I took a seat across from her and set the box of Key lime pie on the table. "I brought pie if you'd like some."

She lifted the lid of the box and gazed quizzically at it. "What is it?"

I forced a smile to my lips. "Key lime pie."

She studied it for another second before closing the lid. "I don't think I like Key lime pie."

My heart clenched with sympathy. I couldn't begin to imagine what it would be like to not know or recognize anything anymore. It was hard to know how to act around her sometimes. The last thing I wanted to do was push and scare her, so I kept our conversation easy and carefree. "It's a beautiful day out. Have you been out for a walk?"

She turned and looked out the window. "No. I need to take care of the lilies."

Though they were some of the hardiest flowers around, I didn't bother to speak up. She'd doted on them, spending hours making sure they were perfect. "I could take care of them if you'd like," I offered.

"That would be lovely, dear, thank you." She seemed lost in thought before she finally spoke. "My Lily adored lilies. Did you know that?"

I shook my head. "I did not."

She smiled softly. "She loved them so—especially the calla lilies. Those huge white ones? He teased her all the time. He didn't like them. Said they reminded him of funerals."

Was the man she spoke about Charlie? "Who made fun of her? Charlie?"

I found myself holding my breath, awaiting Violet's confirmation. She seemed to drift for a moment before giving her head a little shake. "Ironic, isn't it?"

I repressed a sigh. I'd been hoping she would at least acknowledge his presence, if not what happened to him. Shoving away my disappointment, I focused on what she'd said about Lily. I knew Violet had planted the flowers in the backyard in memory of her daughter after her death, but I hadn't realized they were also her favorite flower. "I think it's very appropriate," I ventured cautiously. After all, what else could I say?

"It is, isn't it? I love those flowers so. I always look at them and think of her." Violet smiled broadly. "Well, I think I'll take a nap now," she said as she rose from the chair. "It was nice to meet you."

"You too," I said weakly as I blinked back tears. "Can I come see you again?"

"I'd like that," she said.

I left the room feeling as if my heart was breaking, wishing that things could be different. I cared less about the answers I was seeking than Violet's health in general. As I climbed back into my car and headed home, I let the tears fall. I still felt guilty for allowing Violet to go to the facility. I knew it was what she'd wanted, and

I knew it was easier for myself and Patrick. Mostly, I felt guilty because I felt relief at the fact that someone else more qualified was there to help her. Dealing with a dementia patient was hard; though the doctors and nurses had told me what to expect, I found myself way out of my depth. Sometimes I just didn't know how to respond to her—and that made me feel even worse. I'd known her for half my life, yet she was now a complete stranger to me.

My heart broke as I drove home—for Violet and Lily, but also for myself.

CHAPTER TWENTY-SIX

Clay

Abby had been quiet ever since I got to her house this afternoon, a dead giveaway to let me know that something was wrong. I snuck a glance at her where she stood just a few feet away, sorting things from the closet in the master bedroom and packing them into boxes to be moved to storage.

"How did your visit with Violet go?" I ventured warily.

She paused the process of putting the folded shirt into the box, and she stared sightlessly at it for a few seconds before responding. "Not great."

I hadn't expected much else, to be entirely honest, but I knew Abby was disappointed. "What happened?"

She bit her lip. "She didn't even recognize me. I know there are supposed to be good days and bad, but I just... I guess I didn't expect that. It hurt a little bit, you know?" Her gaze lifted to mine. "And then I felt like an asshole for feeling that way, because I know she can't help it."

"I'm sorry." I abandoned the box of books on the bed and moved toward her, pulling her into my arms.

I couldn't imagine what this was like for her. I didn't have any first-hand experience with anyone who had a form of dementia, nor was I close with any of my family members, save Cole. As similar as our childhoods had been, they were also vastly different. While Cole and I had practically raised ourselves, Abby had had Violet. I knew she was close to the older woman despite the fact that they weren't even related, and I couldn't begin to contemplate a connection like that. Still, I wanted to ease the hurt that Abby was feeling right now.

"I know it's hard for you, but I'm sure it's hard for her too."

"I know," she mumbled against my chest. "That's what I keep trying to tell myself."

She pulled away a little bit. "The doctors recommend just giving her little reminders when she forgets, but sometimes she's just so adamant that it's almost easier to go along with it."

"I don't blame you," I said. "I'm sure she believes whatever she says. Better to just drop it sometimes than get into an argument that she won't remember anyway." A stricken look crossed her face, and I tightened my hold on her. Shit. "I'm sorry, that was—"

She shook her head. "No, you're right. I just feel kind of helpless when she's like this."

"I know, babe."

I hated that she was hurting, and I wanted nothing more than to take that pain away. I squeezed her hip. "The little plastic things on the ends of shoelaces are called aglets."

Abby rolled her eyes, but a tiny smile lifted her mouth. "Distracting me?"

"It was that or sex," I said honestly.

Abby's smile grew and something in my chest fluttered. It was scary how much I liked her. Just being with her made me happy, and the more time I spent with her, the more I wanted to be with her. The only black cloud hovering over our relationship at this point was Con. I felt guilty for not telling him about us, but Abby had insisted she wanted to tell him. I wanted to give her that opportunity—but I hoped she would hurry the hell up about it. I felt like a dirty secret, like she didn't want to admit she was with me. Given my past, the knowledge hurt. I tried not to let it show, but it got harder every day to just let it slide. I wanted to be with her, and I wanted everyone to know she was mine.

She leaned in for a quick, soft kiss. "Armadillo shells are bulletproof."

I wanted to tell her everything I felt, everything that weighed on me, but she'd been through enough today. Instead, I bottled up my emotions and pushed them to the furthest recesses of my heart as I gave a little tug on her hand. "Let's grab some food. I'm starving."

Over dinner we made small talk, keeping the conversation light and steering away from anything that involved either Violet or her brother.

The situation with Trevor hovered in the forefront of my mind. We obviously wouldn't be getting any information from Violet, but the whole thing had stirred my curiosity, especially knowing that Abby was somehow involved. I wanted to get some answers. "Violet has a son, right?"

Abby nodded and swallowed a bite of food. "Patrick."

"How old was he when you lived here?"

"He was older than Lily, so he'd been gone for a while at that time." Abby studied me. "Do you think he had something to do with it?"

"Possibly." I set my fork down and leaned back in my chair. "I don't know exactly what happened to Charlie, but I looked over the backgrounds you printed off this morning. There's no information on him—no vehicle registered in his name, no health insurance, no rental agreement. What Trevor said is accurate—it's like he just disappeared."

"So you really think he's dead?" Abby bit her lip.

"I have to admit it's a possibility. Now, whether it was an accident or intentional, I don't know."

Abby stared at me. "If it were an accident, why wouldn't she have told me about him? Why don't I remember anything about him?" She gestured with one hand. "Not in the entire time I've lived here has there been any evidence of him. Why?"

I couldn't answer that, and I really didn't like the implication. "I'm not sure, babe. I want to help you figure that out, but I don't know where to start. A death certificate was never issued, so there's no evidence that he's actually gone."

"Unless someone admits it," Abby added.

Wishful thinking, but they would be stupid to do so. If someone had killed him, they'd managed to keep it secret for fifteen years. By now they probably expected everyone had forgotten about it. Had it not been for Trevor digging into Lily's past, no one would have been the wiser. "Let's say he is dead. Like you said last night, I seriously doubt Violet would be capable of doing it herself. You were living with her at the time. She couldn't have just killed someone in front of you."

Abby's teeth worried her lower lip, lost in thought. "I—"

She stopped abruptly, her entire body going rigid. "Dr. Vance."

From where I sat watching her, I could practically hear the wheels turning. "Who is that?"

"A child psychologist." She sat forward a little bit.

That was news to me. "What are you talking about?"

"About six months after I moved in, Violet took me to see Dr. Vance. She said I needed to talk with someone about my parents' deaths. But if that were the case, wouldn't she have done that right away? I mean, why else wait so long? I never really thought about it before, but now..." She redirected her gaze to me. "What if it had to do with this instead?"

It made my stomach churn to consider, but I couldn't rule it out. "Do you think you saw something and shut it out, or maybe he helped you to move on and you've forgotten about it until now— until the dreams started?"

She shrugged. "I have no idea. There was another doctor around that same time, too, but I only remember seeing him once. I'd have to look through Violet's things, see if she kept his information."

That didn't help with the situation at hand, and it only left me with more questions than answers. But I wanted a resolution for Abby if nothing else. "If Violet caught Charlie... with you," I said slowly, watching her reaction, "she could have just reacted impulsively. Maybe she was trying to protect you and things went a little too far."

"Then why not go to the police?"

I lifted one shoulder, completely at a loss. "Maybe she felt she couldn't. Maybe she thought she'd go to jail and you'd be alone again. Desperate people do stupid things all the time."

Abby nodded slowly. "She could have covered it up."

"Possible." I nodded. "She'd have reached out to someone she could trust."

Abby's chest hitched. "Like Patrick."

My thoughts exactly. "We should talk to him. Can you call and see if he'll meet up with us?"

Abby nodded her assent, but her face was tinged slightly green like the thought made her sick to her stomach. I couldn't imagine what she was thinking or feeling right now. If this had truly happened to her...

Anger burned in my stomach. I wanted answers on her behalf. I stood and moved around the table to her, then knelt next to her chair. I cupped her face in my hands. "Whatever we find, I'll be right here."

"Okay."

The word was a whisper, but I saw the truth of it in her eyes. She was putting her faith in me—and I wouldn't let her down.

CHAPTER TWENTY-SEVEN

Abby

Patrick had agreed to meet with us under the condition that we do so on his lunch break. He hadn't said as much, but I had a feeling he wanted to keep it away from family so he didn't have to bring up the bad memories around his wife and kids.

Clay held the door for me as I stepped into the restaurant and removed my sunglasses so I could see better. Scanning the small room, I found Violet's son seated at a table in the back corner near a window. He lifted a hand as his gaze met mine, and I offered a little wave in return. Clay fell into step next to me, and Patrick greeted me with a hug before offering his hand to Clay.

"Patrick."

"Clay Thompson."

Patrick waited until we were seated before turning his attention back to me and speaking. "How is the house coming along?"

"Good. Still packing things up, getting them moved to the storage unit."

"I appreciate it," Patrick said with a little nod.

"I actually came across a few of your things too," I said. "I set them aside if you want them."

He smiled. "God, I can't even begin to imagine how old some of that stuff must be. I'll be sure to stop by and get it out of your way."

"It's no problem," I assured him. "There were some yearbooks and things I figured you might like to have."

"Great, thanks." His gaze jumped between me and Clay.

I waited for the inevitable question as to whether Clay and I were dating, but the waitress stepped up next to the table to take our orders. Once she was gone, I looked back to Patrick. "Have you had a chance to speak with your mom lately?"

The corners of his lips turn down. "No, how is she?"

"More bad days than good." I made a little face. "I stopped in to see her a few days ago, but she didn't recognize me."

Patrick's face fell and creased with sympathy. "I'm sorry, Abby. That must be hard for you."

I lifted one shoulder and threw a grateful look Clay's way when he dropped his arm over the back of my chair and lightly rubbed my shoulder. I turned my attention back to Patrick. "I really don't have any room to talk. I mean, you're her son."

"But you're her daughter," Patrick said. "In her eyes, in all the ways that matter, you're just as much a part of the family as I am. Maybe more." He sat forward in his chair and looked at me. "After Lily passed away, mom fell into a deep depression. But having you come live with her changed things. You breathed life into her, gave her a reason to get up every day and go on. I don't want to say that you were a replacement for Lily, because that wouldn't be fair to either of you. But know that I appreciate everything you've done for my mother, and I know that Lily would too."

Tears clogged my throat and stung my eyes, and I took a moment to battle them back before speaking. "She's more of a mother to me than my own ever was, and it kills me to see her like this."

"Me, too," Patrick replied with no small amount of remorse. "I know I wasn't there for her as much as I should have been, and I regret it."

It was a crappy situation all around for everyone, and it was only going to get worse. Before I could broach the subject of what had happened with Lily, the waitress delivered our meals. We made small talk as we ate until, finally, I could put it off no longer.

"So, you're probably wondering exactly why I asked to meet with you," I said, nerves causing my insides to flutter.

Patrick nodded a little. "What's on your mind?"

"What happened with Lily..." I started, then stopped. "We found Lily's diary a few weeks ago when we were packing and—"

"Her diary?" Patrick's tone was ice-cold, his posture rigid.

I studied him. "Yeah, I found it in her old bedroom. I was going to give it to Violet, but I wasn't sure how she'd react. I thought I would ask you first."

"No sense in dredging up bad memories," he said, his voice gruff. "I'd throw the damn thing away."

I paused. He was holding something back, I could tell. I strove for calm as I spoke. "That's fine. I'll just put it with the rest of Violet's things."

Patrick nodded stiffly, and silence descended for a few seconds. My heart told me to leave well enough alone, that Patrick and his family had endured enough tragedy already. But my mind screamed at me for answers. I couldn't just let it go. We'd come this far; I needed to find out if he knew about Lily—and Charlie.

I swallowed hard. "That actually brings up my second question. I was wondering..."

I trailed off, and Patrick lifted a brow in question. "Yeah?"

"Did you know she was pregnant before she—?"

He speared me with a hawk-like gaze, cutting me off. "What?"

I bit my lip, wishing I could read him. Did he know all the sordid details or not? "Well, we found out"—I gestured between Clay and myself—"that Lily had a baby, a little boy, just a few months before she killed herself."

"That wasn't common knowledge." He leaned close, his eyes dark with anger. "Who told you that?"

Clay reached forward as if to physically ward Patrick away, his tone hard. "Let's just relax for a second. We found out because Lily's child—Trevor—tried to break into Abby's house."

Patrick looked absolutely stunned, and he sank back in his chair. "What are you talking about?"

I drew in a deep breath. "A couple nights ago, Clay heard someone outside. Trevor was sneaking around the back yard, so Clay brought him in and we asked what he was doing." An understatement, but I wasn't inclined to tell Patrick the whole truth.

"He explained that Lily had given him up for adoption, and he only found out about her through letters he received much later."

"I..." Patrick's mouth opened and closed. "I had no idea he knew. From what I understood, the adoption was supposed to be sealed."

I shrugged helplessly. "I'm not sure. But that brought up a whole new issue. Trevor is looking for his biological father."

"Couldn't help you with that."

His hard tone and the tic in his jaw told me otherwise, and I pressed on. "You still lived at home when she was married to Charlie, right?"

Resentment rolled off Patrick in waves, and I could just imagine him trying to clamp down on his anger as he responded. "They married when I was in high school, but they separated a few years after Lily passed. She stayed with him too damn long."

"Do you know where he is? Trevor would love—"

Patrick was already shaking his head. "Not a clue. We didn't get along too well, and I didn't bother to keep in touch."

He glanced at his watch, then tossed a strained smile my way. "Sorry, but I have to get back to work. It was good catching up with you."

"Yeah, of course. Thanks for coming."

Unease swirling in my belly, we tossed down some money to settle the bill and headed outside. I somehow managed to curb all of my questions until Clay and I were ensconced in his truck and pulling away from the diner.

"Well that was interesting," I remarked with no small amount of sarcasm.

From my left, Clay let out a little snort. "No shit."

I had to agree. The way Patrick had reacted was suspicious as hell. "Do you think he did it?"

He shrugged. "I honestly don't know. He doesn't seem the type, and there's not nearly enough evidence to suggest he did."

"I know," I lamented. "It's like we're missing half the pieces. But I still think he knows something," I insisted.

"That's a given," Clay replied. "I just don't know what. Is he protecting himself or Violet?"

I thought on that for a long minute, turning the question over in my mind and examining it from every angle. "Maybe both. Like you said, it's unlikely that she would be unable to do anything by herself. Maybe they're both responsible and he needs to stay quiet."

"Definitely a possibility." Clay nodded. "We'll have to see what Trevor thinks. Speaking of..." He passed me his phone as he shifted the truck into gear and pulled out onto the main drag. "Check this, would you? Trevor called while we were talking to Patrick, and I didn't want to interrupt."

I thumbed through the phone, entering the passcode he relayed to me, then pulled up the new voicemail. I turned on the speakerphone function so we could both listen.

"Hey, it's Trevor. I'm up in Ft. Worth right now meeting with a relative of Charlie's. But I've been thinking. Something about Violet and Charlie's divorce was bothering me, and I want to take a look at those papers again. I'll give you a call as soon as I get back into town so we can..." There were some muffled noises in the background before Trevor came back. "He's here, I've got to go. Talk to you later."

The line clicked off, and I glanced at Clay. "Wonder what he found?"

"Not sure. Guess we'll see what he finds up there, if anything."

There were so many questions and not nearly enough answers. I was beginning to feel like we were looking for a needle in a haystack.

CHAPTER TWENTY-EIGHT

Clay

While Trevor was in Ft. Worth, I planned to do a little digging around here. From the papers Trevor had, we'd found an acquaintance of Charlie's, a man by the name of George Grudenfelder. Abby was at QSG, so I decided to stop by and see if the man could shed any light on the situation. From the information Abby had pulled up, the man was single, having lost his own wife several years ago, and he now spent his days primarily playing golf on the private course next to the retirement community where he lived.

After a quick stop at the front desk, I followed directions out to the pro shop. One of the men there confirmed that George had teed off just after 8:30 this morning and should be wrapping up soon. I settled at the small table outside to wait. Within half an hour, a golf cart came puttering up the drive, and I recognized George. He threw a wary glance my way as I stood and lifted my chin in greeting.

"Can I help you with something?"

I held out a hand, and he gave it an abbreviated shake. "Clay Thompson. Hoping I could ask you some questions."

"About?"

"Do you remember a man by the name of Charles Orwell?"

"Sure. Golfed together once a month or so."

"What can you tell me about him?"

"Why?" George raised a suspicious brow. "He done something?"

"Not exactly. I'm kind of worried about him. My girlfriend lived with Charlie and Violet when she was young. Violet's in an assisted living facility now, but no one has heard or seen anything from Charlie for quite a while."

"Not sure I can help you," George replied. "Haven't seen him in... Oh, fifteen years or so? Ever since he and his wife split."

I nodded a little in sympathy. "Did he ever talk to you about Violet and what caused them to split?"

"Not really." George shook his head. "Got the feeling something was going on, though."

"How do you mean?" I asked.

"Just the way he was acting," George replied. "I'd say that started sometime after that little girl came to live with them. Maybe put a strain on the relationship. Especially after what happened to Violet's daughter."

"How did he feel about Lily's death?"

George lifted one shoulder, sympathy creasing his weathered expression. "I don't know. Charlie was a tough nut to crack. Never could quite tell exactly what he was thinking. Seemed to take it pretty hard, though. He seemed mad, bitter, you know?"

"I can understand that," I replied. "What about after Abby moved in?"

"Can't say I remember exactly." George stared off into space as he reminisced on the past. "Come to think of it, I think he was more upbeat than I had seen him in a long time. I think that's what surprised me so much when he left. It was like he just picked up and left everything behind. I thought maybe it was another woman. I never did find out for sure."

A sick sensation roiled in my stomach. I had a terrible inkling that George was partially correct; except the woman in question had been a ten-year-old girl. I didn't want to say anything to George and ruin his perception of an old friend, so I kept my mouth shut. "Thanks for your time," I said to George as I climbed to my feet. "I really appreciate it."

"Let me know if you find anything out, if you would. Be nice to see him again."

I nodded. "I'll do that."

The more I learned, the more I felt we were on the right track.

If my daughter had gotten pregnant, I would want to know who the father was. Had Violet suspected Charlie, or had she trusted him implicitly? Maybe there were old hospital records, something that could help. If we could just determine if Charlie was, in fact, Trevor's father, that would give Violet even more motive to kill him. But why stay with him if she suspected him of raping her daughter? God, it was all so frustrating.

I headed home toward Abby's house with more questions than answers. But the thought of seeing Abby again sent anticipation racing through my veins. When I wasn't physically with her, I found myself thinking about her more and more. I tried to play it cool at work, but it got harder with every day that passed. I wanted everyone to know that Abby was mine, that we were together. Con was going to be pissed, no doubt about that. I just prayed he would accept our decision with as little drama as possible.

CHAPTER TWENTY-NINE

Abby

Clay lay sprawled across the bed sideways, one knee bent and pointing to the ceiling, his head resting on my stomach. With one hand, I raked my fingers through his hair, gently massaging his scalp.

"Did you know the rarest M&M color is brown?"

I laughed when he let out a groan. "Come on, babe, not now. My blood still hasn't returned to my brain."

At that, I laughed even harder. He'd pulled out of me barely ten minutes ago, and we'd collapsed into this position, completely naked and comfortable with each other. But the silence had started to get to me, and my mind had begun to whirl. By now, Clay knew silence wasn't my strong point.

With a resigned sigh, he rolled his head toward me. "M&M stands for Mars and Murrie, the two men who came up with the candy."

"A dentist invented cotton candy."

"Bet that was good for business." He grinned. "Pineapple can be used as a natural meat tenderizer."

"Good to know." I tapped my chin. "Bananas grow upside down."

"McDonald's once tried to make bubblegum flavored broccoli."

"Ewww..." I wrinkled my nose. "That's disgusting."

"So is regular broccoli." Clay rolled to his side so he lay next to me. "I need a shower. Come with me."

"Maybe."

I trailed one hand down his front and over the hard ridges of his abs. God, he was so handsome. Every inch of him was absolute perfection.

He stilled my hand as it traveled south, and he made a little sound in the back of his throat. "Not as young as I used to be, babe. Gonna need a few minutes."

I sighed dramatically. "Always making me wait."

Clay framed my face with one huge hand, squeezing my jaw. "Good things come to those who wait, remember?"

He dipped his head and kissed me slow until all thoughts dissolved from my brain. After a few minutes, he broke the kiss and peered down at me. His gaze caressed every inch of my face and I felt almost self-conscious under the scrutiny. "What?"

"Just you. I'm always amazed by how beautiful you are."

His words sent acute pleasure curling through me, along with a slight tinge of embarrassment. Those golden eyes twisted my insides into knots, sent a strange sensation shooting through my heart. I was terrified to examine it too closely, because I was almost certain I knew what it meant... and I wasn't ready to admit it yet, not to myself and not to Clay.

I swallowed hard and pasted on a playful smile. "I thought you were getting in the shower?"

He tucked a strand of hair behind my ear, a smile curving his lips. "If you help me soap up, I'll return the favor."

I pretended to think it over. "All right," I agreed, bouncing from the bed. "I'll be there in one second."

"Don't take too long." He swatted my butt, then rolled to his feet and strode through the connecting door to the bathroom. His muscles bunched as he moved, and I watched him shamelessly as he flipped on the water, then stepped into the shower. He tossed a look my way as if he'd felt my eyes on him, a come-hither smirk lifting his lips.

I followed him almost immediately, stepping into the glass enclosure already filling with steam. He dipped his head beneath the spray then, as if feeling the change in the air when I opened the door, turned to me. A huge grin curled his mouth as he wrapped one arm around my waist and tugged me inside. Dipping his head, he kissed me deeply, leisurely.

I clutched at his biceps as his hands ran up and down my back, over my hips and bottom, sliding sensually over my slick skin. I broke away, panting, and Clay spun me in his arms until I was facing away from him. I heard the sound of a bottle opening behind me, and I imagined him pouring soap into his palm. A moment later, his hands moved to my belly, and he began to rub, bubbles exploding in their wake. My head dropped back, and I leaned against him as his hands moved upward, kneading and massaging my breasts.

Once we were both sufficiently cleaned and sated, Clay flipped off the water, then grabbed a towel and passed it to me. I quickly dried off, then headed into the bedroom. Snatching his shirt off the floor, I shrugged it over my head.

Clay lifted a brow at me. "What am I supposed to wear?"

I shrugged. "Not my problem. Guess you'll have to stay like that." I gestured to his bare chest, still glistening with water.

"You'd like that, wouldn't you?"

"Absolutely." I grinned, and he let out a little laugh.

"Woman, you're something else."

"I know." I grinned and hitched one thumb over my shoulder as I watched him grab up his boxers. "I'm gonna start dinner. You feeling anything in particular?"

"Whatever you want is good with me." He grabbed the back of my head and pulled me in for a quick, hard kiss, then let me go.

I drifted toward the kitchen, practically floating on air. Just as I cut through the living room, movement from the driveway caught my attention. I strode toward the window and caught sight of a black SUV parked outside.

Shit.

My brother reached the front porch just as I opened the door. "Hey."

His eyes widened with surprise, one brow lifted as he inspected me between the narrow opening. "Hey. You good?"

"Yeah, I'm fine." I leaned against the doorframe, adopting a relaxed pose and hoping he wouldn't see right through me. "Just got out of the shower. What's up?"

"Not much." His eyes skated over me, and I fought the urge to shift under his scrutiny as he took in Clay's shirt hanging to the middle of my thighs. "You steal a shirt?"

"Yeah. You know... marketing," I finished lamely.

My brother threw me a look like he didn't believe me. "Mind if I come in?"

"I'm not really ready for guests." I fought the urge to look over the shoulder for Clay. I hoped he would stay in the bedroom until Con was gone.

"Okay." Confusion tugged my brother's brows together. "Well, I just thought you might want to go look at some flooring."

"Oh, no thanks. I would, but..." I scrambled for an excuse. I couldn't very well tell him I left a man in my bedroom. And not just any man—one of his best friends.

A wary light entered Con's eyes and he straightened a bit, an awkward look crossing his face. "You have company."

If I said yes, would he leave or ask to meet the man I was dating? God, I was in no way ready for that conversation. Not right now. "Um..."

Too late, I heard the soft pad of a footstep behind me, and my stomach dropped to my toes as my world bottomed out.

CHAPTER THIRTY

Clay

I stepped into my boxers, a strange feeling welling up in my chest. I swore every day with Abby was better than the last. I'd never felt more comfortable with a woman. The more time I spent with her, the more I wanted to be with her. From the recesses of the outer room, I thought I heard a strange sound. My ears perked up, and I was instantly on alert. Low voices came from the direction of the living room, and my heart rate kicked up as I followed them.

Abby was partially obscured by the front door, and I swore I heard her hiss the word no. My blood began to boil in my veins as I strode forward. So help me, if that asshole Trevor was back and giving Abby trouble, I was going to knock his teeth in.

Abby stiffened as I curled one arm around her waist and planted myself behind her. "You good, babe?"

Over the top of her head, my gaze landed on Con's face. *Shit.* I watched a dozen emotions flicker in his dark eyes, the initial shock quickly morphing into fury as his face darkened.

"What. The. *Fuck*?" Con lunged forward, and I spun Abby out of the way, already bracing myself for the hit. "You motherfucker!"

I managed to get one hand up, but Con's knuckles landed hard in my ribs, knocking me back.

"Stop!" Abby pulled at Con, who only shook her off. She reached for me next, her voice frantic and pleading, tinged with anger. "Damn it, stop!"

I didn't dare look away from Con, watching every move as he swung at me again. I ducked and weaved, grabbing Abby with one hand and shoving her away again. It left my side wide open, and I grimaced as Con's fist landed in my ribs again.

I threw up both hands but I was a fraction of a second late, and Con landed a hard jab to my chin that snapped my teeth together. I cocked my arm back to return the favor. Just as I did, I felt a whisper of movement behind me as Abby rushed forward again, reaching for me. I couldn't slow my momentum, and my elbow connected with what felt like her face. I snapped toward her, watching in horror as she collapsed backward, her head smacking against the hard floor.

"Fuck!" I dropped to a knee next to her, reaching for her as Con moved to her other side. Already, a red bright hue emanated from her right cheek, and her upper lip appeared puffy and swollen. Christ. My stomach twisted into a tight knot at the sight. "Abilene—"

She smacked our hands away as she gingerly sat up and scooted away from us. I reached for her again, but she shrugged out of my grasp and pulled herself unsteadily to her feet. "Get the fuck out of my house. Both of you."

The abrasion on her face was becoming more prominent, looking worse by the second. "Babe—"

"Now!" I swore I saw tears sparkling in her eyes, but I couldn't tell if she was hurt or furious.

"Okay." I held my hands up in a placating gesture as I stood, feeling sick to my stomach. "I just want to make sure you're okay."

"Then you probably shouldn't have punched me in the face."

"I..." My heart clenched, and my hands fell to my sides as she glared at me. I felt helpless. Full of remorse. Guilt.

"You two are acting like fucking idiots."

Across from me, Con spoke quietly. "Abby—"

"Shut up, Con." Her lethal glare cut toward her brother. "Right now, I need you to leave. I'll talk to you later."

Throwing one last dark look my way, he stepped outside. I looked at Abby, but she just crossed her arms over her chest. "Ab—"

"Get out."

With a low growl of frustration, I followed Con outside. The door slammed behind me, and I leaned against it as I called out to her. "Abilene."

"Fuck off!"

"Babe, I need my clothes."

The sound of feet stomping on the floor moved away from the living room, and I sighed as I turned to face Con. His dark eyes glittered with malice.

"My fucking sister?" Con shoved me, and I fell back a step, expressionless. I wasn't going to fight him. If I were in his position, I'd do the same thing. All I ever wanted was for Abby to be safe, and I knew Con felt the same way. "You fucking tool. I trusted you, and you—"

The door opened, and my jeans came flying at me, followed by one boot, then the other. They hit the sidewalk at my feet, then bounced into the yard. Abby still wore my work polo, but I was willing to part with it for the moment. If she kept it, it would at least give me a reason to talk to her again later.

As if reading my thoughts, she met my gaze and held it for several seconds before grasping the hem. She slowly stripped it over her head, her tits bouncing free as she did so.

"Jesus, Abs." I watched in my peripheral vision as Con whirled away, but I couldn't tear my gaze from the woman in front of me.

The message was crystal clear. She was punishing Con for interfering. For me, it was a display of what I would be missing out on. She stood there for a moment, letting me get a good, long look. Then she tossed the shirt my way and softly closed the door.

Once it was safe, Con turned and scowled at me. "Fucking seriously? You don't have a damn thing to say for yourself?"

I pulled on my pants, then stepped into my boots and shrugged my shirt over my head.

Grabbing my shoulder, he spun me around to face him. "This is fucking bullshit."

"I'm sorry." I met his gaze, still dark with barely restrained fury. "I should have told you."

"You never should have touched her in the first place," he spat, looking ready to swing at me again.

I rocked back on my heels, unable to come up with a good defense. What the hell was I going to tell him? I'd been in the wrong, but I wouldn't take it back. Whatever Abby and I had going—hopefully it hadn't been ruined—was worth his anger.

"This is..." He trailed off, looking ready to tear something apart. "I can't even fucking wrap my head around it. You've been sneaking around for who the hell knows how long and you couldn't fucking man up enough to tell me? Christ."

He was right, but no amount of apologizing or defending myself would change it now.

Con glared at me. "So this is the way it's going to be?"

I stayed quiet, and his gaze took on a calculating gleam that sent my insides tumbling. "Me or her?"

Was he seriously going to make me choose between them? One of my best friends or the woman I... cared for? "Don't do this."

His gaze hardened. "Shouldn't be a difficult choice."

"Goddamn it, Con—"

"Me or her?"

I blew out a breath. "Her."

It would always be her. The single word fell between us like a steel curtain, seeming to freeze time and everything around us.

He stared at me for nearly a minute, his expression still furious and conflicted. Finally he spoke. "Good answer."

I watched as he spun on a heel and strode toward the driveway. What the fuck just happened? "What does that mean?"

Con didn't turn around, just waved one hand over his head before hopping in the SUV and cranking the engine. I stood rooted to the ground long after he disappeared down the street. Well, fuck. I still didn't know where the hell we stood, but I guess it could have been worse.

I threw one last look at Abby's house, then hopped on my bike. I would give her a little while to cool down, but she could be damn sure I'd be back later. Abby and I were far from over. She was upset now, and I would give her the time and space she'd asked for... Then I was coming for her. Because there was no way in hell I was ever letting her go. I headed back toward town, disappointment curling in my stomach, along with a mixture of guilt and dread. I cursed myself for the way things had gone. I knew that she had wanted to tell Con on her own, but part of me still wished I could go back and tell him. Then we could've avoided this whole thing.

Abby seemed furious, but I wasn't sure if she was more mad at me or Con. I still felt like absolute garbage for putting her in harm's way, and the need to turn around and go back to her pulled at me. Knowing Abby, that would only exacerbate the issue. If I pushed too hard, she would just push right back out of spite.

I needed some advice. But from who? Con sure as shit wasn't inclined to help me at all right now, and asking my brother for dating advice wasn't an option. I pulled into the parking lot of a drugstore and cut the engine, then dug my phone from my pocket. I felt like shit for bothering Xander right now, especially after everything that happened recently with Lydia, but maybe he needed a break too. I hit the number on speed dial and waited for him to answer.

"Hey, man. What's up?"

"Wanna grab a beer?"

On the other end of the phone, Xander laughed. "It's 3 o'clock in the afternoon."

I grimaced. "Yeah, I need something right now, though."

"Why don't you come over here?" Xander suggested. "Liddy is resting, so I'm watching Alexia."

"Nah, I'm sorry," I replied. "I won't bother you."

"Come on, man. I've got beer in the fridge, and I could use some stimulation other than the Disney Channel."

"If you're sure," I relented. "I'll be there in twenty."

I stowed my phone in the saddle bag, then turned toward Lydia's house. He opened the door before I had a chance to ring the bell, Alexia propped against his chest. Once we were back in the living room Xander set Alexia down, then grabbed two beers from the fridge and passed one to me. I cracked the top and took a long pull, acutely aware of Xander's curious keys on me.

"You good?"

"I don't know yet," I said. "I think I need some advice."

"What's going on?"

I blew out a deep breath. "I've been seeing this girl."

"Yeah." Xander grinned. "I got that impression. You've been acting shady as fuck the last few weeks."

I scowled at him. "Yeah, well, we've kind of been keeping it a secret."

Xander's brow furrowed. "Why?"

"She wanted to tell her brother in person." His brow rose, and I sighed. "Yeah, I know. Didn't quite work out the way we'd hoped. He showed up this morning while I was at her house, caught me half-dressed after we got out of the shower."

Xander whistled. "Bet he was pissed."

I let out a mirthless laugh. My ribs and jaw still ached from the force of his anger. "You have no idea."

"Can't be that big of a deal, right?" he asked. "Can't you just stay away from him, at least 'til things chill?"

I made a face. Con hadn't really given me an answer one way or the other whether I was fired or not, and I hated to destroy a friendship, but I would do it for Abby if I had to. The question was, would she choose me or Con?

Xander seemed to read the thoughts ricocheting through my mind, because he held up a hand. "Wait. We're not talking about Abby, are we?"

I contemplated playing stupid for a split second, then discarded the idea. "How did you know?"

"Holy shit." Xander laughed. "It all makes sense now. I knew something was going on with you, I just wasn't sure what it was."

"Yeah." I heaved a little laugh. "That's what it was. *Who* it is," I corrected.

"I was at the Hilton one night working the case for Mrs. Morrison, and I met Abby at the bar. We hooked up, then went our separate ways. I knew her name, but I assumed she wasn't from the area. Imagine my fucking surprise when I walked into the lobby Monday morning and saw her there behind the desk."

"Bet that shocked that shocked the hell out of you."

"You have no idea." I explained what had transpired between Cole and me that day, what Abby had overheard. "I tried to apologize, but she wanted nothing to do with it."

"I take it she was more than just a one-night stand?" Xander asked.

I drained my beer, trying to order my thoughts. "I knew after the night in a hotel that something was... different with her. But she was so dead set against me after everything that happened. She went on a date with another guy out of spite, and I may or may not have been waiting for her at her house when she got home."

Xander's eyes widened. "Jesus, dude."

"Yeah, yeah. I know how fucked up it sounds. Anyway, we talked after that—"

"Hooked up," Xander cut in.

I shot him a dirty look. "Maybe," I admitted. "Anyway, we started seeing each other more and more, but she said she didn't want Con to find out before she had a chance to tell him. So... yeah."

Xander stared at me for several seconds before reaching into the fridge and grabbing another beer. He passed it my way. "You're gonna need this."

CHAPTER THIRTY-ONE

Abby

The soft rumble of an engine met my ears, but it stopped just shy of my driveway. Curiously I peeked out the window, but it was completely dark. No headlights. Smart. Several minutes passed in silence, but I knew he was coming; I could feel it.

I hurried through the darkened room, knowing instinctively he'd move to the back of the house. The soft scuffle of footsteps on the back porch was my only warning, and I quickly crouched down out of view, concealed by the corner cabinet in the kitchen. I kept my eyes trained on the back door, watching. Waiting. It wouldn't be long now. My heart raced in my chest, and I tightened my grip on the trigger as the handle jiggled. Blood rushed in my ears, and the sound of metal on metal filled the air as he picked the lock.

I held my breath as the mechanism popped free. The knob turned, and the door swung open an inch. Immediately, it was stopped by the hook and fastener I'd installed this afternoon. A mumbled curse from outside met my ears, and a feral grin lifted my lips. Less than thirty seconds later, a small, thin object slipped through the crack between the door and the frame. I wasn't close enough to see, but I suspected it was a credit card. I waited with bated breath, watching as it slid upward. The object pushed the hook up out of its hole, and it swung down against the door with a gentle clink.

My eyes narrowed. He thought he was so smart. The door

swung inward, and his huge frame filled the space before he quietly closed and re-locked it behind him. As he turned back to me, I rose from my position, finger firmly on the trigger. I flipped the handle on the faucet to full blast, and cold water shot from the nozzle, hitting Clay square in the face.

For a moment, shock rendered emotionless, then he exploded. "Fuck!"

I kept my finger on the trigger, dousing him from head to toe as he stormed forward. "What the hell was that for?" he roared as he tried to wrestle the sprayer from me.

"I told you not to come back!"

Grabbing the sprayer in one hand, he directed it away from his face as he used free hand to slam down on the handle, cutting off the water. Once the water was off, he snatched the sprayer from my hand and slammed it back down into the sink before flipping on the light and whirling back to me. "Christ almighty, woman." Icy water dripped down his face, and anger radiated off of him in waves. "What the fuck do you think you're doing?"

I stared up at the man in front of me. "Waiting for you to break in," I retorted.

"What if it hadn't been me?" He made an agitated, sweeping gesture with one hand. "You just wait in the dark like some fucking psycho, waiting for men to break into your house?"

His lethal gear glare threatened to cut right through me, and I notched my chin up defiantly. "I knew it was you. Who the hell else would park out on the main street, then hike all the way back here in the dead of night to break into my house?"

"In any other instance, I would almost take that as a compliment," Clay said, a smug smile tipping his lips.

"I didn't mean it as one," I snapped. "And the question remains, what the hell are you doing in my house? I told you to leave me alone."

He took a step forward, closing the distance between us with a little shake of his head. "We both know that's not gonna happen."

"The hell it's not!" I exploded. "Do you seriously think you could pull the shit you did this afternoon, then just come waltzing back in here?"

The tension in his muscles drained away, and he lifted one hand to cup my face. "I needed to see you..." His voice lowered, took on a soft quality I'd never heard before. "I had to make sure you were okay."

Anger still crackled through me, and I wasn't quite ready to let go of it yet. "You acted like a fucking asshole. Both of you did. I'm not some toy for you to fight over."

"That's where you're wrong." His fingers speared into my hair, curling around the back of my head. "You're not a toy, Abilene, but I will always fight for you."

The sincerity of his words, coupled with that intense look in his eyes, hit me like a thousand bricks to the chest, knocking the wind from my sails. I should have known my brother would overreact, and I regretted not just telling him sooner so we could have avoided this whole situation. "Did he do anything stupid?"

He lifted one shoulder. "He threatened to fire me."

"What?" My voice rose several octaves. "Are you serious? Are you done?" Clay had known my brother for years. He loved his job here. I would feel terrible if I were the reason he had to leave. "Clay, tell me he wasn't serious."

His mouth kicked up in a little smirk like it didn't matter one way or the other, and I smacked his chest. "If he—"

"Don't worry about it, babe. I think we... understand each other."

I couldn't begin to comprehend what the hell that meant. I would never understand men. I swore to God, one second they were throwing fists and the next they were best friends again. Still, I wasn't completely ready to let go of my anger. "Whatever. Doesn't mean you just get to walk back in here like you own the place."

"You're right," he acknowledged. "I came to apologize."

I lifted a brow. "Feel free to start any time now."

A grin split his face before he could fight it back, and it incensed me even more. "You think I'm kidding? I—"

His hands moved to my face, his eyes turning serious in the dim light. "I would never joke about making sure you're safe."

Disgruntled, I eyed him as he spoke, feeling the gentle sweep of his thumb as it moved over my cheekbone. "I felt like absolute shit all afternoon. Thinking I'd left you here after I hurt you."

"You didn't really hurt me," I said softly. My cheek was still a little tender, a little red, but he hadn't clipped me too hard.

He examined the light bruising under my eye and gave his head a little shake. "Your poor face. God, babe." I went willingly as he tucked my head into the crook of his neck, one hand curved around the back of my head, the other around my back. "I'm so sorry."

"It's okay." He was soaked, but the heat of his huge body radiated through the sodden material, warming me and melting the last of my anger.

"It's not. I should have been more careful. I can't believe that happened."

"Well," I admitted, "I kind of threw myself between you two. I should have let you kick the shit out of each other and get it out of your system."

Clay's chest rumbled beneath my cheek as he laughed. "Probably. I can honestly say that's the first time anyone's ever tried to defend me."

I smiled against his neck. "Just protecting you."

He pulled back and looked at me. "Don't do it again. If you ever got hurt because of me..." He gave his head a little shake.

"I'll try my best," I promised. I knew Clay could handle himself, but the idea of him getting hurt—especially at my brother's expense—unsettled me. I would have done it a hundred times over.

As if he could read my thoughts, he quirked a brow before dropping his gaze to my lips. Head still cradled in his huge hands, he tipped my face slightly to one side as his mouth came down on mine. His lips were soft yet demanding, and I opened willingly, taking the kiss deeper. Clay broke away. "Let me make it up to you."

As if I would say no to that. I lifted my arms over my head and allowed him to strip the tee shirt off of me before dropping it to the floor. I went willingly into his arms, and we lost ourselves in hazy pleasure before falling asleep in a tangle of limbs.

The next morning, I headed into work, butterflies in my stomach. I'd dreaded talking with my brother before; now it was even worse. Not because I was scared of him or what he would do, but because I knew he felt betrayed, and I'd hurt him.

I dropped my stuff off at my desk, then headed toward his office. It was quiet inside, but when I peeked around the door, I saw him seated at his desk, head bent as he studied something on the papers in front of him. I drew a deep breath and stepped inside. "Can I talk to you?"

He was quiet for several seconds before he finally sighed and lifted his gaze to mine. "Sure."

I closed the door behind me, then made my way to one of the seats in front of his desk. His shoulders were tense, and his eyes flitted around the room, landing on everything but me. "I need to apologize for yesterday. I never wanted you to find out that way."

Con raked one hand through his hair. "I just... Why didn't you tell me?"

"I didn't know how," I admitted. "Clay wanted to tell you weeks ago, but I begged him not to. I wanted to tell you in my own time, once I was sure things would work out between us."

"I don't know what I'm supposed to do," Con replied. "You're all I have. It's my job to protect you, to keep you from getting hurt."

"How do you know he'll hurt me?"

His eyes dropped his desk. "Experience."

I understood that Con knew a side of Clay I didn't. He'd seen him as a Marine, as a single man. The Clay I knew was loyal and trustworthy and would do everything in his power to keep me safe and take care of me. "When you were in the service... you trusted him with your life, right?"

Con's expression turned wary. "Yeah. Why?"

"You've never told me a lot of the stuff that happened over there, and I would never ask. I'm sure you guys dealt with some hellacious things. But the whole time, Clay had your back. If you trust him with your life, trust him with mine."

Con was quiet for a solid minute before he spoke again. "I fucking hate it when you're right."

I sputtered with laughter. "You're such a jerk."

"Yeah, but I'm your brother," he returned. "I'm allowed to be protective of you."

"And I appreciate it," I said. "Just... let us figure it out. Nothing is guaranteed in life. We could be together for two weeks or the rest of our life. Only time will tell."

He pulled me into a hug. "I love you, Abs."

"Love you, too." Wrapping my arms around his waist, I returned the hug.

Telling him the truth had lifted a huge weight off my chest, and I finally felt like I could breathe. I had no idea what the future would bring for Clay and me, but I was dying to find out.

CHAPTER THIRTY-TWO

Clay

Con didn't even glance up when I entered his office and shut the door behind me. The sooner I put this shit behind me, the better. "I want to talk to you."

Finally, slowly, his chin lifted and his dark gaze met mine. There was still a trace of anger there and something that seemed a lot like betrayal. He stared at me, and I stared back. "I should cut you loose."

I kept my gaze impassive. "I understand. Do whatever you think is best."

His dark eyes searched mine. "You care about her?"

"Yes."

"God*damn* it." He raked one hand through his hair and sent another lethal glare my way. "Why the fuck didn't you tell me?"

I kept my mouth shut. There was no way I was going to tell him that it was her idea we keep things quiet. "I should have said something," I agreed. "I shouldn't have kept you in the dark."

"She told me it was her idea."

I neither confirmed nor denied it, and his gaze narrowed on me.

"Weeks." He grimaced as he pushed from his chair and moved around to lean against the front of the desk. I balanced on the balls of my feet, ready to move. Here he was within swinging distance, and I wasn't particularly looking forward to getting into it with him again. "You've been together for weeks, and I had no fucking idea. How the hell could I not have seen it?"

I lifted one shoulder at his rhetorical question.

"My fucking sister, man." He planted his hands on his hips and glared my way. "Why the hell didn't she say anything to me?"

I didn't know what to say to that exactly, because I wasn't sure, either. All I knew was, I actually felt relieved as hell that it was out in the open now. "I think she was afraid of disappointing you," I said. "God knows she deserves a hell of a lot better."

He speared me with a dark look. "As long as you know that."

For what seemed like forever, we stood there staring at each other. I had no idea where we stood, either as friends or coworkers, but there were a few things I knew with absolute certainty. Regardless of what happened with Con, whether he cut me from his life or fired me, I still would have chosen Abby. She was more important than all that shit. I could get another job, but Abby was one of a kind.

Con's chest rose and fell. "I'm still fucking pissed at you." He tipped his head toward the lobby. "But you've always had my back, and I trust you to take care of her."

Something flickered in my brain. "Did she tell you that?"

"Yes."

He practically hissed the word, looking disgruntled, and I laughed out loud. That sounded so much like Abby's snarky logic that I couldn't help but shake my head. *This woman...*

I didn't realize I'd spoken aloud until Con replied. "I know. Couldn't even argue with it."

"Haven't won an argument yet," I lamented.

"Don't expect to, either," he quipped.

I snorted, thinking of Abby and her penchant for off-the-wall trivia. Damn, that woman was something else. "I could never be that lucky."

Con stared at me. "You know you're gonna have some serious ass kissing to do."

I cracked a grin despite the situation. Thank God he had no idea what had transpired at her house late last night. I'd made decent headway in the forgiveness department, but I didn't dare say a word to him.

He shook his head. "I should feel sorry for you, but you did this to yourself."

"I'd do it a hundred more times."

"Let's just get one thing straight." Con pointed my way. "Whatever happens between you two—I don't want to hear any of it. She's still my baby sister, and I don't want to have to kill you."

I dipped my head in a brief nod. "I'll take care of her."

"I know you will." He punched me in the solar plexus. "Asshole."

I left Con's office and headed to the bullpen to grab my keys. I wanted to stop by and speak with Harris Grant before I met up with Bennett and Xander for recon. Leaned back in his chair, feet propped up on his desk, Cole lifted his eyes from the folder he was reviewing and nodded my way.

"Hey, I'm gonna go see Dad tomorrow night. Wanna come?"

A hopeful look lit his face, and I fought the urge to groan. Patrick's words from the other day came floating back to me. No matter what else he'd done, the man was right about one thing. If I didn't make amends now, I might not have a chance to later. I swallowed my pride and nodded. "Sure. I'll meet you out there. What time?"

"Six." My brother looked relieved, and it pricked my heart. I had no expectations that this was going to go as well as he hoped, but I needed to do this for both of us.

"All right." I pocketed my keys and phone. "See ya then."

I left QSG, thoughts of Abby, my father, Trevor, and Charlie swirling intermittently through my mind. Just after three o'clock, I entered the welcome air-conditioned lobby of the law office. I threw a smile at the receptionist as I gave her my name, then took a seat to wait. I hadn't told Abby where I was going, and I wondered how she'd take the news. It was nothing against Abby, but I wanted to speak to the man one on one without any distractions.

A slender, distinguished looking older man opened the heavy oak door, and his piercing blue eyes met mine. "Mr. Thompson?"

"That's me." I stood and held out my hand as I approached. "Thanks for taking the time to see me."

"Of course." He shook my hand, then gestured to a conference room in the hallway. "We can speak privately in here."

After he'd closed the door, he took a seat across from me and eyed me shrewdly. "What can I help with today?"

I gave him a brief rundown of who I was and what I was doing here. "It's come to my attention that you filed the papers for Violet's divorce."

He was silent for a moment as he studied me. "May I ask how you know that?"

"I've been pulling some information for a client, and the divorce papers came up—along with your signature."

"That's true," he admitted. "It was a difficult time for Violet, and they were hoping to keep things quiet."

"Was there any animosity between Violet and Charlie?"

He shook his head. "Everything was fairly amicable. From what I understand, Violet was deeply depressed after Lily's death and the marriage began to crumble. They were separated for a good period of time before she actually filed for divorce."

I chewed on that for a moment. "Was that the last time you saw Charlie?"

"I believe so," Grant said slowly. "It's been a while, but I remember he was living up around New Orleans at the time, probably is still there."

"Actually," I replied, "he's not. That's why I'm here. Charlie is an extended family member of my client, who has been trying to reach him. But we've been unable to find any trace—no phone number, no tax information, no DMV records."

"Perhaps he doesn't want to be found." Grant lifted one shoulder. "I think the divorce was hard on both of them, so it wouldn't surprise me if he wanted nothing to do with the memories here."

"That may be," I said, "but I need to explore every option for my client."

Grant stared at me for several long seconds. "And would that be Trevor you're talking about?"

I was more than a little surprised he knew about Trevor, but I tried to mask it. "I'm not at liberty to discuss it. I apologize."

He nodded slowly. "Well, hypothetically speaking, if it were Trevor looking for him, I would tell him the exact same thing I did last week."

He'd spoken with Trevor? "And what would that be?"

Grant sighed. "If you found the divorce papers, you'll also find that I drafted the original trust fund in Lily's name as well. She wanted to be sure her son would be taken care of. None of us knew what she planned to do. I felt so guilty afterward, like I should have known. But she exhibited no signs of depression that Violet saw."

I wanted to argue that her diary was a direct contradiction, but I kept my mouth shut. "So you've known about him all along?"

"I have."

"What about the father?"

A deep sadness filled his blue eyes but was gone a second later as he lifted his hands. "Although I set up the fund for Trevor, Lily never revealed the information to me."

Not the answer I wanted, but it was expected. "Well, thank you for your time. I appreciate it."

"Of course." Harris stood and walked with me toward the lobby. "Tell Abby I said hello."

"I will, thank you." I nodded and headed toward the parking lot.

I still wasn't sure what the hell all this meant. We were getting close to something—to whom or what, I wasn't precisely sure. All I knew was, Abby and Trevor needed answers and I was going to do everything in my power to find them. Then we could put all of this behind us once and for all and move forward with a clean slate.

Now that things between Abby and me were out in the open, I felt freer. Lighter. I couldn't wait until we'd tied up all of these loose ends so she could finally be free of her demons, too. I wanted her to have closure for whatever she'd endured as a child, whether she remembered it or not. I'd encouraged her to speak with the physician she'd visited as a child, but he'd since retired and moved to Phoenix. She told me she'd consider reaching out to him and though I wasn't entirely sure he would have any additional answers for her, I felt like anything could help. She'd only had the nightmare once more since the night she'd discovered Charlie's identity, but she'd woken right away as soon as I reached for her.

I loved being the person she depended on. I loved that she could turn to me when she needed something—anything. She was fiercely independent, but still comfortable enough with me to share her fears and worries. I wanted to be her shelter, her protector, her safe haven, just the way she was for me. I couldn't begin to dissect the feelings that welled up inside me at the thought of a future with her. All that mattered was we were finally moving forward—together.

CHAPTER THIRTY-THREE

Abby

I stared out the window, wondering where we could possibly be going. Con had sounded cryptic on the phone when he called, asking only if I would come see something with him. We had left town and headed southeast, winding our way through the middle-class suburbs. I studied the well-manicured homes on their one-acre lots before turning back to my brother. "Is this your way of telling me you bought a house?"

A smirk lifted his lips, but he didn't tear his gaze from the windshield. "Something like that."

I gave a dramatic sigh. "Just tell me already. You know I hate surprises."

His smile slipped away, and his expression turned serious. "A piece of property came up for sale, and I want your opinion on it. I've been thinking of building a house instead of buying one."

That made sense, especially for my brother. I knew he would never be content in the city, or even in the suburbs. He was the type of guy who needed privacy, space to get away from everything and relax. "How many acres?"

He hesitated. "Twelve."

I froze. Surely there were hundreds of parcels of land that were a dozen acres. But hearing that number dredged up memories from the past that I wasn't entirely sure I was ready to deal with just yet. But when Con flipped on his blinker and turned left onto a familiar old road, I already knew. I sat in silence, my heart in my throat as I watched the scenery pass by my window in a blur. Some things had changed, but in other ways it was exactly the same as it had been fifteen years ago.

The homes became fewer and farther between, and several minutes later, Con slowed and turned into a rutted gravel drive. The grass was overgrown, so tall that it would at least come up to my waist. I could see the familiar roofline of the squat shack where we'd grown up. The wooden clapboard exterior was stained nearly black with age, the windows caked with dirt and dust.

Con parked the SUV, and we sat there in silence for what felt like forever, just staring at our childhood home. Through the tall grass swaying in the breeze, I spied several stacks of tires, and I could only begin to guess at what might be hiding around the property.

Con grasped the door handle and flicked a look my way. "Want to go look around?"

There was a hint of vulnerability in his voice, and I couldn't find it in myself to refuse him. "Sure."

I climbed out of the car, taking care to watch where I stepped as I made my way around the SUV to meet Con.

"So what do you think?" he asked.

"Honestly, I'm not sure."

For the life of me, I couldn't begin to imagine why my brother would want to come back here. I was still young when we left, but whatever bad memories this place held for me, it had to be a hundred times worse for him.

My father had purchased the property for next to nothing back in the early '80s. It wasn't worth much back then considering it was probably as run down then as it appeared to be now. But it had been home, at least when my parents weren't following their favorite band around the south. By the time Con turned ten, I had turned two and my parents had apparently decided that it was safe to leave us for days at a time.

More of my childhood memories consisted of Con than my actual mom and dad. We had spent hardly any time inside, instead wandering around the yard and into the surrounding woods. Even though our house was technically on the wrong side of the tracks, our property backed up to an expensive allotment of homes. The Delacroixs owned a mansion directly north of us, and their only daughter, Grace, and Con had been inseparable despite her parents' censure.

For years, Grace had snuck away from home while her parents were away, and we would spend hours playing in the forest that separated our homes. But everything changed the summer Con turned eighteen. My parents died in a car accident on the way back home from the band's performance. Still just shy of legal age, Con couldn't file to be my legal guardian. Though he and Grace had talked about moving away and getting married, my brother found himself signing up for the Marines the day he turned eighteen. I went to live with Violet, and my brother never saw Grace again.

Although more than a decade had passed, I'd still never been able to learn the whole story. Something had happened during those last couple of days, but Con insisted it was nothing. The look of utter devastation on his face, though, told me otherwise. After that, he was never the same. Not once in the past fourteen years could I remember him having a serious girlfriend. I was sure my brother wasn't a saint, but his heart was still anchored in the past, to a woman who no longer existed. There was no doubt in my mind that part of this was for her—because of her—and my heart ached for him. He deserved to find happiness, too, the way I had with Clay.

I slipped my hand into the crook of his elbow and leaned into him, resting my head on his shoulder. "It won't bring her back," I whispered.

There was a heavy silence, then—"I know."

His tone was bleak, borderline resigned, and another sharp bolt of pain shot through me. "Will this make you happy?"

I was truly concerned for him. He nodded slowly. "I know I can't change what happened, but maybe it's time for this place to have some new memories. Maybe it'll help..."

He trailed off, but I immediately picked up on his train of thought. Maybe if he addressed it, made his own new, happy memories here, it would help him to move on. I squeezed his arm. "I think that's a really good idea. And you know if you decide to cut your lease short, you're always welcome to stay with me."

He glanced down at me, one eyebrow cocked, a wry smile twisting his lips. "And have to watch you and Thompson together? No thanks."

I laughed and swatted his chest. "He's not so bad."

The teasing smile slid away, replaced with his serious expression once more. "He's a good guy. I'm glad you're happy."

"Me, too. If this is what you want, I think you should do it."

Con nodded slowly. "Thanks, Abs."

There was nothing else to be said. I released him, and we climbed into the SUV then headed back to my house. My mind spun as we drove. I'd had so much going on that the ordeal with Trevor and Charlie had completely taken a backseat to the drama of my love life. Something had been bothering me, and I was curious.

"Did Violet ever talk to you about Charlie?"

Con tossed a look my way. "Her second husband?"

"Yeah." I explained a little bit of what'd happened recently, and why Trevor was looking for Charlie. For the time being, I didn't mention my dreams or the situation with Charlie.

My brother shook his head. "I was overseas at the time. She emailed me, let me know that they'd split. She said she wanted you to speak with a child psychologist after everything you'd been through, and I encouraged it. When I next saw you, you seemed fine, so I never brought it up again."

I wasn't entirely sure what I'd expected, but it made sense. Violet had convinced him everything was fine, so there was no reason to think anything was wrong.

Clay was standing next to his bike when we pulled into my driveway, and a smile automatically lifted my mouth.

"Should've known he'd be here," Con murmured from the driver seat. "Guy's totally whipped."

My brother's words made me laugh, and I leaned over the console to kiss his cheek. "Love you. Even if you are a pain in my ass."

"Love you too, squirt."

Clay lifted a hand to Con as he held the door for me and helped me down, then tugged me to his side. "Con."

My brother glanced between the two of us, a smirk gracing his face. "Thompson."

The second Con's SUV turned out of my driveway, Clay scooped me into his arms. I wrapped my legs around his waist and my arms went around his shoulders for support as he kissed me. A moment later, he pulled back. "I missed you."

I was going to joke that it'd only been a few hours since I'd last seen him, but the expression on his face stopped me cold. For once he was being completely open and honest, and I didn't want to belittle his feelings. Something was shifting between us, and I loved it.

I hugged him tighter to me. "I missed you, too."

CHAPTER THIRTY-FOUR

Clay

"So where'd you guys go today?" I asked over dinner.

"To our old house." At my lifted eyebrow, Abby elaborated. "Just outside the city is a tiny little town called Pleasantville. But, trust me, there wasn't a damn thing pleasant about it. Not unless you lived in the mansions on the south side."

"Do you guys still own the house?" I remembered Abby telling me about her parents, but I didn't recall much else.

"It was put up for sale after my parents passed, but Con actually just bought it. You know Bennett Kingsley?"

"Yeah." An ex-police lieutenant, he'd taken over his father's business and now owned a shit ton of real estate in the area. He'd actually assisted on a recent case Xander and I were working, and he seemed like a decent guy.

"Apparently, he snatched up the land a couple years back when the market tanked. When he found out Con was looking to buy it back, he sold it to him. Con wants to build a place out there."

"Good for him."

"I guess." Abby hesitated as she swirled her fork through her noodles. "I'm worried about him."

To hear her say she worried about Con was surprising, to say the least. I expected Con to be protective of her, but I never imagined that she would waste time worrying over him. He was one of the most self-assured men I knew and there were few people, if any,

I'd rather have at my back. "Why?"

"There's a lot of history there." She explained the way they'd grown up and Con's attachment to the daughter of one of the richest men in the city.

It shocked the hell out of me to hear he'd been so crazy about the girl. Dude was straight up cold. Maybe not cold, exactly, but... definitely unreachable. He may as well have been a statue for all the emotion I'd ever seen him exhibit outside of Abby. Though I'd known and worked with him for over a decade, I still didn't know much about him. Some guys kept their love life quiet. Others bragged. Con was locked down tighter than Fort Knox. On the other hand...

A memory from several years ago flickered to life in the back of my brain. We'd been stationed in Iraq at the time, and it was a day like any other—hot, dry, exhausting physically and mentally. We had some downtime that night, and Con had gotten piss drunk. It was the only time I ever remembered seeing him like that. He was always so reserved, so in control of himself and everything around him. But that night, he'd been beside himself.

After countless drinks, I'd taken his service pistol and helped him to his bed. He'd been physically ravaged, at the end of his rope, and the cry for Grace had nearly gutted me. At the time I'd thought nothing of the word. But now... now I understood. It wasn't a cry for salvation; it was a tortured soul's cry for a lost love.

God, I couldn't imagine. If I ever lost Abby... Christ, I couldn't bear it.

"What's wrong?"

I focused on Abby and shook my head a little, forcing down the feeling that had risen in me like a tidal wave. "Nothing."

Her head tipped slightly to one side, the expression in her eyes telling me she didn't believe a single word. "Something's bothering you, I can tell. You can talk to me if—"

I pushed from my chair, suddenly overwhelmed by the need to feel her against me, to hold her close.

"Everything is just perfect." She came willingly into my arms and peered up at me, worry and something else lingering in the dark depths of her eyes. I wanted nothing more than to soothe her fears.

Protect her, cherish her every single day. I tightened my hold on her. "I have you, babe. That's all I need."

We spent the remainder of the evening together, just hanging out and talking. With Abby, there was never a shortage of things to talk about. And I freaking loved it. She was knowledgeable on a variety of subjects, so damn smart and absolutely gorgeous. It still stunned me that she'd chosen to be with me instead of someone else.

After work the next day, I climbed into my truck then headed toward the hotel where Trevor was staying. Although it looked a little better in the daylight, it wasn't much of an improvement. The brick was cracked, and the windows showed a layer of dust, indicating they hadn't been cleaned in quite a while.

The parking space in front of Trevor's room was open, so I pulled the truck to stop and climbed out. I threw a quick look around, then strode to the door and gave a hard triple knock. I heard no sound or movement within, and after about thirty seconds, I repeated the knock. Still nothing. Pulling my phone from my back pocket, I sent him a quick text asking to meet up at some point so he could fill us in on what he'd found up north.

Resigning myself to not getting any answers for the moment, I hopped back in the truck then headed to a fast-food joint. I seriously considered blowing off going to my father's house and spending the time with Abby instead. It was almost surprising how much I enjoyed being with her. After so many years alone, having the steady presence of a woman in my life was as welcoming as it was daunting.

Before I met Abby, I thought I was happy. But I didn't really know the meaning of the word until she swept into my life. I could be myself with her; she didn't push me to act a certain way, and she forgave me when I screwed up. I was still worried I'd fuck up somehow or that she'd wake up one morning and realize how much better she was, that she deserved a better man. I only hoped she could see how much I cared about her. So much so, it scared the hell out of me sometimes.

Abby joked about my rules, but they'd existed for a reason. I'd dated Samantha for years in high school, and she was the one steady presence in my life. After she'd cheated on me, I'd shunned the idea of marriage. Now, though... the idea of having Abby by my side sent a little thrill through me. It was too early to talk that way. Maybe. But every day I spent with her, I became more and more certain she was what I wanted. We hadn't spent a single day apart for the past few weeks, and I realized exactly why I'd resisted a real relationship for so long. I'd been waiting for her.

I let out a sigh. Cole had asked it of me, and I found I couldn't deny him. He was closer to my father than I ever would be, but Cole couldn't see the bad side of him, or maybe he chose not to. Either way, my brother thought our father was dying and deserved a second chance, so I would grant him a few hours of my time. Maybe he'd changed over the past few years. It was possible. Doubtful, but possible.

My father lived in the same house where we'd grown up, located almost an hour outside of Dallas in a dusty little blue-collar town. A majority of the population, my father included, had worked for the local mill for decades. Mineral Forge was quiet and laid back, but it was also the stereotypical small town where gossip reigned supreme. A few weeks after graduation, I'd taken off for boot camp and never looked back. My entire body was coiled tight with tension as the sign for Mineral Forge came into view, and it only increased as I turned off the main road and pulled into my father's drive.

I'd driven the truck today to avoid getting caught in the rain on my bike, and I parked it next to my brother's. I shook my head at the sight of the dark gray Raptor. I was a Chevy guy through and through, but my brother had insisted on the Ford as soon as he laid eyes on it.

Drawing in a deep breath, I climbed from the truck and headed for the back porch. We'd always used this entrance, coming in through the kitchen instead of the foyer, and I gave a cursory knock on the screen door before swinging it open and stepping inside.

"Hey, man." Relief creased my brother's face as he greeted me from his spot at the kitchen table.

My father sat at the head of the small oval table, and I gave him a quick nod. "Hey, Pop."

He grunted a little. "Nice of you to finally show up."

I immediately bristled at the sarcasm dripping from his tone, but I didn't have a chance to speak as Cole cut in. "Work's been hella busy. Clay's been swamped, so I'm just glad he could make it."

I knew Cole was trying to help, and I shot a tight smile his way. Unfortunately, my gratitude slipped away when my father snorted with disdain. "Always trying to fix someone else's life, huh, son? Maybe you should focus on doing something productive for yourself."

"Like work at the same fucking mill for thirty years, then come home and get piss drunk each night?" I shot back.

"I did what I had to," my father snapped. "I put food on the table and a roof over your head. You should be grateful."

"Yeah, I'm fucking ecstatic, believe me." I shook my head and drew in a deep breath. He always brought out the worst in me, and I refused to let him have that kind of control anymore. I'd been away for twelve years, and I wasn't a kid anymore. I'd tried for years to please him, but it was never enough. I'd made a life for myself—a life that I truly enjoyed—and that was all that mattered. His opinion meant less than nothing to me and if he wanted to be miserable, then that was his prerogative. I'd come here for one reason, and one reason alone. "Cole says you're sick."

"Bah." My father took a swig of his beer. "Damn doctor doesn't know what the hell he's talking about."

"Right." I rolled my eyes. "He only spent eight years studying medicine. But I'm sure you know better than he does."

"Don't know why you're so concerned with my health. You can't even be bothered to stop by more than once every ten years."

"Maybe I would if I had a reason to," I countered.

"Bullshit," my father thundered. "After everything I've done for you—"

"Everything you've done for me?" I couldn't hold back my astonished laugh. "And what the fuck have you done for me? Tell me, please, 'cause I can't come up with a damn thing."

"I'm your father, damn it." His face flushed bright red. "Family is supposed to—"

"We're not a family," I snapped. "Never have been."

"Maybe not you," my father countered.

Hot fury raced through my veins. "You got something to say, then say it to my face."

"He didn't mean it that way," Cole said, placing himself in the middle.

"Meant exactly what I said," my dad replied stiffly. "You've never given a damn about anything but yourself."

The thought made me see red. I'd served my country. I'd had the backs of all my brothers and sisters who served overseas. I would lay down my life for them still. For him to throw out a line about me being careless and selfish was more than I could bear. The asshole would never change. He was a prick growing up, and he was a prick now. "And y'all fucking wonder why I never come home. Yeah, Pop, I know. I'm a drain on society. At least you got one good son. I should probably go before my bad genes rub off on him more than they already have."

"Jesus." A grimace passed over my brother's face. "Can't you two stop sniping at each other and just get along for two fucking minutes?"

My hands curled into fists by my sides. "Well, this has been enlightening. Glad to see some shit never changes."

"Come on, man," Cole coaxed. "Just stay."

"Let him go," my father grumbled. "I'm sure there's an empty bar stool calling his name."

For a brief second, the temptation to get blackout drunk out of spite crossed my mind. Almost as quickly as it came, it disappeared again as I slammed out the door and climbed into the cab of my truck. For the first time in forever, I had something I truly cared about. I was gonna grab onto it with both hands and never let go.

CHAPTER THIRTY-FIVE

Abby

Clay's text had told me he was about an hour out, and I waited impatiently for the sweep of headlights to announce his presence. When they finally came, my heart raced with anticipation. From the quiet approach, I could tell he'd brought his truck this time, though with the recent rain it came as no real surprise.

I opened the door, ready to invite Clay inside as he made his way up the sidewalk. Before I could speak, he swept me into his arms and fused his mouth to mine. There was a desperation to his kiss, and I threw myself headlong into it, wrapping my arms and legs around him and holding on for dear life. I was dimly aware of the door slamming closed before my back hit the wall next to it, and the heaviness of Clay's body pinned me in place.

He broke away from my lips, kissing over my cheek and jaw, then spoke low in my ear. "I need you."

I tightened my hold, silently encouraging him, and his mouth found mine again. The pressure of the wall at my back eased and we were suddenly moving. But instead of heading toward the bedroom, Clay sank down onto the couch so I was spread over his lap. His hands moved to the hem of my shirt and yanked it over my head, then tossed it to the floor. I returned the favor then slid off the couch and shimmied out of my shorts, watching as he lifted his hips and shed the jeans he wore. He'd barely gotten them shoved down around his knees when I climbed back on top of him. He grabbed me and pulled me closer, leaving a scant inch of space between us as he wound his hand into my hair and slanted his mouth over mine.

I had no idea what had come over him, but I liked it. Our sex had always been passionate and sensual, but this was different somehow. This was carnal and raw, like he wouldn't survive one more second without me. I loved the feeling of power and desirability that surged through me as he clutched me like a lifeline.

His hands came up and cradled my face, and those honeyed eyes stared into mine. "I want to feel you—just you."

My breath hitched at the implication. I'd never had sex without a condom before; even though I was on birth control, I'd never wanted to risk it. But with Clay... My heart swelled as I stared at him. Clay was my lifeline. My future. I gave a little nod of acquiescence, and his lips were back on mine before I could blink. One hand slid down my spine to my bottom, and he lifted me, fitting the broad head of his arousal to my opening.

The sensation of being with him skin to skin was... incredible. Like nothing I'd ever experienced. I cried out as he thrust deeply, taking over every inch of me body and soul. Everything seemed amplified, and I came in record time. Clay followed seconds later with a ragged groan, his arms banding tightly around my back like he never wanted to let me go.

Afterward, we sat cuddled close together, our hearts beating hard and fast in tandem. His head rested in the crook of my neck, and his lips left a trail of soft, tender kisses along my throat. Something between us was different, though I couldn't quite put my finger on it. The sex had been just as intense as ever, tinged with a sense of urgency. But there was also something more. I felt like this time, for whatever reason, was more like making love.

Whatever had happened tonight had had a significant impact on him. I sensed a vulnerability deep inside him, and I wonder if that had attributed to the change. I had no idea what transpired this evening, but I didn't dare ask him. Though I could talk about anything and nothing under the sun, Clay kept his feelings under lock and key. He traded trivia readily but when it came to emotions, he was a typical guy. I didn't want to risk pressing deeper and pushing him away, even though I was dying to know. Was this a temporary change or the evolution of our relationship? I hope like hell it was the latter.

I could no longer deny that I had fallen for him, totally and completely. With Clay, there was no question in my mind where I stood. I was important to him, and he would always take care of me. I couldn't help but wonder exactly how far that extended. Did he love me back? Was he even capable of doing so? He'd given me no indication in the past that he loved me. I knew he desired me, knew he wanted me on a physical level. But was it a thrill of the chase for him, or... more?

I tried to look at it objectively. He had practically insisted on telling my brother about us as soon as it happened. Out of obligation to his friend, or because he truly felt that deeply for me? I couldn't quite tell. I bit down on my tongue to keep the million and one questions from escaping, to keep from telling him how much he meant to me and asking if he felt the same. I wanted him so badly I could taste it. I had known from the first that Clay was different. I'd never had a man treat me the way he did. He was possessive and jealous, but I truly believed he had my best interest at heart.

I swallowed hard, forcing down the questions and ran a hand over the firm muscle of his upper back. "You okay?"

He lifted his head to look at me, those glowing gold eyes boring into mine. "Better now."

He captured my mouth in a leisurely, sweet kiss, and I felt myself fall a little further. He kissed the corner of my mouth, trailing his lips over my cheek, my nose, until he finally dropped a kiss on my forehead and gave me a little squeeze. His arms were still wrapped around me, and his thumbs stroked my shoulder blades in long, even sweeps.

I dropped my head so it lay nestled the crook of his shoulder and turned so my lips brushed his throat. "Do you want to talk about it?" I whispered.

"Not yet." He shook his head, his hold tightening just a fraction. "I just want this... to hold you, listen to you talk—about anything. Everything. Just being with you makes everything better."

I couldn't begin to describe the sensation that swept over me at his words. They were so genuine, so brutally honest that they brought tears to my eyes, a direct contradiction to the elation spreading through every pore of my body at his admission. As much as I wanted to, I wasn't going to press. Just knowing that he'd come to me for solace spoke volumes. He cared about me, wanted to be with me, even if he couldn't admit it out loud just yet.

I snuggled closer even though he was still inside me. "I don't know how I could possibly come up with anything interesting to say."

He snorted a little, and I smiled in response. We both knew that was a lie; I never tired of talking with him, absorbing every little thing. "I know, I talk a lot."

His lips found my forehead again, and they brushed my bangs as he spoke. "I could listen to you all day. Just hearing your voice grounds me, takes all the bad shit away."

It was so comfortable, and we never ran out of subjects to discuss. There was an open quality to our conversation that I'd never really found with anyone else. Most people were overwhelmed by it, but Clay took it in stride, countering my statements or random musings with something of his own. Even if he didn't have something to say in return, he seemed more than happy to listen, and I appreciated it. "Glad I can help."

"More than you know." He kissed my temple, then gently shifted me off him.

I climbed to my feet and scooped my discarded clothes from the floor, then started to dress. "Have you eaten?"

Clay levered himself to his feet, then yanked on his jeans. "I stopped for fast food earlier, but I'm hungry again."

I couldn't help the smile that formed on my lips, and I paused in the act of pulling my shirt on. "You're always hungry."

A pair of hot eyes swept over my body. "Where you're concerned, Abilene, I'm starving."

CHAPTER THIRTY-SIX

Clay

Cole had called twice since I'd stormed out, and I finally called him back while Abby was getting ready for bed.

"Hey." I could hear the relief in his voice when he picked up the phone. "You good?"

I watched Abby as she moved around the bathroom, brushing her teeth and hair. I'd never been better. "Yep."

On the other end of the line, Cole sighed. "He didn't mean it, you know."

My brother was always playing peacemaker, but I could hear the thread of doubt in his voice. My father would never change, and we both knew it. "He did. But I don't care anymore."

"Just wanted to make sure you weren't doing something destructive."

I stared at Abby, thinking of how easily she'd destroyed my defenses, ripped down my walls and burrowed into my heart. This woman... I couldn't put words to this feeling yet, but I heard the change in my tone when I spoke. "I'm with Abby."

There was a pause on the other end, and I could practically feel my brother's approval singing through my veins. "I'm glad you're happy. You guys are good for each other."

The bathroom light clicked off, and I watched Abby as she stepped into the bedroom. Her curves were outlined in the silvery moonlight, and something flickered in my chest as she moved toward me.

"Me, too," I murmured to Cole. "Gotta go. I'll see you in the morning."

I hung up and tossed my phone on the nightstand without taking my eyes from the gorgeous woman in front of me. Abby crawled into bed clad in a pair of panties and a tiny tank top, and I yanked on the hem. "Since when do we wear clothes in bed?"

A grin curved her face as she curled her fingers into the fabric of her shirt and pulled it off over her head. "What was I thinking?"

Wrapping one arm around her naked waist, I pulled her down to me. Skin to skin, I breathed her in, her presence automatically calming my nerves. Just having her near made me feel stronger. I never wanted to be anything like my old man, I'd known that for years. But I was certain that, with Abby, I'd found the one person who made me a better man.

Her hand drifted over my chest, sliding through the springy hair before moving upward to trace my collarbone. Her hair tickled my chin, and I dropped a kiss on the top of her head. We lay there in silence for several minutes before I finally spoke. "I spent the afternoon at my dad's."

She shifted slightly, tipping her face upward so she could look at me. "How'd that go?"

"It was a fucking train wreck, just like every other time."

She propped her chin on the back of her hand where it rested on my chest. "I'm sorry."

"Don't be. He's just a waste of energy and time, and I'm not going to give him any more of either."

"I fucking hate that I'm even bothered by it. After this long I should be used to being alone."

"You're not alone." She said, her voice fierce and full of vehemence. "You have me, all the guys at QSG... we're your family now. Blood doesn't mean a damn thing. Family is who you choose to surround yourself with. There's no reason to keep toxic people in your life just because they share the same DNA. My parents weren't good people either, and I know for a fact that I wouldn't be the same person I am today without my brother and Violet. So even if your father doesn't want to be part of your life, you'll always have us.

You are—"

She stopped suddenly, and I found myself transfixed, my heart racing as I waited anxiously for her to continue. When she didn't, I felt compelled to ask, "Is that you telling me you care about me?" I infused some levity into my tone, and she lightly smacked my chest.

"I just..." She paused, her teeth digging into her lower lip. I could practically feel the heat of embarrassment radiating from her body where she lay across my chest. "You know what I mean."

I grabbed her fingers and lifted them to my mouth, kissing the tips. "I know exactly what you mean. I'm glad I have you." Shrouded in darkness gave me the confidence to continue, to tell her how I really felt and bare my soul. "Because, believe me when I say this, Abilene. I haven't cared for many people in my life. Cole, sure. My brothers from the Marines, absolutely. I'd lay down my life for them in a heartbeat. But you... It's different. It's like... I feel lost without you. I feel dirty and unworthy but then I see you. I see my reflection in your eyes, and you make me feel whole and good, like I can be better than the man who raised me. I know it's crazy, but I want you more every day. I think about you from the second I wake up 'til my head hits the pillow at night."

"I feel the same," she whispered.

Just hearing those words sent a rush of relief through me and something else I didn't quite know how to identify. All I knew was I wanted more of it. More of her. Abby was the most amazing woman I'd ever met, and at some point, she'd completely stolen my heart.

"Before you, I hadn't kissed a woman in ten years."

There was a beat of stunned silence, and I could feel Abby staring at me. "Really?"

I nodded. "Remember that night in the hotel?"

"The no kissing rule." I smiled at the tinge of disdain in her voice. "Yes, I remember that."

"You should be happy with my no kissing rule." I smiled and wrapped one hand around the back of her head. "I broke that rule for you."

I pulled her down for a long, sensual kiss, pouring every ounce of appreciation and admiration I felt for her into it. Abby lifted her head a moment later. "Since you put it that way... Makes me feel special."

"You are special, babe. You have no idea."

Abby must have heard the seriousness in my voice, and she rearranged herself to see me better in the dim light. "Will you tell me?"

"About the kissing?"

"Yeah."

I turned onto my side so I faced her and sifted my fingers through her silky hair. "You know life with my dad was pretty shitty. I met this girl in high school—Samantha. She came from a good family, helped me with my dyslexia."

"You're dyslexic?"

I smiled at the disbelief in her voice. "I hide it well. Or try to, at least. I still slip up sometimes, but she was the first person who took the time to get to know me, to figure out what was wrong. Her brother was dyslexic, too, and I started doing some exercises to help with it."

Abby gave a little shake of her head. "I never would have guessed."

"Good." I kissed her forehead. "I don't like for people to know. Makes it sound like a handicap."

"How'd you get into the military?" she asked.

"Same as anyone else." I lifted one shoulder. "I passed their tests, which was all that mattered. It wasn't a huge deal. Not like I was a sniper dealing with numbers all day, you know?"

Abby nodded a little, and I continued. "Anyway. So, Samantha and I started dating. She was the first person who really saw me, and I just... fell for it. When I left for the military, I told her I wanted to marry her when I got back."

Abby drew in a sharp breath, and I swept one hand down her spine to comfort her. "Thank God it didn't work out that way. A couple years into my tour, I got a letter saying she'd found someone else."

"Are you kidding me?" Abby's voice rose several octaves. "What a bitch."

Pretty much my sentiment. "Gets better."

Abby snorted. "I don't think there's anything "better" about that situation, except that she's gone."

"That was definitely a bonus," I said, "even if I didn't realize it at the time. Turns out she'd left me for Price."

Abby jerked up to look at me. "Wait. Like... Gavin? Our Gavin?"

"The very same." I nodded.

His girlfriend, Kate, had run into some trouble recently, and he'd hired QSG to do some background on his boss. Gavin now worked for us, doing some legal consultation. Kate was a sweetheart. Gavin... I still wasn't sure how I felt about him.

"I hated that fucker when we were kids. His parents doted on him, gave him everything. He had everything while I had nothing. And then he got my girl."

Abby's body trembled with fury. "Did he know you two were together?"

"No, she lied to him, too. Told him we'd went our separate ways after graduation." I shook my head. "You know what's even more fucked up? He actually served, too. He put in his time overseas, then headed back to the States to study law, just like his old man. So Sam got the best of both worlds—the Marine and the rich lawyer."

Abby thought on that for a second. "They're obviously not together now."

"No, they're not." Gavin had found Kate and they seemed to be extremely happy together. "From what I understand, they dated for a while until she cheated on him, too."

"She played you both. That's why the situation with the Morrisons bothered you so much," Abby said softly.

I nodded. "I can't stand cheaters. Relationships should be built on respect and trust. If you break that..." I lifted one shoulder. "There's just no going back for me."

"I can understand that." She was quiet for a second. "I'm sorry that happened to you."

"I'm not." It had sucked at the time, but I was forever grateful I hadn't married Samantha. "Now I have you, and what we have is a thousand times better."

I pulled her in close, loving the feel of her against me. The sex was good, but this was better somehow. Holding her close, knowing that she was mine and I was hers... There was no better feeling in the world.

CHAPTER THIRTY-SEVEN

Abby

I couldn't get Clay off my mind. After last night it felt like everything was... perfect. Clay had opened up and shown me a side of him I never knew existed, and I'd fallen deeper than I ever thought possible. I wished he were more vocal about his feelings for me, but I knew he would tell me when he was ready. In the meantime, he showered me with attention, showing me every single day how much he cared for me. Actions spoke so much louder than words, and I loved what he was telling me.

I'd decided to meet up with my friend Jamie tonight, and we'd spent the past two hours at a bar downtown. Her boyfriend was a chef, so he rarely got home before midnight. When she'd asked me to come hang out with her, I'd jumped at the chance. I'd needed some girl talk anyway, and I told her everything that had happened recently—meeting Clay at the hotel, finding out we would be working together... and Con finding out about us.

Across from me, Jamie shook her head. "Are you worried about how it will affect you guys?"

"I was," I admitted, "but I think he understands. He's seen us together, and he knows I'm happy. I think he'll always have that reservation about any guy I date, though, you know?"

She nodded. "It's what big brothers do. It's stupid, but they feel like it's their job to protect us from everything."

"Tell me about it." I rolled my eyes. "I just don't want it to ruin anything between him and Clay."

Con knew I was happy, but I wondered if he'd always be waiting for Clay to hurt me. I knew about Clay's past, and I'd be lying if I said it didn't bother me, at least a little bit. I still thought back to that night once in a while when he'd started to leave. I kept reminding myself that he hadn't. He'd come back, and that showed me how much he cared and wanted things to work.

I tried to put myself in his shoes. After everything that had happened with him, I completely understood his reservations. He'd been hurt before, and he was afraid of letting people in. Clay was so domineering that I didn't really think of his being vulnerable. But everyone had fears, and intimacy was one of his. Him being willing to come back to me, even being terrified of what would happen, meant the world to me.

I glanced at my phone. "I should go. But it was great seeing you."

"You too." We headed for the front door, and Jamie turned to me. "We'll have another girls' night soon."

"Absolutely."

I gave Jamie a hug, then cut across the parking lot to my car. The night was warm, and I couldn't help but wonder what Clay was doing right now. I hoped he would finish up his job early so I would have a chance to see him tonight for a while. A tiny smile curved my face. Either way, I knew he would find his way into my bed regardless of how late it was.

Over the past couple of weeks, we'd fallen into a steady rhythm. It probably should have scared me how fast things were moving, but it didn't. I enjoyed having him around and—surprise, I know—I loved talking to him. We talked about everything and nothing, exchanged random trivia and confided stories of our youth. I felt more in tune with Clay than I ever had with another person, like he was a missing part of me.

He could be overbearing and a little arrogant, but a huge part of me acknowledged that I wouldn't have looked at him twice if he weren't. I wanted a strong man who knew what he wanted out of life and would do whatever it took to get it. I didn't need him to take care of me, but I loved that he wanted to look out for me and keep me safe. I loved the way he babied me, and I loved returning the favor. He was everything I could ever ask for in a man and more.

My car came into sight, and I used the key fob to unlock the doors. The taillights flashed twice, the faint red glow illuminating the space around the car. I rounded the rear bumper and stifled a shriek of surprise as a black figure moved toward me in the space between my car and the SUV parked next to me. Immediately, I tried to backpedal, but the man was on me before I had a chance to move or yell out for help. The matte black barrel of a pistol gleamed in the moonlight as he lifted it toward me. My heart skipped a beat, and my breath stalled in my chest as my gaze locked on the deadly weapon, unable to look away.

"Don't make a sound," the man commanded with a low growl.

Oh, God. Every muscle in my body trembled violently as I lifted my hands placatingly. "Please, I'll give you whatever you want—"

"Shut up," he snapped, jabbing the pistol my way.

A soft yelp left my throat and I flinched as my keys slipped from my hand. They hit the pavement with a soft jingle, the sound ricocheting like a gunshot in my ears. Keeping the pistol pointed at me, the man stooped down and scooped them up. My gaze swept over him as he slowly stood. Every inch of him was covered from head to toe in black. A ski mask covered his face, except for the holes revealing his mouth and two dark eyes.

One black gloved hand palmed my key fob and pressed a button. From behind me, I heard the trunk release and pop open. "Back up."

Hands lifted slightly in front of me, I slowly did as he asked, shuffling toward the back of the car.

"Get in the trunk."

My gaze darted toward the trunk, then back to him. I couldn't get inside. If I did, I was dead for sure. My mind seemed to slow down as I fought to figure out what to do. The idea of being kidnapped and tossed in the trunk had seemed inconceivable the day that Clay had come up behind me in the grocery store parking lot. Now I wished I'd paid closer attention. My thoughts scrambled, and my feet remained frozen to the asphalt.

"Get in!" The man gestured with the gun toward the trunk, and I took advantage of the split-second distraction. Thrusting upward, I drove the heel of my palm into his nose. My purse slipped down my arm and hit the ground with a thud, but I paid no attention as I threw myself into action.

He let out a grunt of surprise and pain as he stumbled into the SUV behind him. I took off like a bat out of hell, zigzagging through the parking lot, weaving between cars to put as much distance between myself and my attacker as possible. Heart beating ferociously, I sprinted toward the very same bar I just walked out of a few minutes ago. I was gasping for breath by the time I threw the door open and dashed inside, looking around frantically. Ignoring the surprised looks the patrons inside sent my way, I launched myself toward the bar. "I need help! I... I was attacked outside in the parking lot, and I dropped my purse so I don't have a phone, and I need to call for help..."

I took a moment to drag in a breath as the bartender looked on with concern. "Can I... Can I use your phone?"

He immediately waved me around the bar and into the kitchen area. He flicked a quick look around the bar like he was searching for the man who had accosted me outside.

"You'll be safe in here," he assured me as he led me into a small back room. "This is the manager's office," he explained. "Do you want me to send one of the ladies back here to sit with you?"

It took a moment for my mind to slow down and try to process the question. I appreciated the gesture, but I shook my head. "No. I just need a phone."

He seemed to understand how rattled I was, because he kept a healthy distance between us as he moved toward a cordless phone on the desk. He picked up the handset and extended it toward me, and I accepted it with shaking fingers as he moved toward the doorway once more. He awkwardly rubbed a hand across the back of his neck. "We have a back door in the alley if you could ask the cops to come in that way instead."

I stared at him stupidly for a second, trying to make the connection. "You know." He grimaced. "I'd rather they not come to the front and scare off the business."

"Right." I nodded slowly. "I'll take care of it."

He shot me a grateful smile then disappeared, and I turned my attention back to the phone. I should probably call the cops, but I wasn't sure if there was anything they could do. The only person I wanted right now was Clay, but I couldn't seem to remember his phone number, and my brain locked up as I stared at the keypad on the phone. My fingers started to move, tapping in my brother's phone number from memory. Con would know what to do; he always knew what to do. My entire body shook as I listened to one torturously slow ring, then another. Finally, my brothers voice filled the line.

"Connor Quentin."

"Con, it's... it's me."

"Abby?" His tone with drenched with a combination of worry and concern. "What's wrong?"

"I..." I swallowed hard, trying to remain calm, but I was sure that Con would read right through it. "I'm at Mulligan's Pub. Some-body came after me in the parking lot, and I—"

"Are you safe?"

His tone was strong and clear, and it helped to ground me a bit. "Y-yes. I'm inside the bar in the manager's office."

"Did you call the police yet?"

"N-no." My teeth chattered. "Not yet."

"I'll take care of it," he promised. "Just stay where you are, and I'll be there in fifteen."

"Okay," I whispered. "See you then."

I clicked off the phone and set it on the edge of the desk, then curled up in the chair, wrapping my arms around my legs. The door was partially closed, but clatter from the kitchen provided steady noise, and I felt like an hour had passed before the sound of foot-steps came down the narrow hallway and stopped in front of the door. My entire body tensed, and I looked up to see the familiar form of my brother filling the doorway. But he wasn't alone. Over his shoulder, I spied Clay, his face set in an intense expression.

My brother stepped to the side as Clay moved straight toward me, his gaze sweeping over inch of me from head to toe. He ran his hands over my arms and legs, checking for injuries before slowly grasping my hands and pulling me to my feet. One arm went around my waist, and the other buried itself in my hair as he tugged me into his broad chest. The myriad of emotions swirling inside me finally bubbled over, and the tears I'd been holding back finally broke free as I clung to him.

CHAPTER THIRTY-EIGHT

Clay

I wondered if Abby could hear my heart slamming against my ribs where she rested against me, her cheek pressed to the space over my heart. I was a train wreck the whole way here, driving fifteen miles per hour over the speed limit in my need to see her.

I held her tightly to me as sobs racked her body, the stress of the situation finally catching up to her. "I've got you," I murmured against her hair. "I won't let anything happen to you."

In my peripheral vision I watched Con as he stood off to the side, hands shoved in his pockets, one foot propped on the wall behind him. We hadn't spoken much since he'd walked in on us last week, and I wondered how he felt about me comforting Abby. Not gonna lie, it stung a little that she'd called him first. I'd been sitting in a parking lot waiting for my mark to show up when Con called.

"Whatever you're doing, drop it," he'd said. "Meet me at Mulligan's as soon as you can. Something's happened to Abby."

I didn't have a chance to ask any questions, because Con had already hung up, and I immediately started the engine, threw the truck into gear and headed this direction. I hit the parking lot running, needing to see her for myself. A hundred different scenarios flitted through my mind on the drive here, all of them involving some kind of bodily harm.

I swore I couldn't get a full breath until I saw her sitting in the chair here, looking small and vulnerable as hell. Thank God, whatever had happened must have just scared her, because she didn't appear to be hurt in any way. Whatever it was had to be serious, though—Abby wasn't the kind to make a big deal of nothing. In fact, she tended to downplay things, so it made me even more curious to find out what the hell had happened.

Several minutes passed before her heart wrenching sobs quieted to sniffles, and I ran my hand up and down her spine, offering silent comfort. Finally, she drew back and dabbed at her tear-streaked cheeks, her chest spasming with the occasional hiccup as her breathing returned to normal.

Abby pulled from my arms, and I reluctantly released her as she moved toward Con. She wrapped her arms around his waist, and he pulled her into a brotherly hug. "You okay, squirt?"

She bobbed a nod against his chest but didn't speak.

"Can you tell us what happened?"

She nodded again, and Con shifted her against her side, keeping one arm wrapped protectively around her shoulders. "I..."

A shiver racked her body, and she fixed her gaze to a spot on the floor before continuing. "I was walking out to my car, and I'd just unlocked it when a man came out of nowhere. He was... he had a mask and gloves, and he pointed a gun at me and told me to get in the trunk."

My blood boiled, and a red haze flashed across my vision at the thought of anyone pointing a pistol at my girl.

Con's laser-like gaze met mine, a hardness in their depths that promised retribution, and I watched his grip on her tighten. "What did you do?"

Her gaze slowly rose from the floor, over my feet and legs and finally up to my face. "I punched him."

My eyes widened with surprise, and I saw a tiny flicker of a smile dancing at the corners of her mouth. Her next words were directed at me. "I remembered that day in the parking lot... what you said. I—I punched him as hard as I could, then ran inside."

So fucking brave. Most people, men and women alike, would have followed the man's instructions and climbed right into the trunk, hoping that he would eventually let them go. But not Abilene. "Good girl."

Now that the fear had finally begun to recede, pride glowed brightly in her deep brown eyes, and she straightened away from Con. I held out one hand, and she moved toward me. I stared down at her as she slipped her palm into mine. I squeezed her fingers gently before lifting my hands to cup her face.

"I'm so proud of you." I couldn't stop touching her. I petted her hair, her cheeks, every inch of her pretty face, thanking every deity known to man that she was okay.

"Thanks." A real smile finally broke through, and my heart seized in my chest.

This woman… "I've never been as scared as I was when I got that call from your brother."

Another shudder racked her body, but she managed to keep her chin held high. "I'm okay."

"The whole way here I thought about what I would do if anything ever happened to you." I spoke low, for her ears only. "It would gut me, baby, because I love you so damn much."

Her eyes turned glassy as they searched mine. "Really?"

I was dimly aware of Con leaving the room, quietly closing the door behind him.

"Really." I touched my forehead to hers and tenderly brushed a kiss over her lips.

Her hands curled into the fabric of my shirt. "I love you, too."

I held her for several more minutes until I could put it off no longer. We needed to see if we could figure out what had happened and who'd come after Abby. Con stood next to the bar, and he threw a look our way as we rounded the corner. His gaze dropped to my hand where it was entwined with Abby's before meeting my gaze again.

"Any footage?" I kept Abby's hand wrapped in mine, unwilling to let her go.

Con shook his head. "None on the bar."

Damn. "Maybe we can check the plaza, see if anyone will grant us access."

Con walked with us out of the parking lot. "I'll see if Jason can dig anything up."

I gave a little nod, though I wasn't terribly hopeful. Given what she'd said about the man wearing a dark ski mask, it was unlikely we'd be able to find anything worthwhile. I paused next to her car and used the fob to unlock it, then held the door open for Abby. I hadn't been able to let go of her since we left the bar, and even now, I kept one hand braced on her hip as she slid into the seat. I waited until she was buckled in, then handed over her purse and started to close the door.

"Clay?"

I leaned back inside and rested a hand on her knee. "Yeah, babe?"

"Can we stop for a cappuccino on the way?"

I knew after her scare earlier that she'd be up half the night anyway. "Whatever you want," I readily agreed. If it made her feel better, I'd wrangle the fucking moon for her.

She shot me a little smile, and I shut the door. Con eyed me, an enigmatic expression on his face. "I always wondered what that looked like."

I flicked a look his way. "What?"

"Being whipped."

I rolled my eyes. "Fucking hilarious."

I couldn't deny that it was the truth, though. I would walk through fire for her, and we both knew it.

He paused by the rear fender and tipped his head toward Abby. "She acts tough, but she's still my baby sister."

I gave a little nod, unsure exactly of what to say.

Con's expression turned serious. "I don't know what's going on, but... take care of her."

"I will," I promised. She was so damn strong, and for some reason, it only made me want to protect her even more.

With that he disappeared, presumably to find his own SUV, and I climbed into my truck. I immediately fell in behind Abby as we pulled out of the parking lot, and I kept an eye on our surroundings as we headed to my place. One cappuccino later, we pulled into my apartment complex.

Even though barely a half hour had passed since we'd left the bar, it'd been too long since I'd touched her. Wrapping one arm around her waist, I led Abby up the stairs to the third floor then unlocked the door to my apartment. She'd only been here one other time, and I took a second to clean up the random stuff I'd left lying around the living room. Recently, we'd been spending most of our time at Abby's place, since it felt more like home.

With a little sigh Abby sank into the middle cushion on the couch, and I took the seat beside her, then spread my arm out over the back and around her shoulders. The dip of my weight caused her to lean into me, and she snuggled even closer, her hands still wrapped around the disposable cup of cappuccino.

"Want to talk about it?"

I was always cautious whenever Abby got quiet; I never quite knew how to read that side of her. It meant there was a lot going on in her mind that she hadn't quite come to terms with or didn't know how to verbalize.

"I don't know," she finally admitted slowly. "I feel... angry. Scared, like he's going to pop up again when I least expect it."

I didn't like the way she said that. "I'll keep you safe," I promised.

"I know," she said as she tipped her head against my chest. "It's not that. It's just... with everything going on recently, I wondered..."

I wondered the same thing. I still hadn't heard anything from Trevor, though I had texted him twice more. For something to happen to Abby in roughly the same period of time made me incredibly uneasy.

"Was there anything about the man that you recognized? His build, his voice?"

She gave her head a little shake. "I don't think so. It happened so fast, and all I could focus on was the gun."

The reminder sent a ripple of fury through me, and I tightened my hold on her. "We're going to figure out what the hell is going on."

If someone had indeed killed Charlie and covered it up, then I was certain that he wouldn't like Trevor poking around. He'd dragged Abby into it by proxy, putting her in danger, and I wouldn't stand for it. We were going to figure out what the hell happened to Charlie and who was responsible, then put this to rest once and for all.

CHAPTER THIRTY-NINE

Abby

The first thing I noticed when I woke up was the soreness. I let out a stifled groan as I stretched my legs, all the memories from last night flooding back in rapid succession.

A heavy hand landed on my hip and curled into my flesh. "You okay?"

Clay's voice was thick and raspy with sleep, but I welcomed the way it wrapped around me as I snuggled back into him.

"Good." I cleared my throat. "My body is just a little worn out from last night. I found muscles I didn't remember having before."

Clay's hand slipped from my hip and moved around my waist, pulling me even tighter to him. His lips landed on the back of my neck for a soft kiss before he spoke again. "I'm sorry you had to go through that. I promise I won't let it happen again."

I turned in his arms to face him. "It's not your fault."

He gave a slight shake of his head, his mouth set in a hard line. "I don't care. You're mine, and I take responsibility for that. No one will have the chance to get close to you again."

My heart thudded hard at his proclamation, and I had to fight the urge to melt into him. Dredging up every ounce of willpower, I focused on the alpha possessiveness of his statement. "I'm your responsibility?"

"Yes." There was no remorse in his voice. "You're mine, and I'll always take care of you. And reverse. In a different way, you take care of me, give me everything I've never deserved."

His words struck straight into my heart, and I couldn't help but wrap my arms around him and pull him down for a kiss. What I couldn't give physically, he did. And whatever he couldn't contribute emotionally, I made up for. I freaking loved this man heart and soul, and I wanted all of him for the rest of my days.

I pulled back. "I'm not letting you go. You know that, right?"

A tiny smirk lifted his mouth. "No?"

"Nope." I cuddled closer, sliding one leg between his. "You chased me until I finally gave in. Now you're stuck with me."

"You know, that doesn't sound so bad," he said as he rolled to his back and shifting me so I lay on top of him.

More than an hour later, I pulled on the same tank top and jeans I'd worn to the bar last night. From his spot on the bed, Clay looked at me. "How would you feel about staying here with me for a while?"

I was certain his request had everything to do with what had happened last night, but there was a huge part of me that hoped it meant more. "Because it's safer?"

He nodded slowly. "That... But also because I want you here. With me."

Happiness unfurled in my chest at his admission. "Okay."

He exhaled deeply, then grasped my hips and pulled me close for a kiss. "Thank you."

He released me, and we finished dressing in silence. It felt strange in a way to not be able to stay in my own home, but I couldn't deny that I felt much more secure with Clay. He was taking no risks with my security, and I deeply appreciated it. These were the kinds of things he and my brother were trained for, and I wasn't too proud to fight him. I'd seen all those B-rated horror films. I wasn't going to be the girl who discarded common sense in lieu of pride and got hacked up by the killer at the end.

I didn't know what the person was after, if it was intentional or a coincidence, but I wasn't about to let my guard down. Until we figured out what was going on, I was happy enough to follow Clay's and my brother's instructions. Surrounded by a dozen ex-military men, I knew I would be entirely safe at work. Since I didn't have any clothes here, we decided to head to my house and grab enough to get me through the next week or so.

"I should really stop by and see Violet," I said as I stepped into my shoes. "Would you mind if we made a quick detour to Morningside?"

"Of course."

I grabbed up my purse on the way out the door and checked the battery on my phone. "Have you talked to Jason yet this morning?"

"Not yet." Clay locked up behind us, then took my hand as we headed down to the parking lot. "Your brother was going to take lead on that, see if we could get any info from the cameras of the businesses nearby."

We wouldn't find anything. I wasn't sure how I knew that, I just did. From the expression on Clay's face, he felt the same. "What should I do when you're out working?"

He paused next to the truck and held the door as I climbed inside. "As of right now, I've passed my caseload to Blake. Con is going to handle qualifications for the local LEOs next week if I'm still not back. But my main priority right now is making sure you're safe."

I waited until he was seated before speaking again. "They're good with that?"

"Of course." He threw a quick look my way as he started the engine and put the truck in gear. "You're one of us, and we always take care of our own."

A little flicker of warmth flared to life around my heart, and I relaxed, content for once to just enjoy the comfortable silence flowing between us.

At the red light Clay picked up his phone and studied the screen, brows drawn, before replacing it in the cupholder. I watched him curiously. "What's wrong?"

"Nothing, I hope." He glanced my way and frowned. "Have you heard anything from Trevor?"

"Not recently, not since last week. Why?" Dread curdled my stomach.

"I've texted him several times, but he hasn't responded. I know he was meeting with some of Charlie's relatives, but I thought he'd have checked in by now..."

Clay trailed off and my heart stuttered in my chest. Oh, God. With everything that had happened recently, I was inclined to think the worst. "We need to check on him."

"We'll stop by and see Violet first. If I still haven't heard back from him by the time we leave, we'll stop by the hotel."

We drove toward Morningside, unease and apprehension hanging heavily over us. Less than a half hour later we arrived at the assisted living facility, and I smiled at the nurse seated behind the front desk. "Hi, I'm Abby Quentin. I'm here to visit my grand-mother, Violet," I said as I signed the registry. "Would you happen to know if she's in her room?"

"I believe I saw her go outside not too long ago with Linda."

"Thanks." I turned to Clay and tipped my head toward the hallway bisecting the lobby. "We can head out this way."

He fell into step beside me, and we exited out the back door. As we entered the recreational area outside, I scanned the lawn for a familiar face. A moment later, I found Violet sitting in on a bench in the shade. Tucking my hand into the crook of Clay's arm, I drew him across the yard.

Violet's head lifted when she saw us approaching, and her head tipped slightly to the side in question. Almost immediately, my heart fell in my chest. My fingers tensed automatically where they rested on Clay's arm, and he dipped his head low next to mine.

"You okay?"

"Yeah," I said softly. "I think it's a bad day. Just play along."

I smiled as we got closer, then stopped about ten feet away. "Good morning, Violet."

"Good morning." Her lips tipped into a smile, but I could practically see the wheels turning in her head, trying to remember exactly who I was.

"My name is Abby." My voice broke a little as I said it, and I fought to blink back the tears burning the backs of my eyes. Clay shifted me closer, and I was immensely grateful for the silent show of support.

Violet studied me intently as she repeated my name, testing it. "Abby... You look familiar, but I..." She gave her head a little shake.

"I'm sorry, my memory's not what it used to be."

"That's okay," I assured her. "I hope you don't mind, but I brought a friend of mine."

Clay stepped forward and offered his hand. "Clay Thompson, ma'am."

"Lovely to meet you." Violet returned his handshake, then gestured to the bench. "It's a beautiful day. Would you like to join me?"

"I'd love to." I took a seat on the bench, several inches away from Violet so she wouldn't feel overwhelmed, then threw a look at Clay.

"It's nice to finally meet you," he said from where he stood in front of us. "I've heard wonderful things about you."

"Oh?" She gave a little laugh. "From this lovely young woman here?"

She gestured my way, and Clay grinned. "From her, too," he agreed. "But mostly from your husband."

It was a small test of sorts, and I found myself holding my breath.

A fond smile curved Violet's mouth. "Eugene was a wonderful man."

Clay nodded. "I'm sorry for your loss." Violet tipped her head in acknowledgment, and Clay continued. "You were married a second time, I believe. To Charles Orwell?"

Violet's expression became slightly guarded. "That's correct."

It hadn't hit me before, but I suddenly realized I had always thought of Orwell as Violet's maiden name. I knew it wasn't the same as Eugene's, and I had always figured that after his death, she'd reverted to her maiden name. I didn't know why I hadn't realized it sooner.

"And how did you know Charlie?" Violet's voice sounded tight with tension.

"He was a friend of my uncle's," Clay explained. "They were in the Navy together when they were younger."

Violet nodded a little and offered a brittle smile. "That's wonderful."

"I was hoping to get in touch with him again," Clay added

hopefully.

I watched Violet carefully, and a dark expression moved over her eyes. "I'm afraid I can't help you with that. I haven't seen him for a while."

I couldn't tell exactly how much she remembered, or how clear her memory was, but she obviously remembered the fact that she and Charlie were no longer married. I pressed gently for details. "His uncle would really love to see him again if you have any idea where he may have gone."

Violet shook her head, and her gaze drifted far away. "After Lily..." She gave a little shake of her head. "It's all kind of a blur."

My heart went out to her, but I wasn't quite ready to give up yet. "We've tried looking up his address and phone number, but nothing's listed."

The look Violet leveled at me chilled me to the bone. "I guess some things just aren't meant to be found."

I fought the urge to squirm as Violet rose to her feet. "If you'll excuse me, I think I'll retire to my room for a bit."

I pasted on a smile. "It was nice to see you again. Thanks for your help."

She made her way toward the nurse hovering nearby, and I met Clay's concerned gaze.

"She definitely knows something."

That was certain but I was starting to doubt we would ever find the truth. "I wish we knew who else was involved. Is it Patrick? He's the only one who knew about everything and would have a reason to want to protect her."

Clay slowed his steps, looking thoughtful. "There might be a way to figure that out. Come on."

He grabbed my hand, and I trailed along behind him as he tugged me back inside and up to the receptionist's desk. Though I wanted to ask what he was thinking, I kept my mouth shut as he focused on the nurse behind the desk.

"My name is Clay Thompson with Quentin Security Group." He pointed to the sign-in sheet. "Would you mind if I took a look at your registry?"

Her eyes darted to the insignia on his polo, and she nodded.

"Be my guest. Let me know if you need anything else."

Clay began to riffle through the sheets on the clipboard, and I leaned in. "What are you looking for?"

"I'm wondering who's been by to see Violet." He paused and pointed to a name on the sheet. "Harris."

I checked the date. "That was right about the same time I met with him about the house."

Clay nodded and continued to flip, his eyes rapidly scanning the names on the sheets. He paused again. "Trevor."

I nodded. He'd told us that he'd stopped in but that Violet wasn't able to help him.

"I know he said he hadn't talked with her recently," Clay continued as he turned the pages, "but I just wanted to check because—"

He stopped abruptly. "And there he is."

Almost as soon as the words left his mouth, I saw Patrick's name on the sign-in sheet, and a chill ran through my body. "He told us he hadn't seen her recently."

Clay looked at me, his expression serious. "He lied."

My heart felt like it would beat out of my chest. "Let's go check on Trevor."

We were mostly silent as we drove to the hotel where Trevor was staying, and I felt a prickly sensation along the back of my neck. Something wasn't right. The first thing I noticed when we pulled in was that Trevor's car wasn't there.

Clay noticed the same thing. "Let's go check, just in case."

I hopped out of the truck and followed along quietly as we made our way toward Trevor's room. Clay knocked several times, but inside everything was silent and still. Mouth set in a grim line, Clay turned to me. "I'm going to talk with the manager."

The hotel lobby was located on the corner of the building on the ground floor, and an older man occupied the seat behind the desk. "How can I help you?"

"I'm Clay Thompson with Quentin Security Group," he introduced himself. "My client was staying in room 204, but I haven't been able to reach him for several days. Can you tell me if he checked out?"

The man seemed to consider it for a second. "Sure thing." His fingers flew over the keyboard, and he shook his head. "He's paid up through the end of this week."

Clay turned to me, his face unreadable, and my insides quivered. Where the hell was he?

Clay drew in a deep breath. "Is there any way you can open the room for us? We won't need to go in. I just want to see if his things are there."

The manager finally acquiesced with a small nod, then grabbed up a ring of keys. We followed him back to Trevor's room and stood off to the side. Clay's arm settled low on my waist, tugging me close, and I leaned into him.

The manager inserted the key, and I held my breath as the knob turned and the door swung open. Holy shit. Beside me, Clay swore as he took in the room. Papers littered every inch of the floor, and the mattress hung half off the bed, the covers twisted and lying in a heap next to it. The entire room had been tossed. But why?

Clay thanked the hotel manager, and we made our way to the truck in silence. Once inside, I turned to face him. "Where the hell could he be?" I fretted.

"I don't know." Clay gave a little shake of his head as he cranked the engine and shifted into gear. "I don't like the way this feels. Someone was in that room, looking for something."

"But what?"

"I don't know. But it's more important than ever that we find out where the hell Trevor is."

"Maybe we can get a hold of his parents, see if they've heard from him." I pulled my phone from my purse and brought up the Internet search bar. I began to type Trevor's name as I spoke to Clay. "Do you remember where in Colorado he's from? If I can..." I trailed off as the search populated results automatically.

My gaze landed on a recent headline, and I froze. Oh my God.

I didn't realize I'd spoken out loud until Clay's voice penetrated my fog of disbelief. "Abby? What's wrong?"

I opened the article and skimmed the first couple of lines before lifting my eyes to Clay's. "Trevor's dead."

CHAPTER FORTY

Clay

I wrapped an arm around Abby's waist as she hopped down from the passenger seat of my truck, then led her into QSG, shielding her between my body and the building. I didn't think anyone would be stupid enough to try something here, but you never knew. Desperate times called for desperate measures, and Trevor and Abby's questions had definitely stirred up a hornets' nest of trouble.

Somebody obviously had a lot to lose if the truth came out, and I wasn't going to let him get anywhere near Abby. One way or the other, we were going to find the truth. What happened to Charlie, what really happened to Lily, and if that person was responsible for the incident at the bar last night.

I had texted Con on the way to let him know we were stopping in and that Trevor was dead. Dane sat at the front desk, and he met my gaze as we stepped inside. I tipped my head toward the hallway, and he vacated the seat, leaving it open for Abby.

I moved to his side as Abby settled herself behind the desk. With all of us around, she was safe enough here.

"I need to talk with Con. Can you stay here with her? I don't want her left alone."

"Sure thing." He nodded his assent and moved to stand sentry next to the front door.

Abby's gaze was fixed on the computer screen in front of her, and I knew it was a coping mechanism for her. She was throwing herself into her work, trying desperately to forget about the reality of the situation. I didn't blame her at all. Abby was no stranger to death. She had lost both of her parents at an early age in a tragic car accident, and now Trevor had died the exact same way.

I took a knee next to her office chair, but she kept her eyes focused forward. Placing a hand on her thigh, I gently swiveled her so she had no choice but to look at me. "I'm going to go talk to your brother. Dane will be out here with you in case anyone shows up."

She gave a little nod but remained silent. That was another thing. She'd been quieter than I'd ever seen her since the day we met, and it worried me immensely. It was as if her bubbly personality had been extinguished, overridden by fear and worry, and I hated it. I lifted my free hand and pinched her chin between my thumb and forefinger and studied her for a long moment. I didn't say a word. I didn't need to. She knew exactly how I felt about her; I'd do anything to keep her safe.

I tipped her mouth down to meet mine for a single, soft kiss. Abby pulled back almost immediately, and her cheeks flared pink as her eyes darted over my shoulder. I knew Con was standing there. I had heard him approach just before I kissed her, but I hadn't given a shit. Not bothering to throw a look his way, I levered to my feet then dropped another kiss on her forehead before stepping away. "Yell if you need anything."

She gave a little nod, her gaze landing on everything except me and her brother. I met Con's eyes as I turned around. His face was inscrutable, hands tucked into the pockets of his black slacks. Anyone else would have assumed he was relaxed. I knew better. I was sure there was a huge part of him that still resented the fact that Abby and I were together, but I couldn't bring myself to care. I jerked my head toward his office, and he silently fell into step beside me as we made our way down the hall.

We were silent for a long moment as he settled behind his desk, me into the chair on the opposite side. He stared at me for nearly a minute before speaking. "It's still fucking weird."

I bit back a smile. I sure as hell wasn't going to apologize for it.

"You really care about her."

It was a statement, not a question. "She's everything."

He nodded slowly. "To me, too. As long as you take care of her and she's happy, I don't want to know anything. I'm just going to pretend you're not defiling my sister."

He wasn't wrong. I was no more comfortable telling him about our relationship than he was hearing about it. "No worries there."

He gave a curt nod. "Talk to me. What happened?"

"I haven't spoken with anyone up that way yet, but from the article Abby read to me on the way here, looks like a car accident."

One dark brow lifted. "And your take?"

I didn't hesitate. "Not an accident. I left a message for the lieutenant who handled it, but he was tied up so I'm waiting on a call back."

"Let me know what you find out." Con gave a concise nod. "Also, we've got nothing on the cameras from last night."

Fucking of course not. "All right. I'm gonna wrap up a couple things before we head out. Hopefully he'll touch base soon."

I didn't have to wait long. Not five minutes after I left Con's office, my phone rang. I thumbed the screen and held it to my ear. "Thompson."

"Mr. Thompson, this is Lieutenant Mabry returning your call."

I explained everything to Mabry, but he didn't seem particularly concerned about a man searching for his missing father. To them, Charlie was an adult who was free to move about of his own will. Though I knew they couldn't waste a ton of their time and resources on what appeared to be an open and shut case, I wasn't willing to just sit back and wait for something to happen. I refused to jeopardize Abby's safety, and one way or the other, we were going to figure out who the hell was behind this before he came after her again. Because there was no doubt in my mind that the man who had accosted Abby in the parking lot at the bar was also responsible for Trevor's death.

Mabry made a little sound in the back of his throat. "Are you saying you believe those two are connected?"

"I think it's definitely possible," I offered, trying to be as diplomatic as possible, given the circumstances.

"We retrieved the car from the ravine and had our investigators look it over. So far there's been no sign of foul play."

I could hear the trace of condescension in his voice, and it set my hackles on edge. "Listen, I trust your guys. I'm sure they did a thorough job. All I'm saying is, maybe there's more to the story."

I told him about Trevor going up to Ft. Worth to speak with one of Charlie's relatives. "We tried to contact him for several days but could never get a response. We just saw the death notice this morning, so I wanted to reach out to you. It could be nothing, but I don't believe in coincidence."

The lieutenant was quiet for several seconds before he let out a soft sigh. "I'll have my guys double check, see if they overlooked anything."

"I appreciate that," I said sincerely. "I could just be looking for trouble where there is none, but..."

"Better to be safe than sorry," he supplied.

"Exactly." I hung up feeling not a whole hell of a lot better about the situation, then turned to Gavin and Jason. "Mabry promised to look into it."

Jason stared at me. "Do they have any idea what happened?"

I shrugged one shoulder. "All they know so far is it was a single car accident. Best guess is he swerved to miss something in the road, lost control, and flipped into the ravine. I have a feeling they're just gonna call it a day on this one."

From my left, Gavin lifted one hand in a shrugging motion. "It'll be hard as hell to get them to re-open it unless you have significant evidence indicating it was intentional."

Such a lawyerly response. I narrowed my gaze at him. "I'm telling you, whatever happened to Trevor wasn't an accident."

"Not disputing that, but how do you prove it?" Gavin pressed. "Say he was run off the road. Unless the killer left something behind—paint flakes, tire marks, something—you may never know."

I speared him with a dark look. "You know, Price, I'm starting to remember why I disliked you so much."

He rolled his eyes. "Whatever. It's nothing you don't already know."

No, it wasn't, but it wasn't the answer I wanted. "Who the fuck is this guy?"

"Are we sure it's a guy?" Jason cut in. "Could be a woman."

"I don't think so, not unless it's a team." I thought back to last night at the bar. "Abby was absolutely positive she was attacked by a guy, and after everything that's happened, I'm confident it's the same person. The question is, who has the most to lose?"

"Patrick," Gavin supplied.

Jason shook his head. "As soon as I heard about the ordeal last night, I thought of him. I gave him a call this morning and asked where he was last night. He and his wife were out to dinner with his boss, who verified it."

"Shit. Who the hell else could it be?"

"Could have hired it out," Jason suggested.

"I don't think so." I shook my head. "If this person killed Charlie and covered it up, he would want to deal with this personally.

"Honestly," I said, "I could give a shit less that they killed that asshole. The problem is, he went after Trevor, then Abby. Now I'm pissed."

If he had just left her alone, I would have let sleeping dogs lie. But the moment the killer threatened my woman, he'd sealed his fate. I didn't care what it took, I was going to find him.

CHAPTER FORTY-ONE

Abby

Emotionally, I was kind of a mess. I knew Clay and my brother were doing everything they could, along with the police, to figure out not only who had killed Trevor, but who had attacked me in the parking lot. I felt better knowing I would be staying with Clay, but my heart still hurt for Trevor.

Angry tears burned my eyes, obscuring the view from the windshield as Clay turned into my driveway and pulled to a stop next to the house. "You okay?"

He seemed to have a sixth sense when it came to me and my emotions. I thought I'd been holding it all in fairly well, but I couldn't hide anything from him. I blinked back the moisture in my eyes and nodded as I reached for the door handle. "I'll be fine."

Not waiting for his response and not really wanting to talk about it anymore right now, I climbed out of the car and trudged toward the house. But instead of making my way to the front door, I cut across to the backyard and took a seat on the deck. I had always found peace out here; Violet's backyard was like a tropical oasis just outside the city.

My gaze landed on the lilies lining the fence, and a sad smile touched my mouth. She had seemed so... *different* this morning. I knew she was withholding information, but I didn't have the mental fortitude to confront her right now. Besides, who knew if she would even remember? It was an uncharitable thought, but one

I couldn't help.

"I helped her plant those, you know," I said as I stared at the lilies lining the fence.

I studied the flowers, and Violet's words from several weeks ago floated back to me. The flowers had been Lily's favorites, an ironic namesake, but there was something else. What was it? Suddenly it hit me like a bolt of lightning. I'd been completely thrown by her talking about Lily adoring the calla lilies that I'd almost forgotten the second part of the statement—that he had hated them. Such an odd thing to say. Was it Charlie she'd spoken of? And why bring him up at all unless it was relevant in some way?

My heart thundered in my chest. What if Violet hadn't been talking about Lily at all? I remembered helping Violet plant the lilies the summer after I moved in. If they had been for her daughter, why wait so long? By the time I'd arrived, Lily had been dead for fifteen years. It wasn't out of the realm of possibility, but it was just one more inconsistency that didn't fit.

I could feel Clay's eyes on me. "What are you thinking?"

"Those flowers." I nodded toward the lilies. "I helped her plant those."

"Right..." Though I didn't look directly at him, I imagined him nodding, processing my words.

"That's not what I mean." I shook my head and met his gaze. "I mean, she waited until years after Lily's death to plant the flowers supposedly in her namesake. Why would she do that?"

Realization dawned in his eyes. Though I didn't dream as often anymore, those visions still weren't entirely clear. It had altered from night to night, almost as if my brain was trying to pull memories free a little at a time. Though I never actually reached the end of the dream, there was no doubt in my mind that the two things were somehow interconnected.

"What if..." I tried again. "What if he hurt Lily, then tried the same thing with me? What would Violet do if she found out?"

"I'd have killed him," Clay said quietly.

I drew in a sharp breath before I continued. "And if you killed someone spur of the moment and were afraid to go to the police..."

"You would need to hide the body," Clay supplied, his gaze

sweeping across the yard and over the lilies. "And what better way to do that than bury him in her own backyard?"

He pushed to his feet and strode toward the Cala lilies. "Patrick could have helped her hide the body and get rid of his things."

"Could have." But something still didn't fit. "Why don't I remember any of this?"

Clay shrugged. "I have no idea. Maybe you weren't there that night."

"Maybe," I conceded as I stared up at him. "I know this sounds totally crazy."

"Desperate people do desperate things all the time. I think anything is worth looking into."

Clay turned and headed for the shed, and I moved toward the flowerbed. A moment later, he appeared by my side and passed me a shovel. A twinge of guilt assailed me as I sank the tip of the spade into the earth and uprooted a half dozen bulbs. If we were wrong, I was going to feel absolutely terrible about this. But I needed to know for sure.

An hour later, hot and sweaty, we'd made decent progress. The hole we'd dug was about ten feet long and a foot deep. The deeper we went, the thicker and heavier the dirt was.

"I'm going to grab a water." I set my shovel aside and looked at Clay. "Do you want one?"

He wiped the back of his wrist across his forehead. "Please. I'll keep going."

I headed into the kitchen and poured two glasses of ice water for Clay and myself. Just as I was getting ready to take them back outside, a knock from the front door drew my attention. My entire body went rigid as I froze. It was rare for anyone to show up unannounced, and I knew that Clay and I weren't expecting anyone.

Quietly I headed through the living room, making my way toward the front door at an angle, taking care to stay away from all of the windows. I peeked through the little sliver of glass between the curtain and the window frame, and a man's form came into view. As he turned around, Harris Grant's profile sank in.

I let out the breath I'd been holding and opened the door. "Harris."

He turned toward me, a smile on his face. "Abilene. So good to see you. I saw the vehicle in the driveway, but I thought I'd missed you."

"We're here," I said, keeping my body in the open doorway. "What brings you by?"

"I felt so terrible after that encounter in our office. I just wanted to make sure everything was okay."

"It's funny you said that. Patrick actually stopped by a couple of weeks ago and apologized. We both put it behind us and have moved on."

"Good," he said, his voice full of relief. "I'm glad to hear that."

His icy blue eyes landed on my hand where it rested along the doorjamb, and his head tipped slightly to the side. I followed his gaze to the dirt beneath my fingernails and fought the urge to curl my hand into a fist to hide them from view.

"Looks like I caught you in the middle of something." He chuckled.

"Just doing some landscaping," I said, keeping my voice light.

"I hope you've been taking care of the flowers. Violet loves them."

"I know." I swallowed hard, unease slithering down my spine.

Those eyes turned hard and cold as he studied me. "What are you doing in the yard, Abilene?"

I hesitated, and a frown marred his handsome face. "I really hoped I wouldn't have to do this."

Before I could process his words, Harris lifted a black pistol he'd pulled from his waistband and lifted it to my face.

CHAPTER FORTY-TWO

Clay

I kept digging until the spade pulled up something long and curved. I set the shovel aside and used my fingers to brush off the soil clinging to the object. No more than an inch or so in diameter, long and curved, I suspected what I was holding was a rib bone.

Something was still bothering me. The timeline didn't quite jive. From what Abby said, the lilies here in the backyard hadn't been planted until after Charlie's disappearance. George had said he was under the impression that Charlie and Violet were living together up until the day he left. According to Harris, though, their relationship has been under some serious strain for months prior to the divorce.

Had they truly been separated? And if so, where had he been staying? There were no other residences in his name, not even a rental agreement, and I seriously doubted he would spend money to stay in a hotel, especially for an extended period of time like that. Of course, Harris was only the lawyer who had offered counsel for the divorce. Maybe Violet had told him one version of events, while Charlie had told George another.

Suddenly, I froze as Trevor's last message popped into my head. He'd wanted to look at the divorce papers. Harris had finalized the divorce. But that didn't mean Charlie had actually come into the office. The signature on the papers could be a forgery. Maybe Patrick really was innocent. Maybe it was someone else—like the attorney who'd taken care of Charlie and Violet's divorce. And the trust paperwork for Trevor.

Harris had connections to everyone. I hadn't questioned it at the time but now his parting words came back to me. *Tell Abby I said hello.* How had Harris known about me and Abby? Had she told him? From what I understood, she hadn't talked to him since around the same time Violet has been moved into the assisted living facility. And that had been more than a full week before we were officially together.

A chill moved through my body. I whipped out my phone and shot off a quick text to Con.

Pull everything you can on Harris Grant. Has connections to all the victims.

"Abs," I called toward the house. "I think I've got something."

"That's unfortunate," came a deep, masculine voice.

I snapped my head toward the house, and my blood boiled with fury when I saw the man outlined in the doorway, Abby in front of him, a pistol pointed at her head. Allowing the bone to slip from my fingers, I relaxed my posture and met the man's gaze. "What are you doing, Grant?"

"What I have to do." His gaze filled with belligerence. "As soon as Patrick told me you'd found her diary, I knew I had to do something. All you had to do was stop poking around where you didn't belong. I warned you, both of you!"

My phone was still in my hand, and I held down the side button for several seconds. I didn't dare look at it as I continued to speak to Harris. "Abby has nothing to do with this. Just let her go and—"

He laughed, but it held no humor. "She has everything to do with this."

My phone let out a soft ding, and every muscle in my body went rigid as Harris's gaze dropped to where it rested next to my leg. I didn't dare let go of that button, praying fervently that it would function as intended and summon the authorities.

"Put the phone down and get in the house," Harris ordered.

Fuck. I held on as long as I could, taking a couple of steps toward them.

"Drop it!" he yelled.

Anxiety and adrenaline rushing through my veins, I dropped the phone to the grass at my feet and slowly held up my hands in front of me.

"Good. Get in." Harris fell back a few steps, pulling Abby deeper into the house with him, ensuring I would follow.

I needed to get the upper hand, but I couldn't bear for Abby to get caught in the crossfire. I needed to find a way to get her away from him so I could disarm him. I kept my eyes locked on his as I crossed the backyard, then mounted the porch and stepped into the house. Harris kept one arm locked around Abby's neck as he continued to move backward, maintaining a fair amount of distance between us. As soon as I was fully inside the house, he redirected the pistol from her to me. The way he held it, hand shaking slightly, told me he wasn't proficient with firearms. But anyone could get lucky once, and I was going to make damn sure that Abby and I both stayed safe.

"Why did you do it?" I asked.

"No questions," he ordered. "Get in the bedroom."

I wasn't an expert in dealing with hostage situations, but I knew the more we followed his directions, if we allowed him to take charge of the situation, the less likely we would be to walk out if here alive. "Let's all just calm down for a second—"

"No!" The gun wavered in Harris's hand before he yanked it back then pressed it to Abby's temple again. "Do what I say or I swear to God, I'll kill her right here."

Rage simmered in my veins at the sight of the pistol pressed to the side of her face. I couldn't bring myself to meet her eyes. I knew I had to stay strong, but I could hear her uneven breaths from where I stood several feet away, and I could see her trembling in my peripheral vision. I needed to stay calm, needed to focus on the situation at hand. I couldn't get distracted by her fear or I would snap and do something stupid.

Slowly, I held up my hands placatingly in front of me. "Okay, okay. I'll go."

Not taking my eyes from his, I put one foot behind the other and slowly backed my way out of the room and down the hall toward the bedroom, moving from memory. Harris held the gun trained on Abby, and I kept my movements slow and controlled. The last thing I needed was to spook him and have him pull the trigger.

I maneuvered into the bedroom, speaking as I did so. "Tell me what happened. Did you kill Charlie?"

He shook his head. "You wouldn't understand."

"He hurt Lily, didn't he?" I asked. "And he was going to hurt Abby unless someone stopped him."

Harris's eyes flicked to Abby for a second before returning to mine. His face slowly crumpled. "We didn't know."

"About Lily?"

Harris shook his head. "We never thought... God. None of us ever imagined he could do that. I'd known him all my life, but I still have trouble wrapping my mind around it. But after he tried to hurt Abby..."

A cold wave moved through my stomach at the thought of what might have happened. "You did what you had to do. You stopped him from hurting another innocent child."

"Not me." Harris swallowed hard. "Violet."

Now it began to make a little more sense as the picture became clear in my mind. "She killed him, and you helped her cover it up."

The other man nodded. "I did what I had to do. We couldn't go to the police."

"If you were defending Abby—"

"He wasn't dead when I got here," Harris stated flatly. "She called me as soon as it happened. She was frantic, completely beside herself. I thought he was gone. But that son of a bitch was just knocked out cold. He woke up just after I got here. He..." A muscle ticked in his jaw as he spoke. "I confronted him about Lily. And he admitted it. How could he do that to her? He was her stepfather. He was supposed to protect her, and instead he—"

Harris drew a deep breath. "I was angry. I just... couldn't help it. I remember holding the shovel, then swinging at him. I just... lost it." He blinked, lost in thought. "After I realized what I'd done... I couldn't take it back. I didn't want to. I had to get rid of him. For Abby, and for Violet."

Shit. That put a whole new spin on things. Violet had incapac-itated him, but Harris had taken things one step further by killing him, then disposing of the body.

"And Trevor?"

Harris's lips pressed into a firm line, and he closed his eyes briefly before meeting my gaze again. "I warned him," he said softly. "He just wouldn't let it go. He kept pushing and pushing, and..." He shrugged. "He didn't leave me a choice."

There was always a choice, and Harris had made the wrong one. He'd killed an innocent man to keep from going to jail. Every fiber of my being ached to lash out at him, but I forced my anger down for Abby's sake. I needed answers to all of her questions, and there was something I still didn't understand. "Why doesn't Abby remember any of this?"

"Violet took Abby to a doctor the next day. A hypnotherapist. Then a child psychologist after that." Harris shrugged one shoulder. "Anyone who would make sure it never came up again. We couldn't afford to have her remember and risk us going to jail."

In my peripheral vision, I watched Abby's mouth widen in a little 'O' before snapping shut again. "But... all of his things...?"

"Patrick," Harris confirmed. "While Violet and Abby were out, we erased every trace of evidence that he'd ever been here."

My heart kicked up in my chest, and I mentally calculated how much time had elapsed. "If you kill us, you'll still go to jail, even if they don't find Charlie's body."

Harris was quiet for a moment. "You know, I've loved Violet half my life. When she was married to Charlie, I tried to see her as just a friend. After his death, I still couldn't be with her. She strug-gled so much after that. She regretted what happened, and I knew I was the cause of that. She saw me differently, and things were just never the same after that. I loved her so much, and... he was always between us. Even when he died, he was still between us."

His face creased with defeat. "It's so hard to see her slipping away. Violet doesn't know me anymore—she didn't even recognize me the last time I was there. She was the only thing worth living for and now she's gone."

I saw the intent in his eyes, and I didn't hesitate to lunge toward Harris as he lifted the gun once more. Abby's scream filled the air at the same time the pistol blasted loudly, the sound deafening as it echoed throughout the room.

CHAPTER FORTY-THREE

Abby

Every muscle in my body recoiled as the sound of the gun going off exploded right next to my ears. Had Harris not been holding me, I probably would've hit the floor. Clay's eyes looked positively murderous as he rushed forward, and Harris's grip loosened as he focused on Clay. I threw myself to the ground just as Clay came in low and fast, wrapping his arms around Harris's waist and driving him backwards into the wall with one smooth movement.

I landed hard on my hands and knees, the abrupt movement stunning me as my teeth gnashed together. A second gunshot went off, followed almost immediately by the shattering of glass as the window along the western wall exploded. I cringed at the sound, then threw a look over my shoulder at Harris and Clay where they grappled for control. Muffled grunts filled the air, and it took me nearly a full second to comprehend what was happening.

I watched on with a weird sense of detachment, disbelief warring with fear and worry. Harris was surprisingly strong for his age, and he had no intention of relinquishing the firearm. Clay landed a solid blow to Harris's ribs, but Harris's fist shot upward and the pistol glanced off of Clay's cheekbone. I sucked in a breath as red droplets of blood streamed from the cut, dripping onto Harris where he lay prone below him.

The men ducked and weaved, bumping into furniture and overturning boxes as they evaded each other's punches. With amazing speed, Clay took Harris down, and they landed hard in a tangle of limbs. The sound of shattering glass filled the air as a lamp hit the ground right next to them. But the men were so focused on one another they didn't even notice.

Clay grabbed Harris's wrist—the one that held the gun—and forced it over his head. Harris's free hand came up in an arc, and his fist smashed into Clay's face. I let out a little cry as Clay jerked backward. But he never relinquished his hold. He slammed Harris's hand to the ground once... twice. Finally, Harris's fingers relaxed, and the gun went clattering across the floor, sliding toward the bed somewhere just out of sight.

I had to get that gun. I darted forward to try to find it but the men rolled, knocking me off balance and sweeping my feet out from under me. I went sprawling to the floor, and I landed with a jolt as my chin smashed against the floor. Stars danced before my eyes for a second before I forced myself to move.

Climbing to my hands and knees, I glanced around the room. Where the hell was the gun? I dodged out of the way as Clay and Harris slid on the hardwood, each trying to control the other's movements. The gun had slid away somewhere... Where? I scanned the floor, and a sense of frustration welled up.

Damn it! I needed to stop Harris—but how? My gaze landed on a heavy crystal vase that sat on the dresser, and hope zinged through me. I knew it was one of Violet's favorites, but I couldn't bring myself to care at the moment. All that mattered was it was heavy, and it would at least incapacitate him.

I clambered to my feet and threw myself forward, intent on getting that damn vase. If I couldn't get the gun, it was the next best thing. In my peripheral vision, I watched as Harris brought his knee up fast between Clay's legs. He let out a grunt of pain and the maneuver was enough to momentarily stun him, because all of a sudden, Harris shimmied out of his hold. Instead of standing, he scooted backward several feet, his hand sweeping the floor like he was looking for something.

The gun. Oh, God. My eyes followed his questing hands, and I saw his fingers close around the gun just as I grabbed up the vase. Clay was rising to his feet, getting ready to come for Harris again, when the older man swung the pistol in front of him.

"No!"

A scream ripped from my throat, drowned out by the report of the pistol as it went off. Clay jerked backward, and half a second later dark red bloomed across his chest right over his heart.

Without thinking, I rushed forward. I lifted the vase over my head, then brought it down as hard as I could. The vase shattered as it connected with his skull. Harris collapsed to his back, but I wasn't leaving it to chance.

"Goddamn you!" Driven by anger and fear and a hundred other emotions, I hit him again. Tears streamed down my face, obscuring my vision as I hit him over and over, pummeling his face with my hands.

"Abby!"

The sound of Clay's voice ripped me from my tirade, and I jerked upward. My feet slid on the shards of glass as I launched myself toward Clay. Blood coated his shirt and pooled on the floor around him. His face looked gray, and he winced as I pressed my hands to the wound.

"Oh, God." My stomach dropped to the floor as blood seeped through my fingers. "You're—"

Suddenly a flurry of movement appeared in the doorway, and several officers entered the room, weapons drawn. I'd never been happier to see them in all my life.

"Get help!" I screamed. "Hurry!"

I spared them barely another glance before turning my attention back to Clay. "Don't you fucking die on me!" Tears dripped down my nose and landed on my hands with a small splatter. "I swear I'll kill you."

Clay let out a raspy sound that was supposed to be a laugh. "I knew you were the one for me that night at the hotel."

"It's not funny." The tears came faster, slipping down my cheeks without restraint. "I can't lose you."

Clay covered my hands with one of his own, right over his heart. "Love you, Abby."

"Clay!" A sob escaped my throat as his eyes closed. "Don't leave me!"

His fingers tightened around mine for a brief second, then went slack.

CHAPTER FORTY-FOUR

Clay

I drummed my thumbs on the steering wheel as I headed toward my apartment. My heart beat hard and heavy in my chest, and my stomach twisted the closer I got. Technically I wasn't supposed to be driving, but I'd never been particularly good at following directions. I knew my body's limitations, when to push and when to back down.

My phone rang, pulling me from my thought, and I glanced at the unknown number flashing across my screen. For a second, I considered letting it roll over to voicemail, then decided against it. I tapped the button to answer and lifted it to my ear. "Thompson."

There was a long pause on the other end, so long I thought the person had hung up. I was about to do the same when a familiar voice spoke up. "Son."

Shock rippled through me, and I eased off the accelerator before I realized what I'd done. It took me a minute to find my voice, still not quite believing that my father was calling me. "Pop?"

"I—" He broke off, and the sound of harsh coughing filled the line.

A dull pain twisted through my heart. No matter how much of an asshole he was, he was still my father and I hated to hear him in pain.

"Sorry 'bout that," he apologized when he came back.

"No problem." Silence descended once more, and I clutched the phone tightly. Why the hell was he calling me? My heart thudded hard against my ribs as nearly thirty seconds passed quietly. Finally he spoke again.

"Talked to your brother yesterday."

I stayed silent, knowing instinctively that he had something to say.

"He told me you took a bullet a few days ago."

His voice was thick and gruff, and I cleared my own throat at hearing the emotion in his. "I'm fine."

"Good." He hesitated again. "And your girl? She good?"

"Yeah, she's okay," I said, not wanting to offer too much.

"Good," he repeated. "I'd like to meet her. If you want to bring her by," he added.

I wasn't quite sure what to say. Part of me still didn't quite believe him. "I'll see what we have going on," I said after a few seconds.

"Well, I'll let you go," he said. "I'm sure you're busy."

"Thanks for calling," I offered. The conversation was stilted and awkward, but it was more than we'd shared over the last dozen years. I had to at least give him the benefit of the doubt. "And I'll bring Abby over to see you soon."

We hung up just as I pulled into the apartment complex and I put the truck in park, then sat there for a second, wondering what the hell had just happened. I felt like it was some kind of sign. Maybe it was time to put the past behind us and move on once and for all—and I knew exactly where to start.

I grabbed up the box resting on the seat next to me and stowed it in my sling as I made my way into the building. Inside the apartment, I found Abby in our bedroom, her back to me as she folded clothes and stowed them in the dresser. "Hey, beautiful."

She threw a smile over her shoulder at me. "Hey, yourself. Feeling okay?"

Her gaze dropped to arm, and I nodded. "Good enough."

My shoulder still ached like a bitch, but I wouldn't tell her as much. The sling was uncomfortable, the bandage over the wound bulky and awkward, but the doctor had insisted I wear it for the next couple of weeks. I'd tried to leave it off today, but Abby had made me promise to keep it on. And God knew I couldn't tell her no. Where she was concerned, I had zero willpower.

The fact that I'd almost lost her had shaken me. I still remembered the helplessness of standing there, seeing the pistol pressed to her temple. Fortunately, the emergency function on my phone worked like a charm, alerting the authorities that something was wrong. I didn't remember much after the struggle with Harris, only Abby's pretty face as she hovered over me, doing everything in her power to staunch the flow of blood and screaming for help. I'd apparently lost a fuck ton of blood and passed out, scaring the hell out of Abby.

When I'd woken several hours later, I'd found her perched next to my hospital bed. I was fairly certain security wouldn't have been able to remove her if they'd tried. Thank God, she hadn't been hurt. I couldn't say the same for Harris, though. The blunt force trauma of the blow to the head had caused a massive bleed, and he'd died shortly after arriving at the hospital. Abby seemed to be dealing with it extraordinarily well so far, but I was waiting for it to catch up with her. Either way, we'd take it one day at a time, and I planned to be by her side every step of the way.

The police currently had Violet's house cordoned off and I knew that when they searched the property, they'd found Charlie's remains in the back yard. We'd told them in our statements that Harris was responsible for killing both Charlie and Trevor. We saw no reason to mention Patrick. To my surprise, he'd come to visit while I was in the hospital. He apologized for everything that had happened and offered to tell the police about his involvement. Though I appreciated the offer, I couldn't let him ruin his life like that. He had a family to take care of, and with Harris gone, there were no more loose ends. I understood that Patrick had just been trying to protect Abby and Violet; it wasn't his fault Harris had taken things too far.

Ever since I'd been released two days ago, we'd been staying at my house. It didn't seem to bother Abby in the least, but we hadn't talked about what to do with Violet's place. All I knew was that my future was with Abby, and I needed to lock her down sooner rather than later.

"I have something for you."

"Oh?" A pleased smile curved her mouth as she studied me. "What is it?"

Heart racing, I took the little black box from inside my sling and tossed it to her. She caught it deftly, and I watched a dozen emotions flash across her face as she studied the object in her hands. Her mouth opened slightly, then snapped shut again as her eyes lifted to meet mine. "Is this what I think it is?"

Blood rushed in my ears, and I pasted on a smile. "Depends what you think it is."

"Did you seriously just throw an engagement ring at me?" Annoyance flashed in her eyes and Abby flicked the box back to me with a flip of her wrist.

I snatched the box out of the air, unable to contain the grin spreading across my face. "I'm broken, baby. Aren't you going to take pity on me?"

"Not a chance," she snapped mutinously. "Get down on one knee like a real man and ask."

Damn, I loved this woman. I closed the distance between us, then dropped to one knee in front of her. Maneuvering the box open with one hand, I peered up at her. "If that's what you want, baby, I'll spend the rest of my life on my knees for you."

Abby rolled her eyes, but a smile flirted with the corners of her lips. "You're such an idiot."

"You knew that when you met me."

A grin overtook her face. "True."

"You know..." I stared up at her. "A lot of men say they'll take a bullet for the woman they love. I actually did. You should show me a little extra appreciation for that."

She laughed. "You are absolutely shameless, you know that? Recovering from a gunshot wound and still begging for sex."

"I do not beg for sex," I said stoutly.

"Semantics."

I couldn't help but grin at our banter. I wanted to bicker with this woman every single day for the rest of my life. "I love you, Abilene Quentin. You're quirky and you push every single button of mine. But you also make every day better than the last, and I can't imagine my life without you. Marry me, baby."

Her eyes softened. "Well, how can I resist a proposal like that?"

"You can't." Wrapping my right arm around her waist, I drew her down so she sat on my knee. With my left hand, I lifted the ring from the box and slid it onto her finger. "You mean everything to me, and I can't wait to spend my life with you."

Abby wrapped her arms around my neck and planted a fierce kiss on my lips. The force of it rocked me backward, and I rolled to the floor, taking her with me. A sharp twinge of pain shot through my shoulder, and the edges of my vision dimmed to black before coming back into focus.

Above me, Abby slapped one hand over her mouth to contain her laughter. "I'm so sorry."

"I'm not." I hugged her tighter to me. "I want this every single day."

I couldn't stop thinking about how fucking lucky I'd been to find her in the hotel that night. If we hadn't met outside of work, would we be where we were today? I wasn't sure, but I doubted it. I was so incredibly grateful for the way things had worked out. She meant the world to me, and I would never let her go.

A dull ache radiated through my upper body, but all my blood was starting to flow south, anyway. I grabbed the back of Abby's head with my free hand and pulled her down for a kiss. "Love you, Dallas."

Abby smiled down at me, all the love in her heart shining from those deep brown eyes. "I love you, too... *Johnny*."

EPILOGUE

Abby

I couldn't help the perpetual smile that had taken up residence on my face as I stared at the ring on my left hand. It sparkled in the light, sending tiny rainbows all over the wall as I turned it from side to side, and happiness like I'd never known welled up in my chest, radiating outward. I couldn't stop thinking about him, about us. He was everything I've ever wanted and more. He was bossy and arrogant, but I'd be lying if I said I didn't love those particular qualities. It made me feel important. Cherished. Loved.

The man in question caught my eye as he stalked across the lobby then slid behind the reception desk. "Hey, beautiful."

"Hey." I tipped my head up for a kiss.

"For the love of God," came my brother's voice, "would you two take a rest?"

I grinned, unwilling to let him dim my happiness. "Shut up, Con."

He rolled his eyes at me. "I'll be in my office if you need anything."

He strode away, and I glanced up at Clay, who wrapped his arm around my waist and pulled me close. "I think he still hates me a little bit," Clay admitted.

"Nah, he's just making sure I'm happy."

Honeyed eyes stared down at me. "Are you?"

I pretended to think about it, and Clay smacked my bottom.

"Woman, I swear to God..."

I couldn't help the bubble of laughter that fell from my lips as he let out a little growl of exasperation. "You know I'm just teasing. I'm crazy about you."

"Better be." Clay kissed me once more. "I've got to go. I'll see you tonight."

"Be safe."

With one more kiss, he strode through the door, and I watched until he was gone. It was crazy how quickly things had changed between us. I'd fought it for so long at the beginning, but I wouldn't change the way things worked out for the world.

After all of the craziness recently, I was glad everything was finally back to normal. Clay was healing up well and doing physical therapy a few times a week to improve the function of the damaged muscle. Last week we'd gone to Trevor's service back in Colorado and had spoken with his parents. They were devastated, rightfully so, but at least knowing Harris was gone gave them a small measure of closure.

I still stopped by to see Violet every couple of days, too. Some were better than others, but I was making peace with it. I had considered telling her about Harris, too, but I wasn't quite sure how to even broach the subject. If she did remember him, I wanted her memories to be good ones.

I was rearranging the papers on the desk in front of me, getting ready to run another background report, when the bell over the front door rang. I lifted my head, expecting it to be Clay. "Forget something?"

My gaze landed on the woman who entered the lobby, and I smiled automatically. "I'm sorry, I thought you were someone else. Welcome to Quentin Security. What can I do for you?"

The woman approached the counter silently, then slipped the dark sunglasses from her face. She was blonde, incredibly beautiful, and... familiar. Her pretty blue eyes met mine, and a hesitant smile lifted her lips. "Hello, Abby."

My heart seized in my chest as the whole world came to a jarring halt. Oh my God. It was *her*. "Grace."

Also by Morgan James

Quentin Security Series
The Devil You Know – Blake and Victoria
Devil in the Details – Xander and Lydia
Devil in Disguise – Gavin and Kate
Heart of a Devil – Vince and Jana
Tempting the Devil – Clay and Abby
Devilish intent – Con and Grace (February 2022)
*Each book is a standalone within the series

Frozen in Time Trilogy
Unrequited Love
Undeniable Love
Unbreakable Love
Frozen in Time: The Complete Trilogy

Deception Duet
Pretty Little Lies – Eric and Jules, Book One
Beautiful Deception – Eric and Jules, Book Two
*Each book can be read as a standalone, but are best read in
order

Sinful Duet
Sinful Illusions – Fox and Eva, Book One
Sinful Sacrament (Summer 2021) – Fox and Eva, Book Two
*Books should be read in order

Bad Billionaires
(Novella Series)
Depraved
Ravished
Consumed
*Each book is a standalone within the series

Standalones
Death Do Us Part
Escape

About the Author

Morgan James is the bestselling author of contemporary and romantic suspense novels. She spent most of her childhood with her nose buried in a book, and she loves all things romantic, dark, and dirty.